I0555474

Gaymerica

SCOT FROELICH

This is a work of fiction. Names, characters, places, and incidents are products of the author's imagination or are used fictitiously and are not to be construed as real. Any resemblance to actual events, organizations, or persons, living or dead, is purely coincidental.

Copyright © 2012, 2020 by Scot Froelich (née Moore). All rights reserved.
The author holds exclusive rights to this work. Unauthorized duplication is prohibited.

Third paperback edition: April 2020

For information, please visit: http://scotfroelich.com/

Gaymerica

ISBN-13: 978-1-7347232-1-2

ISBN-13 – 2012: 978-0615564388
ISBN-10: 0615564380

Cover design: Mame Pelletier
Cover photograph: Matt Black, Matt Black Studios
Cover talent: Mariah Christensen, John Zeiler, and Stuart Holland
Author photograph: Heidi M. Garrido, hmphotomn.com

For the voters of Minnesota

1

I'm sitting on the El, riding the Red Line into downtown. A half mile North of the Loop, it dives underground and becomes a subway. Every time the lights cut out and the dimly lit subterranean architecture reveals itself, I hear my mother's voice echoing from our rural Iowan kitchen shouting, "There are no subways in Chicago! The only things below ground in Chicago are crooks and queers!" My mother. Ever the wordsmith.

Beneath the gloomy, steel and concrete surface of Chicago, there really is a subway. It's limited and only runs a couple of lines, but it's there. And while there are certainly crooks, I've never been too sure about the queers. We don't talk about these things and I do my best not to *think* about them as well. Despite the constant warnings on television and radio of far-off lands where our virtue is shunned and how we should resist the urges to entertain such thoughts, they do creep in. Not that I would ever entertain the thoughts themselves, but rather thoughts about the thoughts. For whatever that's worth.

As if on cue, some angular-looking middle-aged guy in a gray suit and tan trench coat is staring at me. Whenever I catch him he looks the other way. "Hey, buddy," I think, "Your type got deported a long time ago. Let it go." But, I don't say anything. Instead, I furrow my brow and go back to reading the morning paper.

I don't actually read all the articles. Too many words. Instead, I buy whichever paper has the more gripping headline or most gruesome image. This means that some days I read the tabloid papers, and they amuse the shit out of me. Last Tuesday, there was a story about a suicide bombing in Russia, the third that week. The journalist kept using phrases like, "some people believe" and "in the eyes of *this* observer" indicating that he'd basically made the story up off the top of his head and didn't trouble to find sources at all. Poor journalism used to piss my old man off something fierce. I try not to think about him, but the image of my dad slamming a newspaper down on a table is somehow seared into my brain.

It's hard to concentrate as the guy in the gray suit keeps checking me out. He's being awfully obvious about it and I'm wondering if he's trying to get himself deported. There are spies everywhere and if they think he's eyeing me and that I'm in the remotest way responding…

The train stops at Lake and I get off quickly. Hoping to put some distance between myself and gray suit, I head up the stairs to Randolph where I hang a left, hurry on over to Michigan and into the lobby of the building I work in. It's an old, ten-story building with about twenty tenants. When I press the button for the elevator (seventh floor) I finally look behind me to see if anyone's following. No shit, Mr. gray suit is standing there by the revolving door trying to look casual. Really?

Seriously?! You just followed a guy from Belmont to the front door of his office building. You don't think anyone's going to notice that?

I step quickly into the elevator when it dings and press and hold the "Close" button, much to the dismay of a hustling young man scurrying toward it with arms full of papers, a satchel, and an extraneous umbrella. Still, I don't let up and he notices, shouting, "Thanks, asshole!" as the doors close. I turn sheepishly to the two others who managed to board and say, "Bad Mexican food," then grab my gut. They huddle into the opposite corner and the rest of the ride to the seventh floor is undisturbed.

Leaping forth from the elevator with my hand firmly gripping my feigned gut-bomb, I turn, inaudibly apologize to my terrified elevator companions and stumble down the hallway to the old wood and glass door protecting Fittzle and Rupert from the public. I slam it shut behind me for effect and turn to straighten up. Chelsea, Katie, and Cassandra are all looking at me as if I'm from another planet. There are times that being the only male employee among numerous attractive female employees has its advantages. This is not one of them. I smile cordially and slink to my desk where I open the window, start the fan and lay my coat over the back of my chair.

Fittzle and Rupert is a personal injury law firm specializing in cases against the former government's public transportation initiatives and welfare programs. When the government was rewritten and all agencies decommissioned, there was a sudden surplus of funds and over one trillion dollars was set aside to cover damages incurred by the socialist regime. So, capitalists like my employers set up shop to profit off the dispensation of said funds. All these years later, cases still roll in as much infrastructure from the former regime is still in use today.

Fittzle lives on an island in the Keys and Rupert lives in his office, pretty much in a constant haze of smoke and coke. We've tried to get him to keep the windows open when he smokes but since the laws banning smoking in public buildings (and public buildings themselves for that matter) have been abolished, he just tells us to fuck off and shuts the door behind him. When it gets bad I usually crack the window near my desk and stick a fan in it to draw the smoke out. I used to smoke, but ever since I got this weird infection in my sinuses I haven't had the urge. I've tried a couple times but it never takes.

My job is to vet incoming claims. See, not everyone who files a claim against the former government actually qualifies. I like to imagine things while I'm at my desk, mostly based on the crap I see on claim forms. Frances deWinter from Pough-keepsie, NY wants one million for having tripped while exiting a decaying city bus. In my head, she was rushing to a Christian rock concert and the bus was going too slowly. "Speed up, driver! I'm going to miss the opening act!" But, while she was sitting there minding her own business, a man sidled up next to her and started making kissy faces and noises at her. Instead of doing his duty and kicking the man off the bus, the driver began laughing and pumping the breaks to slide the man closer to Frances. She screamed and ran toward the exit. The driver stopped, bouncing her off the front window and she rolled out onto the street, her body contorted and twitching from the lurid encounter.

But that never actually happened. The bitch probably turned her ankle as a result of faulty heels on her pumps and is trying to cash in on it. The application makes a delightful crumpling sound before it bounces on the bottom of my metal waste paper bin.

An hour goes by and I daydream seven more claim requests into the bin. Then, a knock rattles the frosted glass in the door. Chelsea and Cassandra bark, "Not it," in childish form and Katie begrudgingly shuffles to the door. It opens toward me and I can't see who's there, but I overhear Katie's half of the conversation, "Hi, how can I help you... Uh-huh? Um, I guess..." She backs up and motions to my desk, "Yeah, he's over there." She shrugs at me and starts back to her desk.

Through the doorway marches the angular man in the gray suit. A chill trots up my spine and I'm suddenly feeling the faux gut-bomb again and am poised to burst from the room to the lavatory in an attempt to climb out a window in search of my own sovereignty. Restraint overrides the urge, though and I remain at my desk, eyeing the man carefully as he approaches. The three Cs as I call them (knowing full well Katie spells her name with a K) pay no mind as a visitor is commonplace enough. None of them see the oddity of this particular visitor and for that I am grateful.

Gray suit sits with his trench coat draped over his arm and an old-fashioned brief case clutched in his left hand which, due to age or arthritis, looks more like a claw. He says nothing. I blink, inadvertently crumpling an un-daydreamed claim form. Realizing it, I unclench and blink again.

"May I help you?" I ask, drenched in sweat.

He leans slightly in, rotates his head to see if anyone's looking, then looks back at me, "Us. You can help *us*," he says mysteriously and returns to his erect sitting position. His scrawny melon shifts back on his neck thrusting out the slightest double chin below his rectangular jaw.

My index finger points unbidden to my chest and my eyebrows raise, "You? Me, help you… Us? Who's us?" My mind races. Am I in trouble? Is he here to arrest me? I draw a breath and my brain slows momentarily. Quickly, I add, "Is this about a claim application? Because, I assure you, I review them based solely on their merits and the criteria set forth by the SGOC!" The Small Government Oversight Committee exists for the purpose of verifying that companies are acting within government regulations so that the government doesn't have to over-regulate. This keeps government small. I've never been able to resolve how that works given the number of government agents I see on a daily basis but I've been told it's much better than it used to be.

Confused, he shakes his head, "I assure you, Mr. Hawley, this has nothing to do with the SGOC."

My bottom lip drops open and quivers. When I see it's distracted his attention I snap my mouth shut and his eyes hastily return to mine. Gathering up my thoughts, I begin, "Mr. Uh…"

"Gray," he answers quickly.

"No shit?" No shit? He shrugs. I continue, "Mr. Gray. I have a very limited scope in my job description. I'm not really able to impact claims beyond the initial vetting process. If you'd like to lodge a complaint—"

The fucker interrupts me, "Mr. Hawley—"

I interrupt him right back, "Corwin, please."

"What?"

"Corwin," I add, "My name is Corwin. Mr. Hawley was my father." Plus, hearing "Mr. Hawley" from this guy sounds like I'm about to be disappeared for crimes against the state... Another shudder sprints up my spine.

He ruffles in his seat, places his briefcase on the floor next to the chair, and leans his elbow on the corner of my desk, "Mr.... Corwin." I shudder and blink again. He proceeds, "I promise this has nothing to do with your job here at Frazzle and Roger."

Before I can stop myself, I blurt out, "I have break in twenty minutes, then. I limit my on-the-clock time to work only."

His head cocks in an irritated fashion and he mumbles something to himself before saying, "Corwin, I have no desire to take you away from your work. I'll be waiting for you in the second-floor lobby in twenty minutes. Here's my card." A gnarled claw appears from under the trench coat and slides the card across the seven square inches of free desk space next to him. I don't reach for it.

We stare at each other for a moment before I utter, "Okay."

Gray shakes his head, gathers his belongings, and sweeps majestically out the door. The three C's can't be bothered to care, not realizing anything abnormal has occurred. I contemplate the card for nearly a minute, moving not a muscle in the interim, before finally picking it up and examining it. It's boring, but concise:

> Joseph H. Gray
> Department of Foreign Affairs
> 77 S Adams St
> Philadelphia, PA 00001

What the fuck? I *am* going to be disappeared! Sweat starts pouring down my forehead, back, and ass making my seat very uncomfortable. I adjust the fan in the window, loosen my tie and begin breathing heavily. Chelsea notices this and says, "Are you okay, Cor?"

Right! The creepy-ass government spook doesn't faze her but a little perspiration and an upped level on my window fan raise her cockles. Annoyed, I reply, "What? No. I mean, yes, I'm fine." Smooth, Corwin.

She shakes her head and returns to painting her nails and tapping her feet to the Christian rock on her mobile device.

What do I do? The lobby on the second floor is completely open to the foyer on the first floor so even if I take the elevator all the way to the first floor, he'll see me as I exit. And, I can't climb out the window since I'm deathly afraid of heights. Now, I could just sit here and do my work, not taking a break all day and hope he leaves out of boredom, but something tells me that with the four miles he's followed me already this morning he won't give up that easily.

Really, how bad can deportation be? I might have to learn a new language, I guess, but learning's never been a problem for me. I hear English is very similar to American and if they send me overseas I might end up somewhere they speak that. A few modifications here and there and voila! I'm English! No one would be any the wiser. Although, what if they send me somewhere else? What if they send me to Iraqistan? Or worse, Afghanistan? I could end up speaking American in a country of people who hate me, shrouded in nothing but some cloth wrappings. I hear they don't even give you a flak jacket.

Truth be told, I don't really know what language they speak in those countries. For our protection, news is limited to only a couple of networks that send specially trained correspondents to report on those meager nations. News from outside America is always grim and even if I could speak the language I can't imagine life would be better. There's always some bombing, terrorist attack, pirate takeover, or Communist agenda waiting for you around every corner. Here, we're safe.

Despite that safety, I do feel like I've been followed before. I'm not sure I have been followed before, but I feel like I have. It's that feeling you get when the muscles tense up in the back and you can almost sense someone's breath on your neck. I turn, but no one's there. In place of the mysterious follower, my eyes scan to find the familiar sign or a poster that reminds us to always be vigilant as there are Communists and Socialists among us. I'm not the most outspoken patriot and I realize that alone causes some suspicion. I suppose that might be as good a reason as any to follow me.

Looking out the window I see the streets lined with dingy, yellowed American flags with their shabby but proud forty-four stars. Posters of patriots past and current and the ever strolling SGOC police remind me that I have limited options.

The sweat continues but the heat which previously accompanied it has now been replaced with a clammy coolness.

Cassandra breaks the silence like a dump truck, "Cor, you wanna close the window?"

Women aren't supposed to be that direct or forceful but the three Cs have come to take a different tack with me and I comply, shutting the fan off and meekly replying, "Sure."

Returning my gaze to the SGOC cop on the corner, I review the alternatives. Meet this guy and see what's up his gray sleeves or attempt to disappear into the walls. Shit.

***

A marble floor and recessed, gold inlay ceiling pockets frame an otherwise drab waiting space in the lobby of the building. The classic old wood furniture was replaced in exchange for boring yet cost-effective upholstered crap. There aren't even any plants in the lobby.

Slowly and cautiously I move across the floor and sit in the wide, armless chair across the seating area from Gray. The barrier between us consists of a low, pressboard table with cheap wood veneer. He sees me looking around, checking for gawkers and sighs audibly, "Mr.—" I shoot a glare at him. "Corwin, no one is watching us."

I almost wish there were. I don't want to disappear without a witness.

"And," he continues, "I have no desire to make you uncomfortable. Please relax and I promise I'll stay over here and you can stay over there."

Please relax and *I'll stay over here*?! What if I don't relax? Will he lunge across the table and strangle me? Will he shoot me? Will he call some behemoth from an unseen doorway and carry me off to the deportation clinic? My panic, manifesting in shaking and increasingly uncomfortable sweating, is likely palpable even to him.

"Will you *please* calm down and focus, Corwin!" he barks, interrupting my frantic notions of abduction. I return my attention to him. "Thank you. Now, before I tell you what I'm here to say I want you to know that you're in no way obligated to agree. You're welcome to choose whatever you want. This is a free country, after all."

A third-grade recitation bubbles up from my past and I almost mouth it as it reverberates through my head, "To be free is to love America. To love my country. And to always do what is in her interest." I have no desire to do something which is not in my country's interest, however free the choice may feel. What will I have the freedom to choose? I give him a listen.

"I have a proposition for you." He leans forward in his chair and peers up at me, "You have a certain…" he pauses to find the right word, "…aptitude that could benefit a growing need my department has over our relations with a particular foreign interest. And, we want you to come to work for us, utilizing the aptitude you possess."

He wants me to work for them? I check myself. Pulse. Breath – bad breath. Flesh still strung taught over my inert mass. Is this code for how they reel me in so they can more easily make me disappear? And if so, for what? I blink a freeze-frame of my life into my head and attempt to digest this new information. Does he want me to be a spy? This is what the Department of Foreign Affairs does (or so I've heard); they train agents to infiltrate other nations and report back to America. But, my logical side says that can't be real, so I furrow my brow in anticipation and lean in a bit – not too much – and ask politely, "The fuck?"

He sighs again. I sense he's becoming irritated with me, which is exactly what I want. If I'm going to have a choice in whether or not I disappear, I either want a more interesting life than the one I have now or to be left alone altogether. If I annoy him enough, I may be able to avoid the possibility of being stuck with something worse. I try to keep reminding myself that I've done nothing wrong and that I can't be deported, imprisoned, or put to death for nothing. But, memories creep in of people I'd once known whom we no longer see. What had they done?

"Corwin, I want you to understand that this discussion is highly classified and that you should take it seriously. DoFA…" he actually pronounces the acronym as if it's a word and I chuckle nervously at it. A brief scowl from Gray returns my face to rapt attention and he proceeds, "The Department of Foreign Affairs is experiencing, as I am sure you are aware, strained relations of late with some of our foreign interests. Your particular aptitude, we believe, could give us quite a leg up with a nation we've been having particular difficulties with…"

Oh, no. Not them…

"With your permission, we'd like to provide you with some

basic training, then implant you in a community within—" his infinitesimal pause feels like a vast chasm of time, yet it's still too short for me to prepare myself for what's on the other side, "Gaymerica."

This is where I disappear.

2

Disappearing is a lengthy, complex process consisting of paperwork, computer files, some IRS worker shredding a bunch of folders, and – astoundingly – the elimination of my debt. Gray said it would be critical that no one be able to trace my original whereabouts. Instead of converting my debt to my new tax identification number, they just pull out a big, magic eraser and make it go away. Not surprisingly, I have no problem with this.

While Gray was unable to clearly pinpoint what my "aptitude" for the work is (it seemed he wasn't fully aware of it himself), he did say I would likely find out not too long after landing in San Francisco. I would be given thirty days to apply for citizenship once there and it's quite possible I might discover it as part of the application process.

I walk through the door of my eleventh-floor studio off of Belmont and Sheridan and suddenly don't care about this special ability. So what if I'm a natural at interior decorating or a genius pastry chef? So what if I happen to have a knack for calligraphy? Let it be known I have no such talents, I'm just postulating. But, let's say that I do. That doesn't make me any less of a man, right? But, as I say, I don't care. I close the door, lock the deadbolt and privacy chain and hang my bag on the hook under my coat.

I crack open a Budweiser and plop into my easy chair under the 46" flat screen television on my wall. Five minutes of Fox News later and I'm out like a light.

Flashback. Iowa 2017.

I'm seven years old, running from the front of the house to the back, my parents grasping my arms so tight it stings. At the front of the house, the police are pounding on the door, "Open up, Mr. Hawley! Don't make us break the door down!" We run to the back and see more SGOC police and agents crouched outside the windows, anticipating our hasty departure.

"This way!" my dad shouts and the three of us bound up the stairs (some more willingly than others) toward a large side window and, just as we're about to open it, a freaking helicopter descends from above with a light shining in and a man on a bullhorn.

The man announces, "Come out! With your hands up!" Simultaneously, the doors downstairs burst open and men come rushing in, guns poised for action. We all raise our hands, but only my father is taken. Mom never tells me why.

***

Shit! The flashback ends as the beer has slipped in my hand from the condensation and spilled a bit on my pants. I get up quickly and dab the chair cushion with a paper towel, holding the beer in the other hand and slurping droplets off the bottom of the bottle. It's getting warm so I chug the rest and drop the bottle in the recycling bin while tossing the paper towel in the garbage.

On the television, actual news has given way to talking heads, though if I were deaf and didn't have subtitles I couldn't tell the difference. They're just heads, talking. What's the difference between that and news?

There will be a briefing next Monday. Until then, I'm to work my day job as usual and not tell anyone about the plan. If I had any close friends I might be tempted to share but, as I don't, I'm in no danger of slipping up.

Mindlessly, the channel flips to a rerun of last night's Ultimate Mixed Martial Arts bouts. I always see guys at bars get terribly wound up and excited about these things when they happen. They fist-bump and high-five each other as if it's some big accomplishment to smash another guy's face in. I guess that just never appealed to me all that much. Still, I cheer along and growl when the blood splatters on the mat. Then I'm wondering how many other men around me are doing the same thing – pretending. While I realize there may be something wrong with me that I don't get so excited about a healthy bludgeoning I know to keep it to myself. Besides, what good would it do to ask these guys, "What if that were *your* face?" I doubt the thought has ever crossed anyone's mind but mine. Shit, maybe there really is something wrong with me. Who knows? Maybe getting your face smashed in isn't all that terrible. It'll heal.

Bam! A swift knee to the jaw and the Hispanamerican dude

drops. Out cold. An excited pang in my stomach rises and falls and my sleepiness takes over again. As I start to shut down I place the beer on the side table and nestle into the chair.

Flashback. Iowa 2027.

I'm at the last high school football game of the season. Our team is being trounced by our rivals from the next county. Something about casino funding and better equipment... I don't care. The boys are getting tired and angry from losing and I'm freezing in the stands next to my girlfriend, Ida. Who the hell names their kid Ida?

A fight breaks out on the field and one of our players kicks the running back from the other squad in the facemask, dropping him immediately to the field. The boy lays, stunned and the fight escalates to a bench-clearing brawl. Ida and the rest of the crowd stand and cheer their boys on as if the 42-13 score means nothing. I reluctantly join them and sense Ida's impassioned excitement as she grabs my hand. Then my groin. "Wanna get outta here?" she asks excitedly. The heat of the sudden violence has gotten her, well, hot.

We hurry back to her parent's basement while they toil away the last quarter and a half of the slaughter and fall onto the couch, turning the television to the loudest action film we can find in the programming. I pull a blanket over us which she immediately flings on the floor. Clumsily, I reach up her shirt and start fondling her breasts under her bra.

Ida gives me a look as if to say, "Really?!" and subsequently flips me off her so I'm in a sitting position, my erection obvious through my loose-fitting jeans. She unclasps my belt, forces my pants and boxers down to my knees and stands up to remove her pink, lace panties. I turn around to see if anyone's coming down the stairs, but she grabs my head and turns it back to hers, sticking her tongue down my throat while her hips writhe over my bulging manhood. Really? Did I just say "manhood?"

Just as she's about to sit on my cock she assertively asks, "You have a condom, right?"

I fumble for my jacket and pull a crumpled condom package out of the inside pocket, ripping it open. I'm about to wrap it on myself, but she snatches it out of my hand and looks at it carefully, "Man, where do you *get* this contraband? Fuck it, who cares. You're the best, Cor!" And she lustfully drops to her knees on the floor to apply the condom. Before she does, though, she begins to play with my cock, stroking it up and down until I make noise. Involuntarily, I let out a slight moan, prompting myself to look behind me again.

She slaps me and mutters playfully, "Eyes front, pussy." Ida then dives head first onto my cock, thrusting it all the way to the back of her throat over and over again in an almost painful practice of what I imagine to be a form of self-flagellation. There's no way gagging over and over like that can be comfortable for her and I know the occasional tooth scraping that accompanies it isn't all that great for me, either. I tell her to stop, "Don't make me cum! I wanna fuck you!" the words blurt out, again involuntarily, and I realize I've managed to get her teeth away from my cock without insulting her blow job skills.

"Man, you're just contraband all around today, aren't you, Cor?" She slaps my cock, then rolls the condom onto it carelessly. Finally, she climbs back onto the couch and wraps her legs around me, slowly thrusting up and down – playing but not inserting. I thrust upward to force myself into her but she stops me, dismounts and lies on her back on the couch, "Let's do it right, mister."

I maneuver between her legs and start fondling her vagina, trying to get it open in such a way that I can get my cock inside of her. She feels wet, but I don't really know what I'm doing. Finally, the thought occurs to me to just point and thrust so I do. The resistance feels dry as I do it and she almost screams. It's nearly painful to me but I'm not mature enough to consider how it may feel to her.

She grabs my shoulder so hard I swear I hear something pop and she covers her mouth with her other hand, not allowing the scream to come out. "Slowly, please… at least at first." This is said with a pleading tone, as if it's not up to her how she's treated. Despite the intimation that it's my call, the thought of doing other than her will never enters my mind, and I gladly welcome the slowing of activities.

"That's good," she whispers, biting her lips and urging me to keep going with her head while her body seems to be doing something else. There is a warm, wet feeling, and very tight. But there's something else, too. On one side of my cock I feel a moisture that's not like the rest of the sensation and is almost grating by comparison. There's a tear streaming down her cheek but a hesitant smile on her face as she whispers, "Yeah, keep doing that." She never seems to really climax or enjoy herself in any notable way, but I eventually come. She's so happy that she clutches me to her, as though she's proud of some accomplishment.

What changed? Before we were having sex, she was all sexy and in charge. As soon as it started, something happened. I pull my pants and underwear up and shuffle to the bathroom just as the garage door opens and a car starts pulling in. Thankful I have my clothes with me I take my time in the bathroom. In the light, I see what the other sensation was; blood gleaming in incandescent light collected in various folds in the condom. Not a lot like there was the first time, but enough. I grab some toilet paper and roll the offending object off my body and into the toilet. I also wash myself in the conveniently low sink and dry off before re-turning to the couch.

Ida is sitting, watching the film with a half smile on her face and her knees pulled up tight to her chest. She grabs my hand, kisses me gently, then nestles into my shoulder to watch the film in silence. We don't talk about what happened. I don't understand.

***

My snoring wakes me up again and I decide it's time to have some dinner. In the refrigerator, there are a limited number of edible items. Eggs, a variety of cheeses in both slice and brick form, leftover pizza, a jar of moldy pasta sauce, and a case of beer. My mother tells me I should have given up living like this in college but, here I am fifteen years later and I can't manage a refrigerator without a case of beer. Mom doesn't visit enough for it to be a strain on our relationship so I don't worry about it.

Assessing my slight paunch, I shrug, stuff one piece of pizza in my mouth and return to the easy chair with the box in hand. It rests in my lap while I open another beer and flip to a live broadcast of a basketball game. The Bulls are having a terrible season, but I watch anyway. I'm part of a poker group that gets together on Thursdays and they talk endlessly about the Bulls and the 'Hawks. I hate hockey so I compensate by knowing every damned stat about every player the Bulls have. I just act like I'm busy eating or drinking when they talk about hockey.

Why do I keep falling asleep while I'm eating?

Flashback. Chicago 2046 (last year technically, but only a few weeks ago).

The guys and I are sitting around the poker table in Chad's rumpus room chugging beer and stuffing our mouths with salted nuts. Chad has never been my favorite person with whom to interact, but this is a really nice basement with a 70" screen blaring the news, a basketball game between a couple teams we could care less about (yet we all know their stats), a sports program about off-season baseball, and some cooking show teaching us how to winterize our buffet-style grills. He has a pool table, ping-pong table, two refrigerators, and a bar with actual taps serving actual beer. My apartment has none of these, save the refrigerator. Whether I like him or not, Chad is the hook up for weeknight entertainment and we all know it. He's younger than me, only thirty-one (I turned thirty-seven in October), but ambitious and successful running the advertising sales for a number of web interests and television stations.

Although, even he admits that the concept of stations may be on its way out.

"We'll all be selecting our own programming soon," he says, and while I've never brought it up, it seems to me that something like this kind of already existed when I was a kid. But, since I can't pinpoint it and never had the urge to dig into the past, I let it go, instead soaking in the ambiance and beer.

"Programming by station is old hat," he continues, "The SGOC has licensed a bunch of companies with the rights to make individual shows available for viewing at *any time*!" He says this with quite a sense of accomplishment as though he's the one that struck the deal, "I mean, restricting access to specific stations ensures that all mandatory viewing is seen, but now the SGOC messages will be input into each individual program!" He slaps the table and turns over his hand, "Pair of eights. What'd'you got, Hawley?"

I lay two sixes and a wild two down next to the seven and the Queen, "Three of a kind, Chad."

One hand follows another and I rack up the cash, as usual. These guys can't read me. I revel in it and usually leave with a thousand or more. Granted, we don't play for much, but some of us are more broke than others. Dave and Rick usually tap out after the first few hands to watch the television, which I would do as well if I weren't so good at the game. I like Dave in particular because he's the only one who's older than me. We maintain our "old guy" group if by no other means than saying on occasion, "You wouldn't get it. You're too young." The jokes are never funny anyway, but it makes us feel better.

On this particular night, though, I'm *really* up. I'm even

taking most of Chad's money. He never seems to lose too much and since he's not very good at poker I've surmised that it's because he cheats. While this likely pisses off some of the other guys I keep my trap shut. Calling someone else a cheat while raking in two grand might seem disingenuous.

He's back on about the licensing, "You know how your station cuts out for mandatory programming, right?"

"Yeah," Riley says, thoughtlessly dropping a chip and upping the bet.

"Well, that won't have to happen anymore. I mean, not with the stations that have the special licensing. Like, you could be watching Fox, or Headline News, or even Murdoch Movies and the station won't change anymore. The programming will just show up in the bottom corner of your screen," Chad chuckles, flipping a chip into the pile.

Without hesitation I meet and raise, asking, "You mean the sound'll keep going on your show and everything?"

Chad belches some of his beer at me and replies, "Don't be stupid, Cor. Of course the sound'll cut out – you have to *hear* the programming, right? Don't be a commie…"

I don't bother to respond despite the fact that this comment raises the hair on the back of my neck. Dave chirps from the pool table, "Be cool, Chad. No one's a fuckin' commie here."

"Besides, the programming's important. You want the sound to not cut out when the commies finally launch the nukes because your girlfriend, wife, mistress, whatever has it tuned into some fuckin' home decorating show?" Chad is disgusted at the thought and I suddenly have the urge to look through the channel surfing history on his remote.

I shake my head, "No, that would be bad. You in or not?"

"Fine, fine," he says, noting that Riley has folded and Steve's watching the game instead of playing cards. "I'll see your two hundred, and raise you another fifty!"

"Call," I say, dropping a chip on the table and laying out my straight – only one wild.

"Goddammit!" he shouts. Everyone in the room makes the sign of the cross on their chest, including Chad. He takes another swig of his beer and starts in again about SGOC regulations allowing flexibility in programming. It's irritating and I start to raise earlier in each hand, forcing him to fold or lose larger amounts.

But, he's had a few too many and is starting to get belligerent. Now, not only have Dave and Rick left the table to play pool, Steve has joined them leaving me, Chad, and Riley to duke it out. The pickings are slim, though as I've got two thirds of the money and Chad and Riley are splitting the last grand between them.

Another hand goes by and I lay down two pair, trumping Riley's one pair and Chad's pathetic Ace high.

"What the fuck?!" Chad blurts out before sloppily taking a pull from his beer. Steve and Rick shake their heads and Dave just shrugs. Chad eyes me for a good minute while Riley is shuffling, taking a swig here and there. I try to focus on stacking the chips but he's become truly distracting and eventually says something, "Why is it you always win?"

"I don't always win," I answer defensively. Half the guys in the room guffaw heartily at this, standing with empty pockets by the pool table. I shrug nonchalantly, "Well, I don't."

Chad leans in, "Yeah, but enough. Like, *half* the time! I mean, you never give anything away. I can always tell when Dave's bluffing 'cause he rubs his nose and shit..."

"I do?" Dave asks, rubbing his nose.

"And the rest of these guys, too, but you. What the fuck is with you?" Some of the other guys chime in, clearly irritated as well by my constant winnings.

I'm confused now and ask, "I thought the point of the game was to be good at it. If you don't like it, get better, yourself," I add, thinking I'll try some of that friendly ribbing the guys engage in.

Apparently, my tone isn't distinctive enough as sarcasm, though and Chad slams his hand on the table, shouting, "Fuck you! This is what it is with you, man. You're always so fuckin' secretive and shit. No one knows what you're up to, you shark us at poker..." All the while, I'm thinking the word is sharp. "...and you never have a fuckin' girlfriend..." I know where he's going with this and so do Riley and the other guys. Everyone looks up knowing Chad is about to cross the line. "I mean, what the fuck, man? You some sorta Commie faggot or something?!"

At this point I completely lose it, pull the table out of the way, strewing the chips all over and knocking a bottle onto the floor. It breaks and spills what's left of Riley's beer. Now, Chad's shorter and fatter than me and I'm pretty sure I can take him. Add to that the fact that he's far more drunk than I am and that I was in wrestling while he and the other guys were playing football and I'm almost positive I can mess him up, even in his own basement.

"You think I'm a commie faggot?" I shout. Dave has left the pool table and stands behind Riley as though he's ready to intervene.

"Well, are you?" he asks, smugly taking another swig of the beer he rescued when I shoved the table.

I calm down enough to not shout anymore, "You know what the SGOC does to commies and fags, Chad?" Seeing the broken bottle, I reach down and pick it up by the neck but leave it at my side.

A couple of the other guys half-heartedly try to stop it by saying things like, "Hey man, that's not cool," and the like, but I can tell they're each secretly hoping I'll mess Chad up. No one likes him. We're all taking advantage of him. I know all this and yet a violent urge is still compelling me to hurt him.

Chad drinks from his beer again. There is fear in his eyes as he does, and he raises his eyebrows. Lowering the bottle, he laughs to himself and says without making eye contact, "Well, now I know what gets to ya." He puts his hand out to shake and the other guys look to see what I'll do. I grab his hand and pull his fat ass up out of the chair. His face is close to mine and he finally looks into my eyes.

I say, "Yeah, that's right," then flick him on the forehead and push him back into his seat.

When he laughs out loud, the tension is broken and everyone uncomfortably returns to what they were doing. Dave helps me put the table back in its place and we re-sort the chips. As we do, a thought enters my brain but it's foggy.

Something my mother had me read in her contraband book collection about protesting too much. I'm bleeding from the broken edge of the bottle and it drips onto Dave's hand while he's picking up the pieces.

"Sorry man," I say, and start toward the bar to get a paper towel.

"No problem," he says and wipes his hand in his pocket. I hand him the paper towel, he cleans off the rest of the blood, and starts cleaning the floor.

Chad kicks at the mess and starts to pull the table over, "What, are you bitches my maids? Leave it." We do and I help him replace the table.

While Riley starts dealing I add, "Now, give me all your fucking money."

***

It's 1:58am when I awaken from my nap, a dried-up headache thumping away at my temples. The television is still blaring late night talk show programming. I have the unit programmed to switch to whatever is the most up to date, live show unless I tell it otherwise. And, half the time that doesn't work anyway. The screen on the remote is small and old and hard to read sometimes, so I end up watching something I couldn't care less about.

A light is flashing on the table under the lid of the pizza box, so I fold it up and toss it on the floor. My mobile device is telling me I have a missed call. A picture of Dave with his face pressed up against a window pane is blinking slowly on and off saying "two missed calls." The second one just thirty minutes ago, so I pick up the device and press his face, initiating callback. I wait for him to answer to the strains of some ancient tune about being "proud" to be an American, the lyrics of which confuse me as I know "America" wasn't a country until after I was born. The song is older than that or so my mother tells me, and in this case I believe her.

One more stanza and I might barf, but Dave finally picks up. "Cor?"

"Win," I add.

"What?"

"It's Corwin... oh, never mind. What's up, man. You called?"

After a momentary and uncomfortable silence, he responds, "You up, man?"

I look around at my room, down at the pizza box and over to the half-empty, warm beer in my other hand and say, "Uh, yeah."

"Can you meet me at Trap's in ten?" he asks, sounding concerned.

Confused but amenable, I shrug. "Yeah, sure. See you there."

***

Trap's is a dive bar a few blocks off Sheridan in the Lakeview neighborhood. It borders a neighborhood that burned down around the time my old man left. They've built some new parks there that consist mostly of basketball and tennis courts. For the most part, it became low-income housing that's gone forgotten by everyone except those who live there.

I don't know who "Trap" is or was, but whoever they were they loved fishing gear, old sports memorabilia, and shelled peanuts. I'm almost positive the floor hasn't been cleaned in thirty years.

Dave is sitting at the bar, one arm propping his head up and the other tossing peanut shells. He drops one more on the floor before taking a pull off his beer. There's loud music, but not so loud we can't talk. The place is nearly empty. He sees me and shifts uncomfortably on his stool. Odd. I take off my jacket and walk over to him, placing the jacket over the seat of a stool, leaving one between us. He looks at me like I've slighted him somehow but shakes his head and goes back to drinking.

"Whatcha want?" the Hispanamerican bartender asks me, "Happy hour's over, so you're at full price."

He speaks American, blessedly. I retort, "That's fine. Give me an I.P.A."

He nods and shuffles over to the tap to pour my beer. Dave looks at me again. I react as if to say, "What?" He turns away again, then begins, "I have to talk to you."

"I know. That's why I'm here. What did you want to talk about? You short some coin again? I told you not to get in with the loan sharks…" a tangent I'm all too used to diving into.

Dave stops me, irritated and unable to mask his desperation, "No! It's nothing like that." I let him gather himself. He leans in, covering half the distance of the stool between us,

"I've been having some troubles lately. You know, with Janice."

"Janice? What's wrong with her?" I ask, adding, "She's hot." And she is. I've always been envious of Dave, but when it comes to Janice even more so. She's one of the most blindingly attractive women I've ever seen and adores him beyond description. I'd kill to have that.

Shaking his head, he continues, "I know! Trust me, I know, and I love her to death – it's not like that either. Look, you're not like the other guys. I called you because I thought you would understand, man!" he says this all with a loud, gritty whisper, wanting desperately to get his point across without arousing suspicions. I keep listening, nodding intently. He breathes heavily before resuming. "We were fucking the other night – you know, really goin' at it, so I figured I'd try something new." I don't know if I'm supposed to be hearing this, but I can't stop or interrupt him so I just try not to get inappropriately aroused. "I grabbed her legs and pinned 'em back over her shoulders and she really started to make some noise. I told her to shut up and she apologized, but she kept makin' noise, so I stopped."

My elbow slips off the edge of the bar and I quickly grab my beer and chug to recover. It's number four tonight and though they've been spaced out I'm feeling a little fuzzy. My prurient interest prevails, "Go on, man. It's okay."

He shakes his head, chugs the rest of his beer, raises his hand to indicate he's ordering another, then proceeds with one of the most bizarre things I've ever heard. "When I stopped, she just kept apologizing, but she couldn't get the fucking smile off her face so I think she's laughin' at me. She told me she wasn't laughing at me, that it just felt really good, but I kept thinkin' she was makin' fun of me. She rolls over and she's facin' away from me and..." He puts his head down, disbelieving what he's about to say. "...then I looked at her. Ya know, I just... she was lyin' there, facin' away from me and she was all... sweaty..." I'm genuinely starting to get hard and I lean my hand on my hip to hide it, nodding like I could care less. "...and there's this little drop of sweat that goes down her cheek and into her ass crack and I couldn't help myself... I just— Please, man, you can't tell *anyone* this! Okay?!"

Dave looks at me angrily, pleadingly and I nod. "Yeah, man, no worries. I won't tell anyone. I swear on my father's grave," which I'm really saying to placate him so we can get onto the part I know I'm not supposed to hear.

"I took her from behind, man." YES! This is exactly what I wanted to hear but know I shouldn't approve of. Fuck. How do I react? I put on a stern face like I'm not enjoying it, but I'm there for him as a friend. Good work, Corwin! "And she starts making the same sounds again, only this time into the pillow so I don't stop her. I just stick my hand over her mouth and she grabs it to make it more tight, you know, so less sound gets out?" I nod excitedly, urging him on. "...until I'm about ready to blow and she starts practically screaming into the pillow. I can't stop and... and..." He can't finish.

"Hey, man, it's okay. You don't have to keep going. I know what you're talking about." I have no idea what he's talking about, but it sounds amazing. And wrong.

Dave looks up, hopeful, "You do?" I nod vigorously while

drinking and bang my teeth on the pint glass. "I knew you would, man. Well, we haven't done it since. We just keep avoiding eye contact. Man, what if they find out?"

"They?" I ask, knowing full well who he's talking about, "What if *who* finds out?"

"Don't be stupid, Cor. I'll get fucking deported, or worse. Look, I told you because, even though I don't know you all that well, you're safe. You never share anything, you're like a wall. Don't hose me now, man."

I relent, "I'm sorry, I know. I just don't think you should worry about it, dude. You trust Janice, right?" he nods while sipping at his beer. "Then you've got nothing to worry about. Plus, you know she's not gonna fuck anyone else with what's she's got at home now, right?" This pat answer is offensive even to me, but doesn't faze Dave at all. He just raises his eyebrows in agreement, knowing that regardless of the pleasure factor, she's just as guilty as he is if not more so.

The whole tawdry scenario is starting to run itself over and over in my head and I have to start talking about something before I get wood in the fucking bar, "Don't worry, man. Just don't let it happen again, right?"

Hopefully, he responds, "Yeah. Yeah, that's the way, isn't it?"

We toast, clinking glasses and proceed to discuss the state of the Bulls and Blackhawks, and what the White Sox are looking like for the upcoming season. But, I can't get my mind off what Dave has said and the image of Janice's naked back and ass, gleaming with sweat and cum writhing underneath me– er, him, is on constant loop in my head.

3

My last week at work went off without a hitch and I'm sitting in a windowless room on the tenth floor of the DoFA building on State Street at 8:00am on a Saturday morning. I stopped for coffee on Belmont before hopping the train as I wanted to stay awake for the indoctrination session. Although, I get the idea there is no danger of that. These people have ways of keeping you awake, you know?

Twenty minutes after I sit down – the interim chock full of paranoia – Gray enters and slaps a mobile PC on the table in front of me, saying, "Sign in, Hawley."

Deciding not to argue the name issue anymore, I begrudgingly open the slender machine and stare at it blankly. "Sign in?" I ask.

"Your palm print, please," he says, irked, and points at the screen. I clumsily mash my palm to the monitor. When I remove my palm, the imprint throbs orange for a few moments before making a bell-type sound and blinking green. It then goes completely black and barks at me, "Establish voice print!"

Gray mouths for me to say my name and I do. "Corwin

W. Hawley." The machine's husky, male voice barks, "Repeat for accuracy!" which I do. An interminable ten seconds pass while Gray and I make uncomfortable eye contact, then the machine continues, "Your profile has been created. Select a password!"

I was not prepared for this. What the hell am I supposed to use for a password? Plus, Gray will know it, so what's the point? He can sense my confusion over the situation and as the machine agitatedly repeats its order he rolls his eyes and points to the keyboard. Sheepishly, I smile and poise my fingers over the keyboard, quickly typing "bulls4ever" and sit back in my chair. The PC then snaps itself closed and shuts down. "Did I do something wrong?" I ask.

"Pansy ass," Gray mutters and takes the machine away from me. I have no idea what just happened, but I keep my yap shut. Gray walks over to the wall on the left and a hidden door opens revealing a panel in the wall where he stashes the mobile PC. Something glows underneath it and the giant wall in front of me lights up, a full-scale screen. "We will now begin your training," a manly voice booms from overhead and the table in front of me descends into the floor, pulling flush and disappearing into the tiles. It's now just me in my chair, Gray, and the wall screen. A droning voice begins:

"*You, Corwin W. Hawley, are about to begin an important mission to ensure the freedom of all Americans,*" my heart beams with pride, "*Over the next two years—*" a timeframe that was not disclosed to me, "*—you will undertake a challenging and dangerous infiltration into known, hostile territory.*" At the beginning of this next phrase, images start popping up with the monolog, "*Gaymerica* [image of a very fit man in leather holding a leash chained to another man, walking him like a dog] *is the bastard secessionist state occupying the Left coast of the American continent. They have initiated strong trading agreements* [image of cartoonish banditos with dark glasses, wads of cash, and bricks of narcotics] *with Hispanamerican enemies of America, and have been amassing an army* [more very fit men, this time in cutoff military dress – how did they get these photos?] *poised to assault America and all she stands for* [image of Lady Liberty with her red, white, and blue torch]."

Referring to the graphic, partial male nudity I lean toward Gray, "Am I supposed to be seeing this?"

"Shut up and listen, Hawley," he snaps and I return my attention to the wall.

"*In your time in Gaymerica you will be subjected to sights, sounds, and activities deemed unpleasant and immoral in the eyes of both America, and God our father,*" I automatically make the sign of the cross on my chest, "*…and your participation in these activities, while not required as part of your contract with the Department of Foreign Affairs, may be necessary to maintain your undercover appearance to those we seek to infiltrate…*"

Suddenly very uncomfortable, I blurt out, "What?!"

"Shhh!" Gray scolds and we continue listening.

"*…Homosexuals…*" I giggle almost uncontrollably every time this word is spoken and Gray becomes increasingly irritated with me. "*…are a blight on humanity. The urge to copulate within the same sex…*" okay, I giggle at that, too, though horrified, "*…is a communicable disease spread between their kind, and to children who attend state-funded schools…*" These images are innocuous enough – oh Christ (I make the sign of the cross), that's two dudes about to kiss! I'm really struggling with this material, "*...who then become the next generation of homosexuals. Gays, lesbians, bisexuals, and transgenders are abominations to God and America. While it is against God's wishes...*" my arm is starting to hurt from all the crossing, "*...to simply eliminate their kind from the face of the planet, Deuteronomy 23:20 dictates that we can enter into financial and trade agreements with other, non-Christian nations...*" I don't remember if that's what it really said, but it sounds familiar enough. I keep listening, continually wanting to cover my eyes, "*...for the betterment of the Christian nation. Still, the Gay nation poses a threat to our sovereignty that must be understood and controlled. Despite their inability to breed, it is estimated that over the last ten years, Gaymerica has increased by more than ten percent in population. We believe they are doing this through unnatural, chemical practices which are also deemed abominable in the eyes of our Lord,*" Really! My arm's fucking tired! "*They are raising gay children, gay teachers, and gay pets...*"

"My God!" That one was my fault. Ow.

"*...There is no limit to their debauchery, heathenism, gluttony...*" the images here are too horrific to tell and I'm really squirming in my seat, "*...and bestiality...*" at this, I almost vomit, "*Homosexuals will stop at nothing to convert the rest of the world to their Gay agenda, and we have been called on by God to stop them. You, Corwin W. Hawley, have been selected to represent America, God, and the very ideals of freedom by making a supreme sacrifice to enter into a life of filth, disease, and Sodomy...*" I knew this, it just really sucks to hear it out loud like that, "*...and you should know that your sacrifice will not go unnoticed by your sovereign government. Our hats are tipped to you. Welcome, Corwin, to the Department of Foreign Affairs!*"

I'm stunned. Never before have I even seen graphic images, let alone in such a barrage as this. Not even in my fantasies (except about Janice) do I imagine women in the way that men were depicted with each other. And, to be clear, some very mannish women, but I'm sure that will be explained. Gray taps a blank spot on the wall and the overhead lights come back up. My expression must be well known to him since he's in no way alarmed by my alarm.

"You've got questions, Corwin. We've got answers. For now, you need to take in the information as best you can, and let the rest wash over you. These images you're seeing now? You will see nothing *but* these images once you enter Gaymerica. We limit travel there under medical quarantine regulations, but those who do visit come back changed. Altered, emotionally and mentally by what they've seen. They have only visited for days or weeks at a time, some less. You will be there, providing reconnaissance for upwards of two years, barring incident."

I interrupt, "What kind of *incident?*"

Gray puts his hand firmly on my shoulder, "Please pay attention Corwin. We have only a week to train you and you must be fully prepared. Trust us when we tell you that if an incident occurs, your safety and the extraction of your physical person from said incident is our foremost priority. We cannot, however, guarantee your mental or emotional sanctity. You will be a changed man, Corwin. After this moment, you cannot go back."

I'm supposed to make a decision now. What am I doing? Am I crazy? I'm signing up to be a homosexual guinea pig for the service of my country, regardless of the lasting effects it will have on me. And I haven't hesitated yet. Am I so bored with my life that I have to do something inhumanely drastic to liven it up? Am I really willing to sacrifice everything I am and everything I stand for? Hello? I could really use a dissenting opinion right about now.

But really, what do I have to lose? I'm nothing. I do nothing and no one. I haven't had sex in almost two years because I can't fathom maintaining a relationship with anyone. I hate my job, and I hate me. This mission will give me purpose. It will give me status. And so what if I can't return to society here as a normal person? I'll be remembered as one who sacrificed for the good of God and America. Perhaps a special endowment will be given to my mother in my honor if I die. As I exist right now, what greater gift do I have to offer? I may be pathetic but I'm not as pathetic as the people I seek to infiltrate and *that* has given me purpose. *That* is why I haven't hesitated. Fine. I'm ready for this.

"Yeah. I'll do it."

Gray exhales and pats my shoulder, "Good! I was worried about ya for a moment there, Corwin."

***

It's two days into the indoctrination and training and I'm already becoming numb to the gay images. The hateful, loud colors of clothing, the lisping accents, the groomed house pets; they all barely affect me now. While I've been viewing the swishy walk and lispy talk I've been instructed not to engage in either activity while here in America or upon arrival in Gaymerica. Gray indicated that they are familiar with deported gays and that we are completely unaccustomed to their ways. If I were to act "gay" upon arrival, I'd be found out instantly. I *really* like this part of the plan.

Among the myriad interesting facts I learned about Gaymerica is that no one there calls it that. "Their charter with the United Nations says 'Gaymerica.' We know – we filed it for them," Gray tells me, "But since then, they've updated their name to something much less accurate – The Western States Republic. Clearly, the name is referential to their previous status as Western states of the United States of America, but it doesn't aptly reference what the nation truly *is*."

The whole thing seems odd and even ridiculous to me as I realize that the abrupt change in how to regard the nation may give me some difficulty. Then again, much of the information imparted in the training results in difficulty, so I try to take it in stride.

I'm allowed out of the compound for lunches to mingle with normal humanity so that I'm not completely cut off from the real world. Today, I make my way to the Wal-Mart boutique luncheonette across State Street. As I exit the building I watch an SGOC police cruiser on the other side of the intersection pull up quietly and two uniformed officers step out. They walk up behind a man in blue jeans and a light gray coat carrying a grocery bag. I don't hear the name they call him, but I do hear them say to come with them. He's being arrested for something, though it's not immediately clear as to what. He's resisting. Why is he resisting?! Before I can think, they tackle him and stun him with the end of their night sticks. We're all stopped, staring at the man, me and twenty or so other lunchtime pedestrians. The officers pick him up by his arms and say something I can't quite make out.

Suddenly, a bystander reaches into the man's grocery bag, pulls out a six-pack of eggs and flings them while screaming, "Faggot! You fucking queer!"

The crowd forms an impromptu mob and begins shouting slurs and threats. The police hold up their arms to protect themselves, but not the man. They fling him unceremoniously into the back seat of the cruiser and drive off. By now, the crowd is chanting "Fag-free America! Fag-free America!" a chant I've all too often engaged in myself. This time, my voice is caught and won't emit sound. I'm frozen in space and time. I can never come back.

The crowd lights his grocery bag on fire, the only available effigy, and continue their chant as they drift away (prompted by two remaining SGOC cops on foot patrol) until it eventually dies off. A cold, January breeze shudders down my neck into my spine and I finally cross the street for lunch. I order a Panini and Coke and sit down at a booth, not caring that I'm usurping a whole table in the middle of the lunch rush. Not that it matters. Even at lunchtime an open seat is easy to find in this town. Hunger won't come, and I can't urge myself to pick the sandwich up anyway. My hands won't stop shaking. I pretend it's due to a lack of nourishment and sugar so I crack open the can of Coke, chugging until my nose fizzes with carbonation and slam it down on the table. I want to get out. I feel stifled and hot, my skin crawling beneath my clothes.

Heartbeats reverberate and rattle in my skull so loudly I almost can't hear anything else. Why won't it stop? Why am I so upset by this?

The man got what he deserved and he'll get what he deserves when he's deported… or the ever-present realization of the phrase, "or worse." But for some reason that phrase isn't an issue for me right now. Somewhere in my gut, something is grinding at me immediately, incessantly, about what *just* happened. Not what's to come. Bile backs up into my throat and I begin to cough uncontrollably, muffling it so as not to bother the other patrons. I grab the sandwich and throw it into the garbage, making a quick exit with my Coke out onto the sidewalk on West Madison and stop in front of the abandoned old Carson Pirie Scott retail store. No one even knows what it used to be and most of these old stores just sit vacant now, but my brain is whirling with what it must have been. Something. Anything to get my mind off the issue at hand.

What were these places? This, Sears, Macy's, and a slew of others all sit dormant, boarded up. Were they Socialist propagandists? Were they run by the Socialist state that preceded the conglomerate, capitalist paradise we live in today? I mean, I know *my* life isn't anything to celebrate, but it would have been worse had we not been saved. These people were leeching off the system somehow and they rightly dissolved. If nothing else, competition proved the superior economic model.

And here I am, unable to breathe. The cold air helps, but my mind is still racing. I glance up and down the street, seeing a few, hard-working Americans hustling from place to place, bracing against the cold and girding up for the second half of their work day. SGOC cops stroll the sidewalks and I can see three from where I'm at. One nods at the other as if to say, "Hello" but it could just as easily mean something else. One is coming my way and looks at me after he finishes nodding to the other. I can't keep myself from shaking and pray I can convince him it's from the cold. Nervously, I tug at the zipper on my jacket, pretending I'm having trouble pulling it up. But, I'm so hot that I go so far as to say, "Fuck it!" to suggest that it's broken and will go no further. As we pass each other, the cop doesn't nod so much as lift his chin in an acknowledging fashion. In counter pose, I bow my head slightly and trudge back toward the DoFA building.

My thoughts whirl from the cop to the graphic images of my training, the previous fears of being followed, Chad's recrimination of me, Ida, my mother, my father, and land back on the pathetic grocery shopper who was just egged and jailed. There's no way for me to come back from Gaymerica into the life I lead now and certainly not a better one. That man and I will share a common fate. Mine by choice, but does that make it better? We're still both exiled to life in a third-world country where the rest of the world hates us. But maybe someday that country won't exist anymore and we can all be enlightened and loved by God. My elbow has healed for the most part, so that crossing didn't hurt.

May God guide my actions. And may God forgive me for the ones I take unbidden.

***

Tomorrow I depart for San Francisco and I'm trying to focus. Today is a lighter day than the rest as my training now consists mostly of what's called "pop culture" references. Since we cut ties with Gaymerica in 2018, Gray admits the material may be dated. However, we are in agreement that simple minds do not progress as quickly as ours and the likelihood of my knowledge being completely outdated is slim, so the info should still be useful. I'm grateful for that as the information I'm already privy to is quite enough for the moment.

Over the past week I've learned all sorts of things the average citizen has never known. I learned the organizational leadership of the socialist regime, who our counterparts are, and the people I'm supposed to report on via any means necessary. I learned how to dance, how to spot a nightclub where gays get drunk to excess and will blab their plans to anyone they meet. And, I learned four new sexual positions I'm pretty sure only me and a handful of people at DoFA have ever seen, and that's on top of the two I learned from Dave and the one I learned from Ida (though we never engaged in, blessedly). In total, I am an expert on now eight sexual positions. I've also been provided brain-searing images of how those positions can be used and I'm confident in saying I will use precisely *none* of them while on this mission. I will find strength with God to ensure this is the case.

The trickier aspect to all this training has not been the information, but rather the reality that I must pretend that the information doesn't exist in my mind. No one who's grown up in America knows these things and it would be too convenient for a new member of the Gay society to be so well-versed in their culture. However, without it, I stand no chance of being able to infiltrate and get the required information: the agenda.

This agenda thing has been a somewhat complex concept for me. As DoFA doesn't seem to know exactly what it is, the concept escapes me as well. Supposedly, the gays have some kind of desire to rule the world. To what end, I have no idea, but in the process they seek to turn as many people gay as possible. Again, we seem stymied as to how other than by transmitting the disease via contact. I am confused by this since, as there has been a lack of invasions in my lifetime, they don't seem to be too focused on touching any of us. Whatever the agenda is, that is my ultimate goal, and just coming right out and asking for it is not an option.

These strands must remain in my head simultaneously, all while my senses are assaulted by the vast cultural differences that will likely shake my being to its very core. Sex, drugs, lasciviousness (a new word for me), loud heathen music, and terribly groomed pets. A cavalcade of imagery constantly flashes through my brain now. My body reacts as it always has – with revulsion – but my brain seems to be numbing to an extent, allowing the imagery to remain unimpeded by my better morals.

I'm sitting in front of the viewing wall, watching some sort of cooking show where a fruity man is teaching me how to bake a cake in a microwave when Gray walks in. He pushes a blank spot on the wall and a chair ascends from the floor. I've begun to ignore all the trickery in this room and expect just about anything to happen. Nothing can shock me now.

Gray speaks, "You've come a long way, Corwin. I want

you to know I'm proud of you."

His tone makes me uncomfortable in a way I can't quite describe, but I smile and thank him, "Oh, it's the training. I couldn't have done it without you and DoFA," I've started pronouncing the acronym now, too.

"You didn't have a father, did you?"

I shrug, nonplused, "I did, up until I was seven. He's dead now, though."

Gray nods. I finish my snack. After an awkward silence, he continues, "Do you know why your father is dead?"

"He was aiding the fags from what my mother told me. Siphoning funds for them or some such thing." I couldn't stomach the thought so I never bothered to ask. Why's he asking me now?

"I know that's the official story. It was easier to keep you and your mother around if he were just a traitor." Now Gray is concerning me a bit. Had my father done something worse? Does this man really know? He takes a breath and adds, "It's time you knew the truth about your father, Corwin. Your father was gay."

My first instinct is to drop Gray like a sack of potatoes and given his advanced years I'm pretty sure I could do it. My mind is slowed by this new information, though and the reality that something in this room could kill me without warning impedes the impulse. "Gay?" I ask angrily, "How fucking dare you! This is my *family* you're disgracing here, pal!"

My body moves to stand up, but Gray manages to snap his arm up and pinch the nerve in my neck until I sit down. Spry old fucker.

"Calm down, now, Corwin," He leans in and whispers to me, "These people don't care about your family, but *I* do. Your father was still your father no matter how perverse he may have been. Your knowledge of that may save you while you're there. Don't ever forget that, do you understand?"

I shake my head inside, but the pain in my neck causes me to meekly reply, "Yes."

Gray gets up and exits the room, leaving me with my training for the rest of the day wondering two things. What the fuck actually happened to my father, and who is that plastic old broad with the black hair asking if I believe in love?

4

My first flight in an airplane since the family trip to New York when I was six has left me nauseated and shaken. Twenty minutes from the border and I can already feel my stomach turning over. The flight itself has been fine, but the obese woman next to me (who happens to be taking up much of her seat and some of mine) and the overly friendly male flight attendant are unsettling. He keeps glancing down at my lap before he turns away, "Do you need another drink?" "No, I'm fine," Glance. Turn and go to the next row. Why is he doing that?

Then I realize I'm sitting with my hands poised protectively over my business and try to shake it off. Don't draw attention to it, Corwin! My training is somewhere out the window with my nerves. I'll be an expatriate in twenty– now nineteen minutes and all I can think about is hiding my privates. Focus. I should go over my history lessons.

Gaymerica seceded from the former United States in 2018, a year after my father was put to death for treason. Taking all of Oregon and California, the gays also obtained parts of Washington and Idaho, and most of Nevada. The part of Nevada they didn't take was gifted them as it contained the nuclear waste disposal site of Yucca Mountain. As far as the American government was concerned, they could have their "clean" power and all mutate into deathly blobs. I wholly concur with this methodology. It seems that hasn't taken place just yet, but these things take time and patience and, as the Lord says (there's very little room to cross myself next to this window), good things come to those who wait.

In 2021 after fierce fighting and a seeming inability to remove the gays – they kept spawning like rabbits – the greater metropolitan area of Miami was also ceded to Gaymerica, giving them their first protectorate on their way to establishing an empire. The Florida Keys remain a neutral zone, entrance to which is closely guarded by security details from both nations.

By 2026 a wall had been erected around Miami and along the border with Gaymerica proper. While most of the border with the bastard secessionists was protected naturally by the Reagan (then Rocky) Mountains, a laser-sighting system was set up to enhance it. This system has caught over fifteen-thousand border jumpers and will likely catch thousands more. Gays cross over hoping to infiltrate our culture and bask in our freedoms. And yet, here I am walking right through their front door, ready to take them completely by surprise.

Gaymerica, or rather the Western States Republic, looks like this:

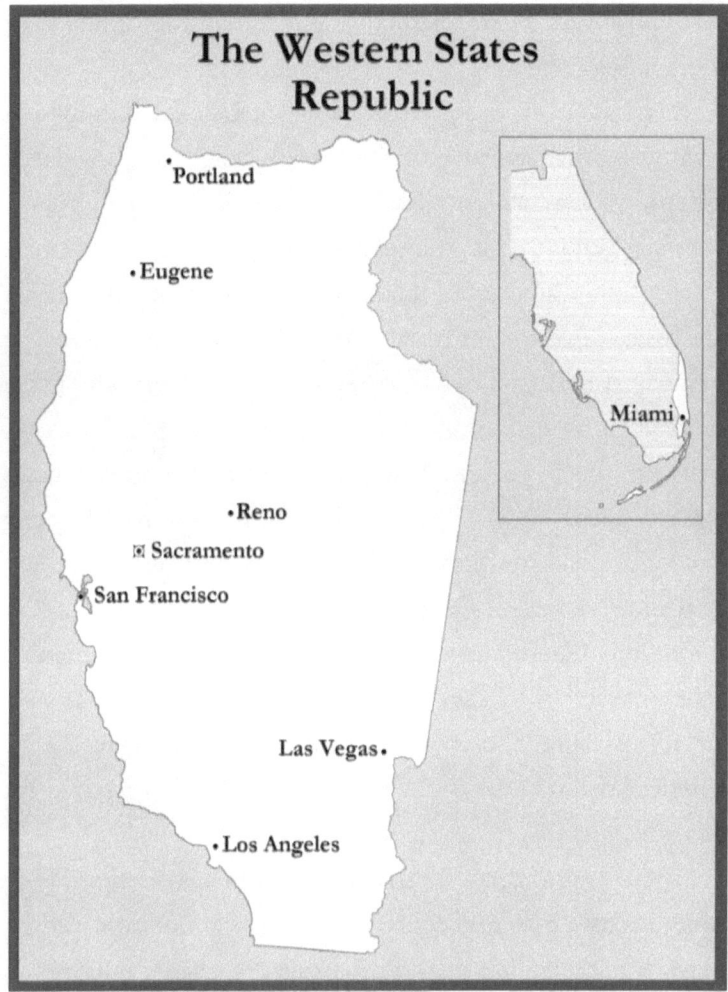

America looks mostly like it did in the past, minus Alaska and Hawaii which were lost to Canada and China respectively due to debt issues and a brief conflict over fishing rights.

I don't recall exactly when it happened as it's been a long time since I took an American history class, but at some point the capital was moved from Philadelphia to Maryland and was called Washington D.C. The new government of America took the opportunity when restructuring to move the capital back where it belonged.

In addition to losing Alaska and Hawaii, the Republic of Texas also seceded but only from an oversight and legislative standpoint. Travelling to Texas is much like travelling to any other state and, despite the separation, they do still participate in a substantial amount of federal funding. The capital of Texas was then also transplanted from the drunken center of debauchery in Austin to the coastal city of Houston. This event I actually recall as there were riots and fires in Austin for weeks until both the Texan and American militaries had to intervene. The city barely exists now and is mostly used for shooting action films and the occasional dystopian mini-series.

Ten more minutes to the end of my freedom.

In 2031 Gaymerica established their first military training facility. Exactly why they need a military isn't known for sure, but it's presumed they began training for an invasion of America. We are ever at the ready and still fully prepared for the onslaught.

There are no open or free elections in Gaymerica. While we return to the polls every two years to elect our holy leaders, they are ruled endlessly by what's called a Queen Supreme, a woman of unspeakable wrath and envy. Her itchy finger poised over their nuclear arsenal is the only impediment to our plans to overrun and annihilate them. This form of constant check-mate is a shadow over our country and our freedoms, and we will never be fully free until we are delivered from the threat of her tyranny. My heart swells at the pride of undertaking a part in this task.

The pilot comes over the speaker and my stomach knots in fear, "Ladies and Gentlemen, we are now crossing the border into the Western States Republic. To the right and left of the plane you can see the Reagan, or Rocky Mountains depending on your nation of origin. We will be landing in San Francisco in about ninety minutes and the co-pilot and I will inform you when it's time to buckle up. Thank you, and enjoy the rest of your flight."

Gray told me that on some flights, the cabin becomes a den of drunken debauchery as soon as the border is breeched. I am prepared for this terrible event, but nothing happens. Five. Ten minutes go by and when I realize it's not going to happen, I relax and rest back into my seat. DoFA managed to get me a safe flight, and for this I am truly grateful. Until the woman starts snoring and rests her head on my shoulder.

***

We initially come up on San Francisco from the South, the plane banking sharply to curl around and approach the airport from the North. Something about wind conditions and flight patterns I don't understand is blathered over the speaker by the far less articulate co-pilot and I fail to pay attention. The view is astounding and despite my gut-wrenching fear of heights, I can't look away from the window. A city similar in size to Chicago with vast bridges leading to and away from it rests on the South side of a massive inlet. The bay beyond is protected by a gigantic red, steel bridge with trains trekking back and forth across it while we fly over. There are no cars on the bridge and I wonder where they've gone.

The view goes away, though and my stomach turns again when the plane rights itself to approach for landing. The view now consists solely of blue sky and the hills around the peninsula. Having not flown in almost thirty-one years, I'm beyond apprehensive since I've been told almost all plane crashes (save those caused by gay terrorists) occur on landing and takeoff.

Despite my fears, the flight lands without incident and before I'm psychologically prepared, I am vomited out into the gate at San Francisco International Airport. The name itself is blasphemous and heathen. All airports are required by the American government to be named after saints. This was an agreement between the Christians and the Catholics when America became a strictly Christian nation. The Catholics were given the cathedrals and airports – the Christians got the rest. Chicago's airport for instance is named Saint O'Hara of the Ascension International Airport, though the three letter call sign is still ORD and I've never known what the letters stand for.

We are at the International Terminal and to exit the airport must be searched – inside and out – before we are allowed to enter the country. This will be my first real test. My fellow international travelers and I are corralled into a large room in which massive "carousels" (I'd always known them as conveyors, but it's the little differences I'll need to get used to) spin our luggage around until we can squeeze through the sea of humanity to grab them. With my carryon in hand, I push my way to the front and await my suitcase, a smart, zipper-bound affair with wheels on the bottom so I can walk long distances without having to carry it. Assuming American technology far exceeds that of the infidels, I stand smiling until I realize almost all the luggage on this carousel looks exactly the same. Having not been prepared for this I am thankful Gray tied a red, white, and blue ribbon on my zippers both to bind them shut and make it easier for me to identify. I didn't realize what he was doing at the time, but I suppose it's impossible to spend a mere week preparing me for *everything* that will take place on this journey.

Forty minutes after I first push my way to the edge of the carousel, the crowd has thinned, I'm fully irritated, and my luggage finally glides toward me. Heaving a breath of relief, I grab it, extend the handle, and depart for the security checkpoint. Now comes the next challenge. I arrive at the checkpoint, consisting of ten turnstiles manned by men and women to my surprise (how they were able to procure security jobs is something of a mystery to me) in sharp, official-looking uniforms. Since most of the other passengers received their luggage before me, the line is short and I'm able to reach the center turnstile – sure to use one operated by a man – in only a few minutes. There is an open turnstile controlled by a woman but I avoid her eye contact and proceed to the one next to hers.

"Passport, please," the man says, using polite phrasing but not in a polite tone. I retrieve my passport consisting of my fully fabricated identity – the only thing that hasn't changed is my name – and hand it to the man. He looks up at me suspiciously, then over to the woman I've shunned. They exchange a glance and I swear I see her nearly smile about something but it all happens so fast I'm not able to follow it before he unleashes another irritated order, "Are you here on business or pleasure Mr. Hawley?"

Remember the training, Corwin. Remember the training, "I am here seeking political amnesty," Good job!

The woman again turns her attention to me and I shoot her a glance to request privacy. She dutifully averts her gaze. He nearly shakes his head but doesn't and instead scans my passport, entering a series of keys on the mysterious console next to the turnstile. For the first time, I divert my focus and take in the gadget the man is working on. Much like the mobile PC Gray used to register me with DoFA, there are no visible buttons or keys, just a pad where information can be entered depending on what the screen looks like. This isn't new. Hell, my phone can do that. What's fascinating is that there is actually nothing viewable on the screen. How does he know where to press? How do I know he's doing it right? How do I know what he's doing at all? I half expect him to accost me for peeking but as there's nothing to peek at, perhaps he doesn't see the need.

He returns my passport to me and though he's touched it with no device or stamp, an image has been emblazoned into the first empty page of the visa section. Flatly, he recites, "Congratulations, Mr. Hawley, you've been admitted on a thirty-day visa to apply for amnesty. If, at the end of the thirty-day visa you have not applied for amnesty, you will be asked to return to your nation of origin, or apply for an extension. Please note that some fees may apply for an extended visa.

Welcome to San Francisco and the Western States Republic."

Confused, I stare at him blankly. He adds, "You may enter now, sir." I don't move. The woman sees this and chimes in, motioning to the turnstile which I finally notice isn't a genuine metal turnstile at all but a holographic, laser-sighted barrier much like the border walls I'd learned about. Uncomfortably, I rush through it fearing it will burn or shock me somehow. There is no sensation, however, and I'm on the other side in an instant.

"Enjoy your stay here, sir," the man jabs, rolling his eyes and turning to the next person in line.

I am now thoroughly confused. Gray said there would be an interrogation and possibly an overnight detention. At the least would be the search – inside and out as I was told. I try to get his attention, "Uh, sir? I don't understand what I'm to do next."

Sighing audibly, he rotates to face me, "What?"

"Now? What do I do now? Where do I go for the questions?" Is that how it was worded? My brain is failing me.

He squints at me and shakes his head as if to rattle something loose, "Huh?"

I put my carry on down and start over, "Aren't I supposed to report somewhere? Or, talk to someone?"

Shrugging, he puts his hands up. "I guess if you want to you could do that now, but you have thirty days. Go, see the sites first, I suppose."

"No, now!" say, becoming more flustered by the moment, "I was informed there would be some sort of debriefing and a…" I lean in, "…search, if you understand?"

He's terribly irritated and says, "That's already been done, you're free to go now." He then returns to his station, adding to himself, "Honestly, where do these people come from?"

The woman then touches my shoulder to get my attention. I really don't understand why a woman would have such an official position, but as I'm confused and don't have the intellectual wherewithal to combat the concept at that moment I allow her to address me, "The search is virtual, sir. It happens when you walk through the turnstile. Since you didn't set off any alarms, you're free to go. Head that way," she says pointing behind me. I follow her gaze, "…to the main terminal and down the stairs to the arrival area when you see the sign that says 'Pick-Ups,' okay?"

While I wouldn't normally take a woman seriously in this official capacity, she is more friendly than the man and certainly more informative. I nod my thanks and proceed through the terminal. Despite warnings to the contrary, the SFO terminal looks mostly like an airport terminal ought to. There is security everywhere, shops to purchase food and disposable goods, and all means of people. One major difference I notice, though are the women. Not that they look any different *as* women, but there are many more of them than there were in the business and travel districts of America and they are dressed far less appropriately. Many are wearing jackets with shirts underneath plunging well below the neckline and even more are wearing pants.

Again, these are all things I must adjust for. I realize I'm not going to understand everything I see or hear, and so I will come to treat the presence and dress of the women here as if it were an everyday occurrence. Because, well, from now on it will be. Actually, as I look at that woman by the magazine rack with the very tight jeans, the fitted v-neck t-shirt and satchel (the strap cleverly positioned between her supple breasts) I'm thinking I shouldn't have too much trouble getting used to—

"Can I help you?" she turns and asks me in a sharp tone.

Stunned, I reply, "Huh?"

She smiles bemusedly, lowering the magazine she's perusing and continues in the same tone, "You wanna ask me something? You're uh, staring."

Shit. She's right, I have been staring. I'll need to watch out for that.

"Hello, you need something, pal?" she asks, becoming more irritated.

Before I can respond, the vendor levels his own annoyance at her, "Hey lady, you gonna read the whole thing, or you gonna buy it?" His accent doesn't sound Hispanamerican, but his skin is somewhat darker than mine and since I can't place it, I assume he has some form of ethnicity and pay him little mind.

Still looking at me expectantly, the woman shakes her head, then says to the vendor, "This thing sucks anyway." Slamming the magazine back onto the rack, she brushes past me and through the concourse to the right of the International terminal I've just exited.

Deciding to start digging early, I walk up to the vendor, who is shaking his head, and start the small talk, "She's uh, traveling light, huh?"

The man shrugs, opening a box of magazines and replies,

"She's a day-tripper from L.A. I see her in here all the time on business, but maybe she never stays overnight – no need for luggage, I guess."

Confused, I ask, "On business?"

"Yeah," he says, still focused on his box of magazines. He can sense I'm staring at him now and looks up, "So? You know her or somethin'?"

The man is much older than me, maybe twenty years or so, and his accent is throwing me. Suddenly, I recall where I've heard it before. It sounds something like how the out-of-town associates of Rupert's. They're from New York and New Jersey as I recall. Perhaps this man was deported from there at some point. My curiosity heightens as I realize there are probably stories like that all over this country.

Sensing his growing annoyance, I answer, "No, just curious. Hey, I'm new here," He rolls his eyes and nods. "And, I'd like to get more acquainted. Do you have anything that might prove good reading material for that?" I'm leaning in, trying to be casual.

He locks eyes with me for a moment with a "bullshit" look on his face. Normally, I would avert my eyes and just leave, but I'm on a mission here, and if I run at every sign of adversity I'll never get anything done.

"Right," he says, adding, "Look, the only things in print in this country are periodicals. Newspapers, books, anything else you wanna buy new goes on your mobile instrument – now, I can hook you up with that, if you want. There's a browser over there," he's pointing to a tiny station near the entrance to the stand that looks like an ATM. "Otherwise, *all* this stuff is for travelers. Whatcha here to do?"

He's right. I didn't notice it before, but there are no normal magazines in this place. Instead, these appear to be trade publications and the like. I ignore him and walk over to the rack the woman was at and pick up the publication she'd been perusing. "Graphics Today" is the name of the magazine and on the cover is a photograph of a woman in slacks, a less than conservative top, and an up do squatting down towards the floor where the camera is at. She's smiling suggestively and while one hand is positioned on her knee, the other appears to be playing with a black, plastic, donut-shaped device I don't immediately recognize. To the right of her head in the blank space, it reads, *"Bridget Merriman is the queen of Interactive Holographics* (Ah, that's a holographic projector! I've heard of these but never seen one). *Read how she turned a fledgling imaging business into the nation's leading engineering firm,"* then below that in smaller print, *"Plus: This Quarter's China Projections."*

Holy shit! Right here in the airport, they sell material about Gaymerica's international relations. Maybe I won't have to be here two years if everything's this easy to find. I start to drift away and the man barks at me, "Hey, pal, you gotta pay for that!"

"Right! Sorry, I don't know what I was thinking." I hurry back to the counter, dig in my trousers for my wallet, and ask, "So, this says quarterly projections. Is there anything more current?"

Stunned, he stares at me momentarily and says, "No one prints monthly or weekly anymore buddy. Where have *you* been? Look, if you want something more current, just sub-scribe on your mobile. Now, gimme your hand." He reaches over the counter and grabs my wrist. I resist feebly, realizing he's moving my hand toward the tiny screen on the counter and panic overtakes me. Why is he doing this? He'll have my identity on his system! But, if I fight him I'll make a scene. I'm trapped and out of indecision inadvertently allow him to press my thumb to the screen. It instantly glows orange. What does that mean? Releasing my hand, he then takes the publication and waves it over the same spot, then hands it back to me. Finally, he asks, "Anything else?"

I'm too disoriented to shop any further and the encounter has left me overheated so I shake my head and exit quickly. He shouts after me, "Have a nice day..." then something less audible I can't discern but I keep going.

Vaguely remembering the security woman's instructions, I proceed to the end of the terminal. There, I see another security checkpoint for non-international travelers entering the usual concourses. It appears just as smooth and seamless as the international one that baffled me so much. No one is being patted down or detained. No one is arguing or stopping, just passing through and showing their mobile devices to the workers at the checkpoint. Aside from the presence of the security personnel, this has all the calmness and serenity of communion at church.

I move along to the "Pick-Ups" sign and take the escalator to the lower level. As the exterior comes into view I'm stunned by what I see. Beyond the glass doors is a train – like the El in that it's a train, unlike it in every other way – and various other vehicles quietly parked, waiting for passengers. Occasionally, one goes by, and for the most part the entire picture is moving, but quiet. At first, I assume it's because the doors are closed. The noise outside Saint O'Hara is deafening – trucks, cars, buses, and plenty of security personnel shuffling people along.

When the doors open, the cause of my curiosity is confirmed. There is almost no sound. Sure, there's the sound of people coming and going, and the sound of tires on pavement and wheels on rails, but I can't hear a single engine – just the occasional jet wash overhead. A car pulls up in front of where I'm standing. It's painted bright yellow and has "Speedy Rickshaw" inked in neat letters across the front door. The vehicle is tiny and silent. There are four doors, but the back ones are smaller than the front and behind that only a hatchback and meager trunk space. The driver lowers the window on the passenger side and shouts at me, "Where you off to, mister? Need a ride?" She is dressed in a t-shirt and jeans with a light jacket and a chauffeur's hat and is leaning her right arm on the passenger seat so she can see me. How are so many women in the workforce? I suppose this particular woman being in the work force makes some sense as she's technically doing a service job.

"Uh, yeah. I need to head to the Estate Hotel on Dolores and Nineteenth – is there room in that trunk for this suitcase?" I interrupt myself genuinely concerned about the petite nature of this vehicle.

She looks down at my suitcase, then back at me, "If you put the carryon in the backseat, sure. You might want to sit up front, though. More leg room."

This whole situation sounds troublesome. First, it's a woman driver. Second, she wants me to sit up front, and third, where's the frickin' engine? I do as instructed when the hatch opens and place the suitcase in the trunk. The hatch closes itself, the back door opens for me to put the carryon down, and I finally situate myself in the front passenger seat.

"Buckle up," she orders, and I look around for the straps only to realize they're in front of me. I reach for them and she giggles, "I'm just fuckin' with ya." She then pushes a button on the dash and the seatbelts automatically strap me in.

The vehicle takes off silently. We roll past the giant glass exterior of the terminal on one side and the train on the other before curving left and away from the airport. A quick turn and we're going North on Highway 101. It's cloudy out, but even with the overcast skies I can tell this place is terribly clean. The highway is neat and manicured with easily viewable lines and signage. A train glides past us down the middle of the highway, then rolls up to an overpass and stops to load and unload passengers as we overtake it again.

Once I've settled a bit, I take stock of the vehicle from the inside. Just now I notice the dash has no buttons or knobs on it. It's almost completely blank save for a touch screen in the center, a touch screen in front of me, and the wheel and controls on her side. Confused about how it all works I turn my attention back to the road.

There are very few other cars on the road, which is probably for the best as there are only two lanes either direction. However, there are two sets of rail lines in the median – two North and two South – with enough traffic on them to accommodate for the passengers who are clearly not driving.

A couple miles later and we pass over a long bridge that cuts off a large inlet. I look past the driver to the far side of the inlet and see a park, a rail line pulling up, and hills in the distance. On the other side of the inlet, things begin to get more industrial. When land emerges to the right of the vehicle again, the first thing I see is a rundown old stadium, overgrown with vines. There is no parking around it, just grass, vegetation, and beaches leading up to the bay. The driver notices where my attention is drawn and speaks up.

"That's the old Candlestick Park – the stadium."

"Oh yeah?"

"Yep. They removed all the seats, planted some grass and removed the whole East side of it. We only use it for concerts and conventions now."

I'm still staring at the complex as we go by and ask, "But where does everyone park?"

"Park? Man, only cabbies drive cars nowadays. Where are you from anyway?"

Still staring out the window I mumble, "Chicago."

All but silenced by my response, she mutters, "Oh." Several uncomfortable moments pass and the stadium curls off behind a hill before she says anything else. And, she does, "You here on business or uh… pleasure, then?"

"Why does everyone keep asking that?"

"Everyone?"

"Well, you and the security guy, yeah."

"Well, the security *guy* asked it because it's his job. *I* asked it because, I guess, it's part of my job, too—"

I interrupt her quickly, "It is? Do you work for the state or something?" I realize only after I've asked this that it sounded way more panicked than I intended.

"Slow down, there, man. I'm not interrogating you. It's part of my job because I'm a cabbie. That's what we do – we try to make you feel welcome. You don't have to answer, though, if you don't want to."

I'm annoyed with this woman. Why the need to talk? I'm clearly disoriented and out of my natural surroundings. It would be nice to just—

"We could talk about other things too if you want. Do you like baseball?"

I shrug. "I suppose."

"How many games did you go to last year?"

"None. I just watch 'em on TV. Besides, it's basketball season anyway."

She nods approvingly, "Oh, so I bet you're quite the Bulls fan, huh?"

Why does she know about this? I answer, "Yeah, I guess. Do you watch the Bulls?"

She buzzes her lips in an emphatic negative, "Hey, I have enough trouble keeping up with the teams in *this* country. Nah, my old man was from Chicago and he used to rave about how when he was a kid the Bulls won practically every championship they played in – the golden years, he called it…"

I'm comfortable enough with this conversation and allow it to continue. As we roll along, the scenery becomes more and more dense with architectural smatterings of at least a dozen eras painting the hillsides and neighborhoods. Brand new steel and glass structures coexist alongside ancient brick buildings much like the one I live... *lived* in in Chicago. The buildings aren't all skyscrapers, but it's clear this area was built up for population consolidation. Gray and the training taught me about how people are herded into dense metropolitan areas for easier social control. People don't have room to breathe or think and will swallow whatever you throw at them, and this is clearly a highly dense area. All of these sheep being processed and brainwashed to bend to the will of the state.

The car makes a sweeping turn to the West and eventually exits onto a broad boulevard bisected by yet another rail line. On either side are a number of taxis and even more buses, but what's most shocking is the number of pedestrians. There are people *everywhere*, walking in the fifty-five-degree chill. They're interacting, milling from one shop or business to another and not a single individual-owned car in sight.

"Where are all the cars?" I ask.

"I told you before, man, no one owns cars anymore. You have to get a special license and even then, it's only so you can be a cab driver. Like me," she adds, grinning from ear to ear.

"You like it?"

"Man, I *love* it! I'm always drivin' somewhere new or different. I've lived in this city for twenty years and I still haven't seen everything. I'll drive a fare to some club or restaurant and think, 'You know? I should check that place out.' I get off my shift, hop the bus or the train and I'm seein' something new. I'd *never* know that stuff if I didn't do this job."

I latch on to one particular piece of information, "Wait,

you take the bus? Why not just drive your cab?"

"Drive? Hey, it's fun and I'll do it for work, but there's nowhere to park these things anymore 'cept the company garage."

"Not the state garage?"

"What?" she looks at me like I'm from another planet, "I don't work for the state at all. I'm a private contractor. I pay to rent this thing from the company that owns it."

"But you don't own it yourself?"

"Listen, my life is complex enough as it is. I don't need maintenance and repair on something like this. Besides, the thought never crossed my mind. You can get around fine without one. The only people that own vehicles of any kind these days are farmers. Even then, they're only used for transporting food or growin' it. Or, other things."

At this, I let her be and don't push further. Does the state really tell these people they can't own cars? I can't get the thought out of my head about how happy this woman is to be told she can't do something. She's brainwashed to be genuinely happy at her lack of freedoms – it's disgusting.

The ride ends when we reach the hotel and she says, "Stick your thumbprint on the dash and we're all good. Although, we do accept tips," she adds, smiling politely.

I look, bewildered at the dash and ask, "How do I do that?"

"Just press your thumb for payment, the option will come up."

I do and it does. I tip her fifteen percent so as not to be a cheapskate and ask, "Will I get a receipt?"

"You bet. It's probably already on your mobile. Thanks for

riding with me and don't hesitate to refer to that receipt whenever you need to schedule another ride. You can even ask for me – I'm Andrea." She sticks her hand out assertively and I shake it, albeit begrudgingly.

The doors and hatch open and I exit, retrieving my luggage. Silently, Andrea's car pulls away and down Dolores St.

The Estate Hotel faces a quaint park in the middle of what is otherwise a strictly residential area. Normally, hotels reside in business districts, but this one seems to be its own animal. While the architecture isn't the same as the surrounding buildings, it somehow manages to fit. Only three floors tall and utilizing a combination of glass, steel, and brick, it is nestled amongst the trees with every effort made by its designers to be unobtrusive.

I climb the steps into the lobby and wait for someone to come to the desk. Nothing seems quite like I was told it would be. This place is unique, to be sure, but they've got the debauchery far more hidden than I was anticipating. While their reading material may be readily available, the behavior will be harder to come by. This could take a very long time indeed.

After a few moments a man comes to the counter and checks me in. He tells me the room number and to press my thumb on the plate next to the door to enter. While I may disapprove of the lifestyles and dress codes here, I have to admit that being able to go everywhere and do anything without carrying one's wallet is very handy. Upon checking into the room, I begin unpacking and set up the mobile PC on the desk. DoFA assured me that no one would be able to use it but me as the password is required for it to start up. Still, I plan on stowing it away in my luggage every night until I can secure an apartment. But, to get an apartment I first have to find a job. This is the priority.

I order a pizza – you would be amazed how difficult it is to find a plain cheese and sausage pizza on one of these menus – and start up the PC to have my first video conference with Gray. I tell him essentially what I've seen, or *not* seen for that matter, and he seems unfazed by the debriefing. We sign off and I sit back on the bed to watch the television, scanning for sports channels. The only live event at the moment is soccer, which I'll have to suffer through for half an hour until a basketball game between two teams I've never heard of starts at eight. Ugh.

As I'm lying here, a couple thoughts start rumbling through my head. First, who were all the other people on the plane? No one talked to each other and everyone seemed pretty calm, but if travel is so limited to Gaymerica then why was the flight so full? The thought has occurred to me that perhaps only one or two flights a week actually depart from Chicago to Gaymerica, but even if that's the case, there are certainly a lot of travelers to a place deemed to be on medical quarantine.

Second, since my departure from St. O'Hara, I haven't heard nor seen the term "Gaymerica" anywhere. Not at SFO, not at the entrance to the highway… nowhere. I didn't ask either of the questions to Gray as I don't want him or DoFA to think I'm questioning their methods. Anyhow, I'm really just curious. It's been a long day and between the exhaustion and the soccer I'm starting to fade to…

5

I've been here a week and haven't been subjected to sodomy, yet. I'm not complaining, mind you. In fact, I'm rather pleased at the generally cordial nature of the citizens of Gaymerica and their willingness to let me get settled first. Although, even during the training I found it difficult to believe that people in this or any other country just ran around subjecting each other to unsolicited anal penetration. The term "sodomy" comes from the Old Testament, and is named after the heathen, debauched city of Sodom, whose sister city Gomorrah was equally wicked. I assume that the reason the term is "sodomy" instead of "gomorry" is because "gomorry" just sounds ridiculous to say, and combining them into "sodogomorry" sounds like someone sneezed while reciting Genesis.

In the holy book of Genesis, two angels come to town (disguised as travelers) and are put up by some guy named Lot. According to DoFA, the city of San Francisco is much like Sodom was. The neighbors dropped by and demanded to fuck the visitors, but Lot would have none of it. Instead, he offered them his daughters. Now, in my estimation I see no difference, if you're going to anally violate someone, between a man and a woman. If anything, I would assume the lack of body hair would make a woman more pleasing as a victim, but that didn't stop the men of Sodom.

So, the girls were spared and escaped with Lot, his wife, and his guests. After that, things get fuzzy. There's a pillar of salt, some incest, and a truckload of booze – at least according to my mother. To be honest I've never read the Bible myself, but it's one of those books, the content of which is so universal and ubiquitous, that it's difficult to understand how one can't learn from its lessons. Clearly, if you try to have sex with another man against his will or engage in incest, you'll get drunk and turn into a pillar of salt. What's the difficulty here?

The Bible is replete with these sorts of moral warnings. Leviticus tells us that if two guys get it on, they are to be put to death. In 2016 after the new government was passed, I'm sure we would have eventually finished that edict except for the Queen Supreme and her itchy trigger finger. Now it falls to me and other operatives (I've been told there are many others engaged in various forms of espionage) to help get the job done.

Despite my initial impression that Gaymerica's international relations were printed simply and plainly in quarterly reports, I've discovered otherwise. At least, the *Graphics Quarterly* publication I picked up had very little to do with actual international relations. It seems the graphics industry has been reliant for decades on the manpower the Chinese possess, and that the suggestively posed woman on the cover of the publication has single-handedly brought much of the work and business back to the Western Hemisphere. The projections the magazine promised were not Earth-shattering tell-alls about how Gaymerica relates with China, but rather a grid showing which parts of the industry were still trying to wean themselves off of Chinese processes, manpower, machinery, etc. The graph also indicated which parts of the industry Ms. Merriman personally helped to influence, and included a descending red line of Chinese involvement and ascending green line of Gaymerican independence for each corner of the market.

The information is mildly useful in that I see these people are trying to do as little business with one of the world's superpowers as possible. However, the information is incomplete as the only motivation for these actions seems to be something about human rights violations and until I can dig farther into the actual causes of the rift I'll still be in the dark.

In an effort to embed me as deeply in the gay fold as quickly as possible, Gray managed to line up an interview for me with an organization that, ironically enough, helps expatriates find employment. The work seems similar in description to what I do... well, *did* at Fittzle and Rupert. As a side note, Gray never managed to learn the actual name of my employer for the entire time I was in training.

If I land the job, I'll be reviewing submissions completed by the expatriates and assigning them to job counselors who are then tasked with finding jobs for these people. That's about all Gray was able to tell me about the position. The interview is today at 10:00 AM, and I'm more than a bit nervous.

As it turns out, the job is a state job. If I get it, I'll have access to millions of files and documents that could help to turn the tide in the war against the Queen Supreme. Above all else, I must remain calm. Any suggestion that I'm not on their side and the entire operation could be compromised. So, no pressure, right?

***

After a couple days trolling around town I finally got the nerve to strike up a conversation with a bitchy male barista at a coffee shop in The Castro neighborhood. When I say the word "Gaymerica" I usually get a bit of a scornful look, but when I let it slip this time, the barista corrected me quickly, saying, "Okay, I guess you're probably new here, but please don't call it that. I know that you folks from *America…*" he said this with quite the tone, including air quotes, "…like to call us that, but it's basically slanderous, so please don't…" A couple people applauded his ridiculous tirade and I exited swiftly after getting my coffee (no tip) to avoid further assault.

After picking up a small dark roast from a different coffee shop, I make my way to the address on the interview confirmation. It's a very tall building near Union Square Park. The lobby faces out onto the park, which is a nice thing to have in the middle of a business district. From what I understand, Chicago used to have an enormous, remarkable park not far from the building I worked in, right on the lake. This seems a strange notion to me, since the area is now filled in with a run-down theme park, a small airport, some factories, and numerous condominiums. How the site was ever useful as a city park I'll never know, but Union Square seems compact and pleasant enough for a town like this one. And, it's not the only one. There are myriad parks tucked away throughout San Francisco.

Over the last week, I've become more accustomed with the city, riding buses and trains which are much the same as they are in Chicago – just cleaner. The major difference on the transportation front is the number of cars. I still can't get over the fact that no one drives here. They've completely foregone their right to own a car at all. True, I didn't drive in Chicago but for a couple particular reasons. Primarily, I'd had my license revoked, so there's that. But, the price of fuel had gotten out of my price range. So despite the fact that I occasionally ran a red light or hit a stop sign while digging for a donut in the passenger seat is beside the point. I couldn't afford to drive and if things are close enough, a person doesn't really need to anyway.

But here, people can't even go for a drive if they want to. Sure, the buses and trains run on time and get you there safely and smoothly, but I can see the meandering highways along the coast and desire nothing more than to stomp my foot on the gas and take the turns at something beyond a responsible speed. I mentioned I had my license revoked, right?

A slender woman in a smart vest and tie with her sleeves rolled up clicks across the tile floor toward me and stops, saying, "Mr. Hawley?"

Shivering, I answer, "That's me."

"They're ready to see you now," she adds, and turns away from me indicating I am to follow. Doing so, we cross behind the front desk and up a flight of stairs to a small conference room on the second floor. Beyond the glass doors I can see two women and one man sitting at a wide table with a chair on the other side. The woman opens the door then walks away as I enter. To my surprise, all three get up from their seats and come around the table to shake my hand.

"Hello, Mr. Hawley!" they grin alternately, seemingly happy to see me. The women's hands I shake with slight trepidation as I still have not acclimated to seeing women in authority roles. The man is another story. While he's not lisping terribly or wearing a sequined ball gown, he has a very effeminate demeanor and bows his head oddly when saying, "So nice to meet you, Mr. Hawley."

What Gray trained me for was dealing with men like this– Wait, so does this mean the women are overt lesbians as well? As the man turns away from me and they go to take their seats, I do a quick check for sandals and leg hair, but see none as both women are wearing professional looking heals and... pants. In the week I've spent here, I've discovered very little about the female dress code. There doesn't seem to be any rhyme or reason to what women wear at all. I've surmised that the women who wear pants are the more "butch" lesbians, and the ones who wear skirts are the "lipstick" lesbians. One problem, though, is that these two women and a number of others I've seen over the past week fit neither description. Sure, they're wearing pants, but the shoes are definitely of a come-hither variety and their hair and lips are made up as per the distinctions Gray set forth for the "lipstick" variety. I'm thrown, but I try not to let it show.

After the awkward handshaking, I'm pointed to a slender,

simple-looking chair on the near side of the table while the interviewers return to their seats. The chair looks narrow and breakable and I'm shocked at the firm level of support I receive upon sitting. One of the women speaks first.

"My name is Chandra, this is Lewis, and this is Althea," She motions down the table to each of the others. Althea?! What the hell kind of name— "Thanks for coming in today, Corwin."

I shrug, "Thanks for having me."

Lewis pipes up and I try to ignore his slight lisp, "Now, we see you're an expatriate of America. How have you been liking your stay in the Western States Republic?"

I almost freeze. They're all staring at me and I have to make something up. Aside from the name sounding ridiculous – fags can't deal with their country being called what it is – I have to actually make them believe I like it here. So, I decide to start with the few things I *do* like, "Well, I'm impressed at the cleanliness. Your public transit is, well… clean. Oh, and the wharf. I don't think I've ever had seafood as good as you get it here."

Althea seems to be the seafood expert of the group and responds, "I suppose since the food doesn't have as far to travel, we've got a bit of an advantage here. But I love it, too."

They all seem very happy to be here and the pressure on me to feel the same is daunting. I continue, "And, your program surfing is much easier and user-friendly here. It took me a night or two to get used to, but I think it's neat." Neat? Where did that come from? I think these people are wearing off on me.

At this point, Chandra steps back in to take over the conversation, "Well, we're glad that you're enjoying your stay. And, I hope you're able to stick around. Now, in the interest of full disclosure, and you're receiving the documents on your mobile device as we speak…" she's pressing an unseen button on the table as she relays this information, "…we can only hire you on a temp-to-hire basis. The citizenship process takes up to twelve months, and we would not be able to hire you as a permanent employee with benefits until you're a full citizen. We can, however, offer temporary benefits with your union membership should you be hired. Would you still like to proceed with the interview?"

Benefits? Union membership? What on Earth are these people talking about? I'm thinking as fast as I can. I know I need this job and that I should just suck it up and take whatever they offer me. "Yes, I'd like to," I blurt out, comprehending precisely nothing Chandra has just said to me.

"Great!" Lewis blurts out. I'm thankful for his candor.

Chandra smiles at Lewis and refers to her notes, "So, Corwin, today we're interviewing you for a position as an application reviewer with the Federal Employment Administration. So, just to get warmed up a bit here, I see that you've been working with a private practice in Chicago, focusing on liability claims, is that right?" I nod. "Why don't you tell us a little bit about that?"

This part I can keep mostly honest since my job there was very similar in practice and scope to the one I'm inter-viewing for. I bypass the parts about how I dream up scenarios counter to the ones claimants invent in the forms and move right on to where I know what the federally mandated procedures are. They nod, sometimes smile, and mostly just listen intently.

After a few moments, Althea stops me, "Now, Mr. Hawley, when you say 'forms' you're talking about actual, *paper* forms?"

They stare at me, anxiously awaiting a response. Whether good or bad, it isn't my fault we still use paper. People like to write things and get carbon copies for their records. I'll admit that all these e-receipts I've been getting the past week have jacked up my inbox. I have to set up a separate folder system just to save them so I can see where people would prefer paper. Then again, I'd have to have *actual* folders for that, too. Sheepishly, I shrug and say, "Well, yeah. I mean I use a PC at work for entering information and at home for videos and the like…" I'm blathering now and it's getting hot. Here comes the sweating again.

"Wow," Althea finally lets out, "Weird."

"Sorry," I add automatically.

Chandra looks quickly to Althea, who sits back in her seat, then back at me, "No, you have nothing to apologize for, Corwin. We're just getting a gauge of where you're at. We don't use paper at all here so it comes as a bit of a shock that anything other than a book or print-periodical comes in actual paper…" that lousy magazine, "…but it's certainly helpful that you've had that depth of experience."

Nice. She managed to sell my deficiency as a plus. I grin weakly at Chandra for this and she smiles back at me, then refers to her notes for the next question.

The interview meanders along for more than half an hour

and I do my best to focus. Regardless of the effort, though, there are many things I just don't understand. Primarily, the concepts of benefits, unions, and subsidies – although I think that last part means I get a free federal transit pass due to being employed by the government. It's the next best thing to actually owning a car (if the things they have here can be called cars) so I respond favorably.

At the end of the interview we all do the awkward dance again where they come around to my side of the table and shake my hand. As if summoned somehow, the same woman from before shows up to escort me out of the building. I glance at the magic table on my way out and see no buttons, bells, or whistles. This technology is well beyond my under-standing and I presume that if I lose the position to anyone else, a large part of the reasoning will be that. Still, it's pretty neat to see.

***

My mother spent a lot of time telling me about the world before the secession of Gaymerica. To this day, I don't know it like she did. Then again, how much stock can you put in the memory of one person? She told me that employment was a constant struggle, particularly for my father. It's never been an issue for me, so I tend to feel something of a sense of superiority over him.

The split between the two nations highlighted the flaws inherent in the socialist system of Gaymerica, and to a lesser extent the socialist regime of the former United States. In

Gaymerica, citizens were given jobs based on the fact that they had a pulse, and the ones who couldn't work benefited from state-sponsored subsidies called "Unemployment" or other such programs. I always thought that if you didn't have a job, you were just in a state of "unemployment" but these people felt (and still feel) that being in that state entitles you to remuneration.

Mom taught me to type, read, study, and take care of myself. True, I don't... *didn't* make a lot of money, but I've always been able to retain employment because of my skills and education. Those were things I chose to do on my own. No one gave them to me. Here, you get by on your will to live alone, not on the sweat of your brow and it's perturbing at best.

Upon further review of the documentation provided me during the interview, citizens of The Western States Republic have free healthcare. Not kidding. It's free. This is one of the benefits Chandra referred to in the interview. Because the citizenship process takes so long, and I can't have the free benefits in the process, newcomers to Gaymerica are forced to join a union.

From what I can tell, a union is a group that provides all the benefits (health care, life insurance, representation in salary negotiation) that one would have automatically if they were a citizen. This comes at a price of eight percent of my income. That's on top of the taxes that come automatically out of my pay, which means I go home with a whopping 79% of what I actually earn. In America, there is only sales tax. I take home everything I make and then purchase only the services I need after that. I haven't added up what health insurance costs on a percentage basis and I don't recall it being cheap, but at least it was a choice. This system forces me pay into things I won't even use, like Unemployment. What the fuck?

I have to keep reminding myself that this is all for the good of my country and of humanity as a whole.

*****

When I get home from the interview, I call Gray and give him the rundown, including my experience being dressed down for saying "Gaymerica." Oddly, though, when I ask him why I wasn't taught anything about unions, benefits, or really any of what Chandra talked about in the interview, he hesitates.

"I guess it just wasn't one of the priority items we had time to train you for. It could also be a training gap."

"A training *gap*? What does that mean?" I ask, suddenly wondering how many other "gaps" there are in this thing.

He shrugs, "Oh, I don't think it's anything to worry about. Remember, they'll expect you to be ignorant of a few things. Now that you mention it, though, I could see how that might be useful information. I'll make sure we uh… you know, add it to the training."

The debriefing ends without further incident, but I'm left wondering if there are any other gaps in my training that could lead to more embarrassing moments. I suffer a restless night's sleep before waking at 9:30am to the sound of my mobile ringing. It's the Federal Employment Administration. I got the job.

6

I've been working my new job for almost three weeks now and still don't fully have the grasp. Fortunately, the training has been rather comprehensive on the computer stuff so I don't feel like a complete buffoon. My trainer and manager have worked with a special training department to get me up to speed on the technology.

Here's what I do. Whenever someone like myself comes to Gay– the Western States Republic they file a job assessment with the Federal Employment Administration. One of the laws of the Queen Supreme (whom I reference here though I've learned they actually call her "Prime Minister") is that everyone must have a job or be actively seeking work. Otherwise, they can't apply for assistance with the government. I asked at one point about people who are independently wealthy and was informed that as long as they don't file for Unemployment coverage, they're entitled to remain out of work for as long as they like. The rules are in place so people don't abuse the system, supposedly.

I review the applications and match up the identity the person enters into the system with the Interpol identity provided by their nation of origin. This is somewhat ironic considering my personal circumstance, but I digress. Once that's done, provided the person checks out, I forward their assessment to the employment counselors who get these people interviews. In America, a person is responsible for getting their own job. If you can't do the work to *get* the interview, then why should you be trusted to do the job? Still, at least I have something to do and it pays well enough.

My feelings about union membership are mixed, much more so now than when it was first brought up. Initially, I thought it was pretty useful that the union took care of all the things it was designed for. However, on Gray's urging, I read up on the history of unions in both Gaymerica and America and discovered an unsavory history. For now I'm using DoFA's library of information accessible on my mobile PC but intend to cross-reference native information to Gaymerica to see how forthright they are with their version of the same stories.

I discovered that unions initially were utilized as a way for opportunistic men (and some women) to take advantage of workers by pocketing the dues and stalling negotiations with employers to push pay higher and higher, thus lining their pockets further and further. The union I'm now a member of seems to have little local representation and runs itself as a more streamlined version of the same thing. However, one upside to this particular union is their disclosure. The income of union representatives is disclosed to all members of the union. And, since union members are frequently only members for a year at a time while they procure citizenship, there isn't as much opportunity to take advantage of the system. Also, many of the reps are recent expatriates as well. There are monthly statements (I started in the middle of a cycle so I actually just got my first) that show exactly what the revenue for the union is and where the money is spent. It's all accounted right down to the penny including money that goes into a "retirement program" people can transfer funds out of once they achieve citizenship.

All in all, the union appears completely functional and I can actually see the benefits I receive from it. There are other unions in this country, though, and other unions throughout the world that have entirely different motivations, and I have to be careful with what I say and do so as not to fall victim to them.

***

Today, I've been given the morning off to bus down to the government center and complete my amnesty processing. This is the appointment at which I'll officially file my request for citizenship. I've discovered that the state has a test they can run to decipher whether or not someone is gay and possibly whether it runs in their family. As it's a communicable disease, I'm not sure how it "runs in the family" but as it was explained to me, it may be possible to discern from my blood whether or not my father was gay. The test is voluntary, but I've decided to go through with it along with the rest of the citizenship processing because I can't bring myself to reconcile what Gray told me the day before I left America. It still bothers me and

I'd love nothing more than to be able to tell Gray to his face…
well, via videophone at least, that while my father may have
been a traitor, he was *not* a faggot.

In addition to knowing some of my own medical details, I
can also voluntarily allow them to upload my information to
the state database for quick reference in case of emergencies.
The database is said to be confidential and has been known to
save lives. What they do is record blood type, known diseases,
and biological history so that if someone is killed in an accident
of some sort, their organs can be harvested and sent
immediately to sick people on a list to receive transplants. It's
completely automated and the compatibility of donor and
recipient is analyzed within seconds of deter-mining the
decedent's identity. I had no idea this could be done and, the
way I figure it, as long as it's confidential and someone can't
just look up the size of my penis while scanning the menu at a
restaurant, it could be very useful. Long story short, I'm
signing up for that, too.

The government center is actually a massive complex of
buildings on the East side of the bay in Oakland. There is a
commuter train I take across the Bay Bridge that stops right in
the middle of the complex. For a commuter train it's a great
deal faster than the ones in Chicago and I'm dropped off at the
complex within 20 minutes of leaving my apartment.

I head toward the Immigration building a block and a half
from the stop. Here, the sights become a bit more familiar to
me. For the first time since arriving in Gaymerica I spot signs
of poverty as a homeless couple is sitting in front of a coffee
shop playing guitars and singing blues music. There's a small

crowd, but people mostly come and go.

There is no paper money in Gaymerica – everything is either credit processed off thumbprint identification or, on rarer occasion, coinage. Coins come in denominations of $5, $10, $20, and $50. Not huge stakes, but people like this won't pass up an opportunity to shuck the citizenry (or rather the unsuspecting *un*citizenry) out of a coin or two.

As I pass by, I see there are a number of coins in the guitar case with denominations all the way up to $50. One of the crowd breaks off and starts walking along next to me and I decide to strike up a conversation with him.

"Damned homeless, right?" I ask.

He gives me a confused look, "What are you talking about?"

I look back and motion to the two playing guitar, "The beggars. Pain in the ass, right?"

Still confused, he shakes his head, "Whatever, I guess. They're just troubadours. They travel around, sing some songs, babble about political stuff... They're harmless, man."

Not knowing what to say, I slow down and let him walk ahead of me. He looks back once, shakes his head again and keeps going. What did I miss? There are homeless people begging for money and irritating passersby. I've always known that to be a universal annoyance yet this guy seems to think they're harmless.

I gather my thoughts and continue to the Immigration building. Inside, it is crowded but not to excess. There are sectioned waiting areas based on nation of origin. I check the board near the entrance and am presented with a screen that has the word "Enter" written dozens of times in myriad languages. I look around for American but am astonished to discover it's not an option. What the fuck? These people speak the same language as me, how could *our* language not be an option. I scan further down the list and find "English." I recall having been told of its similarities to American and check to see if anyone's looking before pressing it. A brief moment after doing so an attractive woman of indeterminate ethnicity appears on the screen in front of me and says politely, "Good morning, and welcome to the Western States Republic Immigration Administration center. How may I help you?"

How on Earth can it be remotely affordable to staff someone for something this simple? As I'm puzzling over it, her image seems to flicker momentarily and she asks again, "How may I help you today?" It's a recording. Now I get it. It's a very sophisticated recording, but a recording nonetheless. I'm fascinated by the interface and answer, "I have an appointment to file for citizenship."

"I can help you with that," the woman assures me, smiling and adds, "Please press your thumb to the plate at the bottom of this screen and I can point you in the right direction." An area below her left shoulder glows orange and I do as she says. Though the screen doesn't flash my info (likely for security reasons), it does present a map and set of instructions which she kindly spells out while I'm reading, "Please proceed to the escalators in front of you and continue to the second level. On the right, look for the second hallway and proceed to room 205A. Press your thumb to the plate next to the door to gain entrance. Please feel free to refer to any of the information screens in the building if you have any further needs. Is there anything else I can help you with?"

"Uh, no," I answer, stunned by the conciseness and simplicity of the instructions.

"Thank you for your time and we look forward to serving your needs," and with that her face disappears from the screen and the menu of languages appears again. Turns out, English sounds *exactly* like American. Huh.

I do as instructed and proceed to the second level where I see another set of waiting areas. The designated waiting area for America is smaller than the rest and empty, so even though I'm early I continue to room 205A and press my thumb to the plate. A previously unseen light glows green above the plate and what was a frosted glass door becomes clear and opens, sliding into the wall. I pass through and watch the door close behind me. Once closed, it turns opaque again. Cool.

A receptionist begins speaking behind me, "The door's transparency is adjustable for security purposes. Pretty neat, huh?" I turn around and see a young man in tight slacks, a white shirt, and a tie sitting at a mostly empty desk save for a large, touch-screen monitor and a pair of matching plants. He is looking at me intently and eventually adds, "Are you Mr. Hawley?"

Looking around, I notice this is a relatively small room nowhere near the exterior of the building, yet it's lit with natural light and has a bright, welcoming feel about it. The receptionist and a light, classical strain of music are the only signs of humanity within. I answer, "Uh, yes. Is that okay? I'm a little early."

He shakes his head and snorts. "Oh, that's okay! We only get a couple of you Americans a day around here. In fact, I work the other half of my shift in the European rooms."

Most of the people I've seen in Gaymerica (or met on the job) have been some hybrid of the caricatures I witnessed in training and the normal people in America. With the exception of the average female wardrobe (something that continually baffles me), people seem mostly normal. This receptionist is something entirely other. Initially, I think how odd it is that a man is a receptionist. On top of that, though, is his wardrobe. The tight pants, even while seated, reveal a sensual curve in his hips and accentuate the bulge of his ass. The white shirt is a T, with the shortened sleeves folded neatly above the elbow with a button above, and have a purple flourish nestled into the fold. His hair is sticking straight up, though cropped short, towards the middle with waves curling up his head toward the peak. The tie is fashioned more like a cravat, and hangs loose below the second button of the shirt, which is open on top revealing a tank underneath. He has a wide, purple belt with a buckle shaped like a face on one side and the prong protruding through… the mouth. I get it. Calm now, Corwin. This man is the enemy.

"So!" he starts with gusto and a bounce on his chair, "You have come to partake in the vast cultural shock that is The Western States Republic or, as you've come to know it, Gaymerica. Yes?!"

He said it! He fucking said it! I'm so completely thrown that all I can utter is, "Uh, yeah."

The man nods his head and presses the console near him.

The counter of the reception desk in front of me lights up in the middle with a menu next to a touch screen. "Great! Press your hand to the screen for three seconds, then lift," he says with great joy, as if he relishes every registered candidate. Once I've finished scanning he continues, "Fabulous! Now, have a seat over there…" he motions to the slender, ergonomic bench not three feet behind me, "…while I review your info and then we'll get started."

"Get started?" I ask. Isn't there some supervisor or skilled government official that should be processing my request?

"Uh-huh. We'll begin the questions in a moment."

"*You* will?" I ask.

He nods dramatically, "Yeeaaaahhh," and makes a grand gesture out of pressing some unseen key on his console, returning his attention to the screen in front of him.

Is this "man" really going to be questioning me about my citizenship request? I try to fortify my confidence for intellectual battle, knowing somewhere in the back of my head that I'm superior to this queer and that I can manage anything he throws at me.

Mere seconds later (and before fortification of any kind has taken place), he proceeds, "Okay, Mr. Hawley! Can you see me okay?"

The counter of the reception desk rests at the center of his chest in my field of vision and, considering his distracting wardrobe, reveals just about enough of him, "Yes, I can see you fine."

"Excellent. If you could look at the top of the desk please," he starts. I do unwittingly and am about to ask "why" when a flash blinds me and he continues with the statement, "I'll just get your photo…" I don't see how telling me what's happening *after* it's happened is quite fair, but I then remind myself that fags can be shifty fuckers. "Very nice, sir. Now, I do have a number of questions for you…" he starts while I'm still reeling, "…It says here you were born in Mason City, Iowa, is that correct?"

"Uh, yeah – yes," I try to be as direct and affirmative as possible.

"And your mother's name?"

Surprised, I ask, "Don't you already have…"

"Thank you, Mr. Hawley, *I'll* be asking the questions," he interrupts, brandishing an almost delighted, sarcastic smile, "What is your mother's name?"

"Betsy Hawley."

"And your father's name?"

Reluctantly, I abide, "Percy Hawley."

"Do you have any siblings?"

He's moving very fast and I'm having trouble keeping up, "Um, no."

The fag grins devilishly and asks, "You sure about that?"

"Yes," I say firmly, "I'm an only child."

As if he knew what my answer would be, he continues hot on the heels of my response, "Have you ever travelled out of America before?"

"Once, when I—"

"And where did you go?" He's pissing me off.

"Canada."

"For how long?"

"A week, maybe two."

"Were you ever convicted of a crime in America or Canada?"

"What? No!"

"Not even a little one?"

"No."

"Not a teensy, weensy little infrac—"

"NO!" I say assertively. Realizing I've let him get to me, I take a breath and try to sit casually in my seat.

He grins and looks back to the screen for the next question, "Do you have any affiliations with known criminal organizations?"

"No."

"Is this your first time filing for amnesty or citizenship in a foreign nation?"

"N- Yes. Yes, it is."

Grinning as if this whole thing is some fabulous game for him, he asks, "Are you sure?"

Irritated, I reply, "Yes."

"Okay. Now, Mr. Hawley. We, here in the Western States Republic welcome all people and wish to provide a safe, nurturing environment for you in your quest for citizenship. Therefore, the next few questions you are under no legal obligation to answer. However, your responses may factor in your application for citizenship."

I bristle, "Positively, or negatively?"

Pursing his lips, he leans forward, "Well, we won't know until we hear the answers, now will we?" The man's smile almost never leaves his face and it's becoming clear to me that he enjoys this process. Are they like this to people who emigrate from other countries as well, or just Americans? Straightening up, he begins the questions anew, "Have you ever been part of a political dissident group?"

Delighted I'm able to keep my answers honest, I say, "No, sir." Yuck. I called that fag "sir."

"Have you ever been recruited by a group or entity whose intent was to subvert the government of your nation of origin?"

"No."

He waits for the sir and when it doesn't come, continues, "Have you ever partaken in illegal activity with the intent to subvert your government though not part of any group or entity?"

Catching up to the convoluted wording, I muster, "No."

"Before defecting to the Western States Republic, were you approached by any group, entity, or individual with solicitation of intent to harm any other sovereign nation?"

The question chills me to the core but because I'm already in a pattern of saying "no" it comes out as if by rote. "No." The answer surprises even me but I try to remain calm and react as little as possible.

He doesn't notice anything amiss and merely enters the answer in the computer like all the others. I'm so focused on the aftershock of the question and the new bead of ass sweat that I almost don't hear the next question.

"Since your arrival in the Western States, have you been approached by any individual, entity, or group with solicitation of intent to harm any other sovereign nation?"

"Not at all," I say proudly.

He raises his eyebrows as if to say, "I don't actually care" and continues, "Do you harbor any ill intent toward America, the Western States Republic, or any other nation?"

"No." I'm becoming uncomfortable.

"Do you swear that for the duration of your probationary citizenship – not to exceed twelve months from the date you entered this county – you will act with the same loyalty and conduct becoming of a true citizen?"

"I do," I answer, but not as quickly as I wish I had. Again, he doesn't notice (or care) and simply presses a couple more spots on his console. A door opposite the one I entered clicks, unlocks, and swings open. Beyond, there is a hallway similar to the one that got me here.

He clears his throat and announces, "Congratulations, Mr. Hawley, your application for amnesty has been approved, and your application for citizenship has been accepted. Go through that door, down the hall to the right and you'll come to our medical exam room. I have marked here that you would like to volunteer for our medical alert scanning program. The medical exam room is where that scanning will take place. please note that you'll be contacted with further citizenship documentation as time goes on, so please try to remain current with the process. Thank you, and have a nice day."

I don't want to talk to him anymore, so I give a quick, "Thank you," and stand to exit. Once through the doorway, the door closes behind me and I turn back to look into the room. The door is clear at this point and I see the one on the other side still frosted with a red light blinking above. The interrogator turns to me, presses something on his console, and the door becomes opaque again.

***

Five minutes into the medical exam and I'm already bored out of my skull, ready to pull the hair out of my head. A dreadfully nerdish woman with glasses and a limp is chatting my ear off about the brilliant technology they have with stem cells and regenerative healing processes and the like. She's espousing the virtues of a system I couldn't care less about that, from what I heard from Gray and DoFA, goes against the Bible in every possible way. Still, I grin and bear it.

One thing she mentions that piques my interest is this DNA thing. She sounded it out for me but I told her I'd rather stick with the acronym. Supposedly, they have a way by which they can look at the code of a person's "genetic" makeup and tell all sorts of things about them. Eye color, hair color, height, predispositions to certain illnesses… the works.

When I ask about how I would be able to know about my father's sexual orientation she wavers a bit, "Well, it's a recessive gene, so it can be passed from generation to generation without ever presenting. Or, it could present in *all* blood-related members of an immediate family. There's a lot of chance involved in it."

I've been scanned externally and had blood drawn and now she enters information on a console and I'm annoyed when I ask, "Chance… or maybe God has something to do with it?"

She shrugs nonchalantly and replies, "I don't know about that stuff. I just work the math. Twenty percent of people have the recessive gene and about half of them present with active traits. In a family where multiple individuals have the gene, the percentage of offspring presenting with active traits goes up. In a family where only one does, the odds are lower. It's all statistics to me, but certainly some people believe…" she's still talking long after I've stopped listening, "…and my father was a Catholic. Well, the church is a lot smaller here in the Western States…" and still talking, "…but eventually the math wins out."

Oh, thank God! She's taking a breath! "How much longer?" I ask as politely as I can muster.

"Actually," she starts. Christ, please let her not go on like that again. She clicks something on her console and a screen next to her lights up. She turns to me, motioning to the screen and adds, "We're done! Would you like me to send this information to your mobile device?"

"Sure," I shrug and walk over to look at the screen.

She leans in look at it with me, "Would you like to know if you possess the gene? It seems important to you."

I stiffen at the question. On the surface and even quite a bit below I really *don't* want to know if I have the "gay gene" as it's called. Before I answer I ask another question, "A gene is something you're born with, yes?"

"Correct. It's inherent in your make up."

"Because, I had always heard that being a fa… homo-sexual," she closes her eyes and reopens them with a slight irritation at my faux pas, "…was a disease transmitted through contact with another person."

She sits casually on the counter next to the screen, "Mr. Hawley, I'm not here to question how you were educated or to try to change your mind about anything. This is a voluntary process and you should know that you still have the choice to opt out of it."

I look to the screen at the statement saying "Press thumb here for results" and the throbbing orange spot below. I press my thumb to the spot and a page scrolls up from the bottom of the screen with my results. Most of it's complete gobbledy-gook but at the bottom I see a section marked "Specially Requested Data." Underneath that, there is a section that reads:

Presence of gene marker Xq28 – **Positive**   Click **here** for more information

I press it, now thoroughly aware of the accumulating sweat but no longer concerned about my smell or appearance. Another screen pops up in front of this one displaying the following:

Human genetic marker Xq28 (commonly known as Rainbow Gene #2) is the gene that governs a human male's orientation in seeking a mate. Presence of the active gene indicates that the carrier is predisposed to select mates of the same sex. As it is a recessive gene, it is only active in 50% of carriers.

Related genes include...

I've stopped reading. I think this fucking thing says I'm a

faggot. I turn to her, visibly perspiring and ask, "Does this mean I'm gay?"

She shrugs again, "Only if the gene is active. You'll have to find that out on your own."

I sense that she's holding something back, but given her official position I can see how she might have been instructed to keep quiet about certain things. While I realize I should be actively questioning *any* piece of information provided me by a known hostile government, I can't help but be struck by this information.

After I leave the room I notice I have two new messages on my mobile device. The most recent is the bizarre news I've just heard and the next is a citizenship packet bearing the identification photo snapped by my interrogator. I look like a complete ass.

***

I'm furious when I get back to my hotel room and call Gray instantly on my PC, wanting to see his face. When he answers, I skip the formalities and bark at him, "Why didn't you tell me about genes?!"

"What?" he says, waylaid by my outburst.

"And DNR! Why didn't you tell me about DNR?!"

"DNR? What's gotten into you, Corwin? Are you talking about DNA?" he asks, trying to play off my concern as lunacy.

"DNA, DNR, what's the difference? Why didn't you tell me about this stuff? These people think I'm queer!"

His reaction is pronounced but he attempts to veil it as

calm, "Do they?"

I retort, "Yes! They're telling me that I'm predisposed to be gay! They've got all this damned science and tests and *bizarre* information you never damn told me about. Is this another *training gap*?!"

"Okay, now calm down, Corwin."

"I *am* calm!" I say, almost shouting.

Gray starts to say something but pauses and starts again, "We've known about this information for quite some time—"

"Quite some time?! When were you gonna tell *me*?!"

"Just let me speak for a minute, okay? Now, think about it. What good would it have done to tell you about these things in advance? To frighten you? To make you afraid to assimilate? We wanted you to know the things you *needed* to know to complete the tasks assigned to you. But, the other things, the cultural things that would have only alarmed you, well, it was important to us for your compliance and to you for your safety that you be completely in the dark about this information before you experienced it. It was important that your reactions be honest. If you had known all of this in advance and reacted falsely, don't you think they'd have noticed that?"

A long silence passes between us and I glare at him through the PC. He can see me and when I sit on the edge of the bed, he nods his acknowledgment of my concern.

Almost near tears I ask, "Is this my 'aptitude?' Is this why you picked me? Because I'd be *gay* enough to fit in?"

"You do have the gene, Corwin, it's true."

Another silence passes and I laugh disgustedly, "Well, I guess it's about time I went out and gay-ed it up, isn't it?" and

I stand to shut off the PC.

"Corwin," he starts soothingly, "Don't judge yourself for this. Remember that you have no control in the matter – you don't have any choice in what you are."

"No," I reply. "I have some." And I shut off the PC.

7

My job is getting under control as well as the progress on my citizenship. I've moved into a studio apartment upstairs from a hardware store a few blocks from the hotel I was staying at. I know that all seems cursory but these are big steps for me since I've been completely uprooted from my former life. Since I don't own any furniture I was sleeping on the floor the first couple days until I could have a bed delivered.

I managed to obtain two chairs and a nice table from a community bulletin board posting similar to the one we have in Chicago. The table and chairs are now by the window and the bed is in the middle of the wall between the window and the door. There's a small kitchen with a refrigerator and microwave. The bathroom contains an antique claw-foot tub but modern sink and toilet. The medicine cabinet over the sink appears to be just as antique as the tub and is built into the wall.

As for progress on citizenship, I've been doing quite a bit of reading from the materials provided by the state. Citizenship requirements include language proficiency, suitable levels of education, knowledge about the Western States Republic,

licensure (if necessary) in your desired field of employment…
the list goes on. The information seems somewhat consistent
with what I was trained by DoFA, but there are certainly
differences.

For example, the timeline of how the Western States
seceded is precisely the same, but the circumstances
surrounding it are different. DoFA records show there was a
month or more of fighting that led up to Miami becoming a
protectorate of Gaymerica, but the required reading for my
citizenship shows that the land was actually gifted to the
Western States as they could find no local governing body that
wanted to follow American rule. Plus, the gay to straight ratio
was so high that a forcible takeover of the area seemed
impossible without significant loss of life on both sides. While
I'm skeptical that it happened this way due to the contradictory
nature of the information, it actually makes some sense. I've
never been to Miami, but I heard stories both here and back
home in America about how the area was just too far gone –
taken over by gays – to be worth fighting over.

There are other differences as well. Where DoFA indicated
that the walls separating our nations were erected by
Gaymerica to keep people out, this material says the opposite,
and instead warns its citizens against crossing the border
illegally as America has strict entrance policies and stricter
punishments for violating them. Sometimes I get angry and
have to put the material down before I start shouting too
loudly at it and disturb my neighbors.

***

I don't have any real friends per se, but I do have a couple of friendly acquaintances at the Employment Administration. There's Travis, a gay man who works as a job counselor and occasionally freaks out over the fact that he'll be turning thirty at the beginning of next year. He was born here before this was a country by only a matter of months. He tells me that he's one of a small percentage of people whose parents were given the option of making their children American citizens and allowing them to be raised there instead. He indicates that his parents were "activists" against the American regime and chose to make him a citizen of the Western States instead.

Michael is a different story. He's young – twenty-four or thereabouts – and works as something of an executive assistant. He schedules appointments for management and keeps the office running efficiently and on time. Occasionally, he can be quite dramatic but he's very good at his job.

The two of them have taken pity on my inability to socialize (something Gray has criticized me for a number of times) and invited me to go to happy hour with them after work on Friday. Since I realize I have a deficiency in socializing myself, I'm grateful these two queers managed to initiate some of it for me. When I informed Gray of the event, he backed off, saying only that he expects a full report when I return that night.

It's a bit before 4:00 pm and Michael sashays over to my desk in a pair of tight pants and a very fitted button-up shirt. He's also wearing a light scarf and a pair of horn-rimmed glasses. He taps on my cubicle wall and asks, "You ready to go, Corwin?"

Michael always makes a point of fully pronouncing my name. Granted, almost no one here shortens it to "Cor" like they did in America, but Michael is very particular about how he pronounces it. Something about accentuating the "win" part is enjoyable for him. He's equally particular about his name. I made the mistake of calling him Mike once and am fairly certain I saw a vein pop out of his head. Since I'm no fan of "Cor" I respect his wish not to be called "Mike." As a result, we get along much better now than when I was first exposed to his swishy demeanor.

"Yeah, I just have to schedule this batch and I'll come over to your desk."

"Right on. Don't make us wait, I don't wanna miss the drink specials," he adds.

I smile and nod. "Don't worry, I don't either."

He taps on the cube wall again and returns to his desk.

A batch is really just a fancy term for a folder of files. Where I would have taken a folder into my boss's office in Chicago, here I mark a series of files based on the representative who will be managing them and, at the end of the day, submit them all in a batch. I love this part of the day because I can look at my desk top and see both how much work I've done, and where I'm at overall. Admittedly, I was behind for a while, but have pulled some extra hours and got caught up. Now, I can look at my work queue at the end of the day and know that I'll be able to stay caught up.

Travis swings by after finishing a call with a candidate and says, "You done?"

I press the "Batch" button and the entire window I'm

working on shrinks up, sending itself through an animated tube, and leaving my desktop clear except for a few program icons and a stock picture of the Golden Gate Bridge. "Yep," I answer and press a series of secure keys to lock the console.

"All right, all right!" Travis says excitedly, shimmying in place. He's by far the more masculine of the two and I see myself having more in common with him than with anyone else at work. Well, except for that curmudgeonly sixty-year-old guy who works with Italian expatriates, but we think he's a little weird and is speaking in Italian half the time anyway, so we ignore him.

As we breeze past Michael's desk, he mutters, "Geez, finally," and the three of us head out onto the street, walking toward the bar. Travis and Michael swap stories about people they've worked with throughout the day and engage in the usual gossip about co-workers. I wonder what they say about me when I'm not around.

The bar they're taking me to is one I've never heard of called Quantum. They have nightly jazz bands and attractive happy hour specials, I'm told, so at least I know I won't go broke. That being said, we're meeting some of Travis' friends there and for all I know this could be one of the awful gay bars DoFA's videos talked about.

In preparation for the evening's festivities, I went shopping for some decidedly more fitted pants (though I stopped short of the style some men wear) and a tighter t-shirt with print on it of some band I've scarcely listened to. From what I can tell, I look appropriate enough as neither of the men comment on it and I feel like our outfits are comparable.

Quantum inhabits the basement in one of the older office buildings downtown. It's a bricked-over steel structure with stairs leading up to an arched entryway. Inside the lobby there is a maze of staircases and we take the one to the right down a level. There, we come to the entrance of the club.

It's a mid-grade establishment with a restaurant and a bar. Between them and tucked into an alcove is a small stage where the jazz band is hammering away on a fast piece, working up to a drum solo. The audience is applauding the solo as we sit three to a two-top in the bar. The place is busy, but not packed yet. We sit adjacent to some of Travis' friends who are droning on about their jobs. The conversation rotates around the crowd and eventually to me. Ill-prepared to complain about my job in mixed company I simply relate, "I'm liking it so far. It has its challenges, but I think it's a good gig."

They shrug, and continue their discussion without me. I chime back in on occasion, asking about what people do and who they work for. I know I'm not getting the dirt on the empire just yet, but learning how to interact is an important part of my infiltration. At one point while I'm watching the jazz band, one of Travis' friends leans over to him and appears to be saying something about me. He giggles, shakes his head and says, "No."

I have no idea what they're talking about and I don't want to be left out of the crowd so I speak up, "So, is this what you guys usually do on Fridays?"

Michael answers, "Sometimes. This place is pricey and I'm cranky so I prefer more of the dive bar scene. These old fogeys like the classy joints, though."

Travis slaps Michael on the arm, stating emphatically that he isn't old *yet* and that he's got another eight months before he's thirty. I keep my mouth shut about how old I am and just let the age discussion go by.

Finally, Travis answers my question as well, "We don't always do the classy thing. There's a place over on Mission—"

The friend that whispered to him earlier – Kevin – smacks him and says something about me being a square. Travis replies quickly, "He is *not!* Look, some of us are going there after we finish up here. You wanna come with us?"

Kevin looks at me expectantly, clearly anticipating I'll say no. I'd expected this place to be the den of debauchery I'd heard about and used up a large amount of my courage getting here. So, I have to gulp down trepidation again to answer, "Sure! Why not?!"

Kevin rolls his eyes and says, "Okay…" in time with Travis answering, "Great! Let's settle up and head out, then."

Travis hails the waitress and we pay our tabs. A couple of the men break off and go home, but five of us continue on to a place called The Work House, a gay club several blocks South. Ten foot, red Gothic doors are propped open under a stone arch. In front of them is a large, muscular but friendly bouncer manning the entrance and making sure everyone checks their age by thumbprint on the plate he's holding. Mostly, he's just socializing, not doing much bouncing.

Beyond the doors is a spectacular night club, designed for… I have no idea. There's a cage in one corner, a massive dance floor on one side, a 360° bar on the other, a fifteen-foot ceiling sporting dozens of flashing, oscillating lights, and in another corner (inexplicably) a shower stall. On two sides of the room, doorways exit into other parts of the club.

We make our way around the bar on the side opposite the dance floor, which isn't very full yet. I take stock of the myriad people here. For the most part, they're dressed much like we are, but I focus harder and begin to see the differences. There are fewer women than the previous club and the men here seem to move and dress in a more effeminate manner than average. Many are wearing jewelry, bracelets (though frequently made of leather), heeled shoes, and the occasional collar. I shit you not, collars.

Finally, we arrive at a table near a back corner and deposit our respective satchels and bags. My heart is pounding and the music is loud – I can barely think for all the noise – and Travis leans over to me, "Whatcha think?!" I simply nod weakly and he throws his head back with laughter, "You'll get used to it! Come on, let's get a drink!"

On our way to the bar I am almost run over by a… man of sorts, wearing what appears to be a black leather harness, a pair of very tight (and short) black boxer briefs and calf-high black leather boots. Nothing else. "Sorry, sweetie," he barks, apologizing for nearly running me over and pats me on the cheek before moving on. I try to shake it off and stumble the rest of the way to the bar. Travis is already mid-order when I hear him say, "And for my friend…"

The bartender is wearing rainbow suspenders, a tilted chauffeur's cap, and a tight t-shirt with some symbols on it I don't recognize. Weakly, I say, "Uh, gin and tonic?"

"It's two for one on rail drinks. Do you want 'em both now

or do you wanna come back for the second?"

Looking around at the patrons of this remarkable den of sin, I nearly make the sign of the cross, but stop myself, reducing it to mindless chest rubbing and answer, "I'll take both now."

He smiles broadly and taps the bar. Travis pats me on the shoulder, allowing his hand to linger a little too long and tosses a $20 piece on the bar. The bartender finishes pouring our drinks and starts the next set of orders. I grab mine immediately and start drinking one of them, only to realize too late that it's mixed *very* strongly.

Returning to the table, I sit on the stool in the corner and take stock of the establishment and its inhabitants. There are maybe a hundred people in here at present, approximately twenty of them female, the rest male. However, sex doesn't seem to determine dress code at all. There are jeans, leather (though I eventually discover this to actually be something called "pleather"), canvass shoes, suspenders, tights, skirts, tube tops, hair ribbons, high heels, stiletto boots, corsets, harnesses, hats of all shapes and sizes, wigs, and some motherfucker with a whip wearing sunglasses. At night.

There are drinks of all kinds – fruit punch mixed with hard liquor, beer, scotch, martinis, something called Appletinis, lots of tropical-looking things with umbrellas and rain forests protruding from them. All are mixed with a generous portion of liquor and in generous sizes and volumes such as two-for-ones, three-for in some cases.

The walls are adorned with all fashions of decorations. There are explicit posters advertising different beverage companies, some of which I recognize, some of which I don't; paintings in oil, watercolor, and acrylic mostly of a very gritty, dark aesthetic; the hanging cage in the corner; a blank wall with projections of videos for the music pumping through the speakers; a giant speaker box with men and a girl dancing on it... The list goes on. Unlike any bar I've been in before, there are no dartboards, video games, or pool tables. It seems that the life here is sustained almost strictly by socializing.

At one end of the room is a raised platform that protrudes into the dance floor like a narrow stage. The wall behind the platform is obscured by a large, black curtain. Michael's sitting closest to me so I nudge him and ask, "What's the stage for? Do bands play here?" It would be an awkward stage for a band, but it's the only thing I can think of.

"Bands?" he shouts quizzically. I shrug. He looks at the stage, laughs to himself then looks back at me, "Honey, that's for the drag show."

"Drag show?" I ask, perplexed.

His eyes bug out of his head with shock, "You don't know what a drag show is?" Two of the other men turn their heads in surprise and I start to feel ostracized and warm. "Well, looks like we're stickin' around for the show tonight, boys," Michael adds before turning away from me again. They're pleased with this and as they've all seen "the show" before, I resign myself to remain.

After the first two drinks at Quantum and now the two very strong gin and tonics here, I'm starting to feel a little bit drunk. Perhaps it's because I'm used to drinking beer, but this shit's strooooong. Anyway, Michael's friends look like children to me and they're getting more giddy by the minute for the "drag show," whatever the hell that is.

Travis has been turning around and checking on me every once in a while to make sure I'm okay, but I raise my hand and shout over the din, "I'm *fine!*" He chuckles and goes back to his almost completely drowned-out conversation with a tall, strapping young man in a t-shirt and jeans. Other than being gay, he's awfully masculine-looking.

Up until now, the music's been loud, but as the lights come up on the stage area, the crowd on the dance floor cheers uncontrollably and a rumbling audio track kicks in slowly underneath. After a few moments, when the lyrics start, a tall woman in a dark robe and sunglasses steps out from behind the curtain and I can see her lips mouthing along with the track. The song picks up a bit and her hood comes off to reveal a bleached, short, spikey hairdo. At this moment I realize the woman is dressed to emulate the man on the video screen – a rather gaunt character with slight facial hair. Aside from the facial hair, she looks just like him from the neck up.

Now that I'm focusing a little harder on the differences between the actual artist and the woman on stage, things are becoming fuzzy. If I'm not mistaken, that woman has some interesting cheek bones, a rather large nose, and… something funky about her throat? Still, though somewhat mannish, she's quite attractive.

The music ramps up quickly and suddenly, and simultaneously with the first line of the chorus, the woman rips the black robe off to reveal her undergarments, blindingly white; a corset, thong, stockings, garters, 4" stilettos, elbow-length gloves, and a white pleather collar. The first line of the chorus is a deafening roar from the speakers and the crowd of "I'm Afraid of Americans!"

Travis leans over to Michael and has to shout, "That's a pretty shabby tuck-job!"

I look to the woman in response to Travis' comment and almost instantly see the bulge in the panties and realize… that's not a woman.

The man dressed up in women's clothing, the music spouting anti-American sentiment, and the crowd screaming along with it is all too much for me and I have to get up to leave. Not caring or realizing which direction I'm going, I stumble through a back hallway to a fenced-in patio, gasping for air and sit on a low concrete wall under the fence. I might have also had too much booze.

After a couple moments catching my breath a young man and woman come over to me, drinks in hand and ask if I'm okay. I nod and smile as much as I can, saying, "Yeah. I think I just, uh… I think I might have hyperventilated a bit. You know… claustrophobic, I guess."

The woman nods emphatically, piercings jingling in her nose, lip, and ears, "Yeah, man, I hear ya. It can be rough during drag shows, that's for sure."

I take a closer look at the two club patrons hovering over me and assess their appearances. The woman has tattoos on her neck and some on her face, piercings everywhere, a t-shirt for some band or club or other, and pants with more pockets than are remotely necessary.

The man speaks next, "And, we've all seen it before. No

need to get trampled to see a tired act." He's black and dressed more conservatively than the woman. His t-shirt also has some design on it, though I have no idea what it is and the shirt is cut short – just barely covering his stomach. The pants aren't as tight as many I've seen and his shoes are dark and unobtrusive. His hair is the only thing about him that stands out, as most black men in America have either shaved their heads or at least cut their hair *very* short. It isn't huge, but it's enough to grab my attention and he notices, "You like it? I just had it trimmed."

Careful not to offend him I quickly say, "Oh yeah! It's great." The woman is nodding in agreement – I don't think she's stopped since she first saw me – and I look quickly to the long dreadlocks protruding from her skull and add, "I like yours, too."

She snorts and smiles at me, "Hey, thanks man! I've been growin' these babies for years."

The man scoffs at her, "Baby, we know." They laugh at each other and the man sits next to me on the concrete. She grabs a chair from a nearby table and pulls it over. Holding out his hand, the man says, "I'm Victor. You can call me Vic."

"I'm Rhapsody, but you can call me Rap," she's still smiling and nodding. With that hair I have no idea how she's not getting whiplash.

Burping inwardly, I extend my hand and shake Vic's first, "I'm Corwin and, uh… Yeah, I'm Corwin."

Vic responds first, "Happy to make your acquaintance Corwin. I don't think I've ever met a Corwin before."

Sheepishly, and more and more cognizant of my level of

intoxication, I shrug, "Hey, I guess I'm one of a kind."

"Far out, man," Rap replies gleefully. After we shake, she searches through her pockets and continues, "Hey, do you party?"

I'm confused by her question. Isn't *this* a party? Aren't we partying? And if *we* are partying, then aren't *I* a part of *we*? It's drunk logic, but it's logic. I look at her confusedly and ask, "Party?" Burp.

She giggles at the burp while Vic shakes his head at her. "Of course you do, man," and she begins assembling some concoction out of a piece of glass and some leafy dirt.

"So, where are you from, Corwin?" Vic asks to fill the time.

I hesitate, then relent, "Chicago."

"WHOA!" they both emit in prolonged gasps.

"A couple months ago, yeah."

"Wow," Vic adds, "So, this is like, culture shock for you, then, huh?"

There's that phrase again. It's no less true, but still. I respond, "That's certainly a way to put it," though I'm not responding well.

"What made you give up all that *freedom*?" Vic asks sarcastically.

I'm too drunk to actually be offended by Vic's question, and sober enough to know I have to deal with it so I answer, "I guess it wasn't quite... free... I guess." Even as I say it, something breaks loose in the back of my head. What just happened?

"Hey, man, I know it's a big change, so good on you for getting' out there and being a part of the community," Vic continues, "I've met lots of people that defected and sure, a few of 'em are straight up freaks, but most of 'em just kinda keep to themselves, pretending they're still back home."

Rap inhales deeply off the concoction she's mixed up and hands it to Vic. While he takes a lighter to it and inhales, she slowly exhales while saying, "I think it kinda depends on why they're here, ya know? Like, the people who got *kicked* out versus the people who like, *left.*"

Vic has inhaled and is holding in the smoke while pounding gently on his knee, nodding in agreement, and holding the glass pipe out to me. This is drugs. These are drugs. Fuck, I may be drunk, but I'm not too drunk to tell that whatever's in this glass pipe is an illicit substance of some sort, so I weigh the pros and cons very carefully. I could smoke it, get high, and accidentally give up my entire mission. Or, I could refuse and be spotted as a square.

Flashback. Two months ago, January 2047.

Gray puts on a video and leaves the room. "*Drugs. Drugs are the driving social force in Gaymerica, inducing behaviors and attitudes that promote lasciviousness, apathy, and anti-government sentiment…*" the video displays clips of people smoking, injecting, snorting, and all forms of imbibing, "*…Drugs are illegal in America because they cloud the mind, reduce motor functions and in general, reduce the user to a blubbering puddle of idiocy…*"

This stuff smells sweet but kind of skunky. I hear the video in the back of my head warning me there could be all kinds of bizarre chemicals in this, but I realize the gravity of what could happen if I refuse…

"*…If you are offered drugs, do your best to placate the person offering,* *but do as little as possible. If you refuse, you could be deemed a traitor and taken in front of the Queen Supreme to be dealt with at her discretion…"*

With this in mind I put my mouth on the end of the pipe and inhale. And, I inhale. And… nothing's happening.

"Lost your cherry. Here," Rap reaches over and hands me a light, "Fire it up, man." They are apparently both aware that as an American I'm unskilled in the art of smoking drugs since they're watching me intently to see how I do it. I start the lighter and hold the flame to the bowl at the end of the pipe, then breathe in. Just as I finish, Rap adds, "Now, you gotta hold it!"

"What?" I inadvertently ask. In doing so, I cause myself to cough.

"Or cough! Yeah, that works, too, man! You wanna make sure it saturates your lungs!" she's very excited for me and is nodding again. Her explanation sounds terribly scientific and logical and I don't completely follow due to my current level of intoxication. So, I continue to cough. Then, I try to stop coughing. And I try again, but I keep coughing.

Vic hands me his beer and says, "Here, have a swig. That oughtta help."

I take a swallow, then another and the coughing seems to subside. For what seems like the rest of the night, I have the occasional mini-coughing fit, but not the big one again.

We talk about random things – where we grew up, what our jobs are – and after a few minutes, I start to notice things change… and change again. I feel like I'm blanking out, not *blacking* out, mind you, but *blanking* out.

Vic says, "We should hit the pancake house after this!" and

I feel like I've faded away, gone somewhere else for a while but I have no idea where. When I shake my head, I come back and Rap is only just responding to Vic saying, "Yeah! That sounds like a blast..." and completely against my will, I blank out again... disappear for what seems like a long time.

I turn to Vic who's only just looking to me for my response and I say, "Sure! That would be cool."

"Awesome," he says after another blankout.

We make our wayWemakeourwayWe make our way...

...to the exit and wait outside for a bus to come by. And now I'm rhyming.

***

Pancakes taste awesome. I like them with syrup and blueberries. The blueberries here taste fresher and crisper than they ever did in America. Vic is sitting next to me and our legs are touching. It's a small booth with Rap on the other side, so it makes sense we're squished next to each other like this. I think he's swaying his leg back and forth on purpose, though. I'm way too drunk and high to protest, though – these pancakes are SOOOO good! Blankout.

***

Rap lives only a few blocks from my apartment, so Vic is going to crash on her futon and stumble home in the morning. My apartment is between the pancake house and Rap's "pad" (I made that word up... I think) so they're walking me home.

We reach the front door of my apartment building and I stumble onto the concrete stoop to rest for a second before getting back up, saying, "You know, I had a great time tonight. I came with some other people but I have *nooo* idea whatever happened to them. But this is cool."

Rap and Vic both agree, saying, "Yeah! For sure…" and the like. Rap slaps Vic on the ass and starts slowly meandering down the sidewalk in the direction of her apartment, which is apparently some form of co-op, whatever that means.

"So," Vic says, his hands in his back pockets, looking down at the ground then back at me, "I had a great time, too."

"That's cool," I reply.

"Soooo…" and without further warning, he swoops in and plants his lips directly on mine. My reaction time is understandably slow, so instead of pushing him away or recoiling in horror as I might have had I been sober, I merely push back with the slightest pressure, assessing the situation. He hasn't shaved for almost a day now and neither have I, so there is a slight sandpaper effect as our skin connects. His lips are soft but firm and it appears he knows what he's doing. As long as I keep my eyes closed, it's not that bad.

While this has been taking place, I've inadvertently moved my hands up to grasp him at the elbows and slowly moved him away from me. As the kiss ends, I open my eyes amid a torrent of confusion and drop my hands to my sides.

Vic nods understandingly and takes a step back, "All right. We'll do better next time."

"Next time?" I ask, on the verge of passing out.

He takes his mobile device from his pocket and taps it.

Apparently, I've given him my phone number at some point. Vic smiles and ambles down the street toward Rap who jibes at him, "Come on, pokey! Heh… pokey…"

I watch them go, the look of utter confusion still plastered on my face. Vic only turns back once, blowing a kiss as he does. Blankout.

Stumbling up the stairs I search for my keys out of habit only to realize after what feels like hours that I just need to press my thumb to the plate next to the door. It takes longer than usual to register but eventually lets me in. When I enter my apartment, there's a blinking light coming from my PC. I open it and see there's an urgent message from Gray saying I was due for my Friday check-in hours ago. Looking at the status bar I see it's 4:37 am and mumble, "Fuck it," slamming the PC shut and falling face first into my new bed.

I kissed a guy.

8

Blink, blink, blink… My phone and PC are now both blinking with frantic messages from Gray. What the fuck time is it? The alarm clock next to the bed (an antique electric model I picked up at a secondhand store down the street) says 8:45am and there's sun beaming through the window. I believe it, but I don't feel like I've been in bed for four hours. Rather, it feels like it's been an eternity, my brain sloshing around from moment to moment, merging actual events with dreamed-up ones. All are disjointed and prolonged due to considerable chemical influence.

I can't face Gray right now. How do I explain that I got very drunk in mixed company, stoned, and kissed a man… all in the same night?! It's too much to face at the moment, and I have the urge to scrub my skin clean. But first I need coffee… and painkillers – my head is throbbing.

Every cupboard seems to be completely empty. I have a coffee maker but apparently no coffee. I quickly change out of last night's clothes, scrub my teeth and wash my face, and grab my jacket to head down to the coffee shop.

Once outside, I realize (as I would have earlier this morning had I been remotely sober) that it's unseasonably warm for late March and I don't need the jacket. Instead of running back upstairs, I take it off and carry it to the coffee shop.

Beane Wilde is a trendy establishment on the first floor of an old brick building about three blocks from my apartment. It looks busy from where I'm at as people are out in droves to enjoy the weather, most of them in dark glasses. Taking their cue, I search my jacket pockets for my sunglasses and am thankful for my wardrobe error when I find them. Ah, much better.

Just as I'm donning the sunglasses and about to cross an intersection, a woman walking at high speed darts out from around the corner of a white-painted brick building and plows into me at full force.

"Shit!" I yelp and fall – too hung over to fight gravity – to the pavement, my sunglasses and jacket landing next to me. The woman also yelps, but doesn't fall over. Instead, she stands on the street corner staring at me with her hands over her mouth.

"Ohhh, fuck! I'm so sorry!" she gasps from behind her clasped hands, finally extending one to me, "Are you okay?"

I take her hand, knowing she's likely too weak to help me up and press my other hand to the concrete to help myself up. I'm mistaken, though, and she yanks me up off the ground before retrieving my jacket and sunglasses. Hiding my surprise, I mutter, "Yeah, I'm all right."

"Shit, dude, I'm really sorry. You sure you're okay?"

I brush myself off and reapply my sunglasses as she hands them to me. I answer, "Hey, no problem..." and finally look at her. She's beautiful, but not in any way I've ever found a woman beautiful before. She's wearing a rumpled hat perched over middle-length auburn hair that's bound in a loose ponytail. A plain t-shirt covers a thin, long-sleeve thermal shirt and mid-thigh cutoff jean shorts overlap dark green tights tucked into tall, striped socks. Her black, canvass shoes have holes in them and I can see her toe through her shoe. I don't know why, but this is devastatingly attractive to me. She has a slender, but firm figure and a sculpted face made up of dark brown eyes, a slight nose, and un-painted lips graced by a lip ring.

The wind has left my lungs but I manage, "Yeah, I'm good." A few pedestrians have slowed to make sure every-thing's okay and we both blush with the attention.

"Are you sure? You look a little stunned," she adds and puts her hands up to steady me.

My hand goes up to meet her and I touch her arm for just a second. The passersby are now confident that everything is all right and have moved on. I answer, "Yeah, I just, uh… Just need some coffee – one of those nights, I guess." I laugh, trying to make it sound better, but it fails and I feel like a moron.

"Hey, I understand. Say, I was thinking of getting some coffee a little later, too, but I could go now and buy you a cup," she suggests, motioning toward the coffee shop.

"Oh, you don't have to do that—"

"If nothing else, it'll make *me* feel better," she adds smiling.

I shrug. "How could I possibly turn that down?"

When we order, the barista knows the woman and

addresses her pleasantly, but barely acknowledges me. She orders some exotic drink – soy, Irish Crème, extra espresso – and I order a dark roast, black. It's too crowded so we step outside.

Admittedly, it's been so long since I spoke with a woman to whom I was remotely attracted that I've completely forgotten the protocol. Mostly, I'm just trying to get out of this situation without making an ass of myself. Once we're clear of the crowd and part way down the block I say, "Well, thank you for the coffee. I'm sorry if I made a scene."

"Oh, it's really no trouble. I'm sorry I almost killed you," she adds, laughing enough to show she realizes she didn't almost kill me but that she does have a good sense of humor. How can this woman be a lesbian? She seems to be giving off all the common signals that she's attracted to me.

Finally, I realize we haven't exchanged names and state, "Oh, um. I'm Corwin."

"Corwin," she repeats, holding out her hand, "I'm Hannah."

"Hannah," I repeat. "Hannah, it's a pleasure to meet you. I should probably get headed back, I have a…"

"Wait, you can't drink coffee alone. There's like, a rule about that or something."

Seriously! She cannot be a lesbian! This is truly baffling. I play along, "Oh, it is?"

"Yes," she smiles, proud of her logic, "It is. Look, I'm headed down to Duboce Park to stalk other people's dogs. Why don't you come with me?"

"Stalk?" I ask, perplexed.

She nods with a faux serious look on her face, "Yep. They don't allow dogs in my building so I have to get my canine fix watching other people's dogs. They're usually pretty cool about it. Some of 'em even let me pet their pooches."

"Huh," I shrug and point my coffee toward the park, "I guess let's do it then."

We walk in silence momentarily before Hannah starts by asking, "So, are you from San Francisco?"

If she has to ask, that means I'm fitting in. Awesome. Proudly, I answer, "No, actually I'm from Chicago."

"I kinda thought. You've got that newcomer look about you." Well, shit. There goes that theory.

"What about you? Where are you from?"

Hannah sighs, "Well, it's kind of a long story if you're ready for it."

"Fire away."

"Okay. I'm from Columbia, South Carolina—"

Shocked, I stop in the middle of the sidewalk, "Wait, what?!"

"Hey, *you're* a defector." She smiles, politely urging me to listen, and I do. "I was born a couple months before the U.S. split..." She doesn't look thirty, by the way. "...and my dad didn't want to leave America. Him and my mom fought a *lot* about it – 'course, I don't remember any of this 'cause I was like, a couple months old. And, my mom wanted to leave. She always used to tell me about how she couldn't live in a country where entire segments of the population were persecuted for who they were..." I've never heard a woman speak so openly and frankly before and... it's strangely captivating to listen to her despite the fact I completely disagree with her. "My father used to call her a goddamned hippie and all sorts of stuff... and worse, I guess. Well, after a couple years – and I don't remember this at all – my mom had had enough and she packed me up while dad was at work and hooked up with a couple old friends of hers. Women aren't allowed to travel alone, as I'm sure you know, so her friend's husband had to claim her as family. In those early years as things were settling down, they weren't as restrictive about travel between the countries so they got across the border just fine. Back then, you used to have to go to the capital in Sacramento to file for amnesty and apparently it's a long drive from where they crossed. Then again, I guess it's a much longer drive from South Carolina to the Western States in general..."

She trails off and I take this opportunity to ask a question I've been wanting to ask for a long time, "Okay. This 'Western States' thing – when did that name come to be?"

She nods in an exaggerated fashion and makes a sucking sound with her mouth. "Western States, right. Yeah, you Americans don't call it that, do you. You call it *Gaymerica*!" She sounds it out with gusto, pretending to be an announcer of some sort. When I respond quizzically, she proceeds, "Yeah, we can't help that. They like to claim that's our official national moniker, like it's chartered with the U.N. and, to be honest I used to believe that. After all, we're a bastard child of America anyway, right? Well, whatever the genesis of that name was, it doesn't exist anymore. At least not here. Plus, it's not accurate. I mean, hell, less than half the people in this country are gay anyway, why would we put that in the name? It certainly doesn't speak for everyone here…"

MIND. BLOWN. I trip and almost fall over. I'd like to imagine it's on a crack in the sidewalk, but upon review, that's not the case.

"Are you okay?" she asks, reaching her hand out to steady me. Luckily for me, I'm too shell-shocked to respond in any way but a nod. She continues her tale, "My mom met a couple guys when I was younger, but it never took. They were jerks anyway." There is a long pause and she laughs, shaking her head, "Oh my god. I can't believe I just droned on like that, I'm so sorry."

"No, that's totally okay. I like to listen," I say, trying to keep her talking. I loudly slurp some coffee.

Hannah takes her hat off and shakes her head, her auburn hair shining in the late morning sun. She holds her hand to her forehead and sighs, "Tell me about yourself, Corwin. I love that name, by the way. Corwin. Do you go by Corwin, or Cor, or something like that?"

"Corwin," I answer politely.

"Corwin is better. Cor sounds childish and… incomplete." This woman summed up in one second the reason I've always hated "Cor" as a nickname. I'm pleased that she respects that.

"Well, uh…" I start slowly. Basics, Corwin, "I was born in Mason City, Iowa. I won't tell you, but it was quite a while before you—"

"Aw, it can't be that long. You look young!"

I'm blushing but I continue, "My dad…" I pause uncomfortably. "…He was branded a traitor, I guess. I never really knew what happened to him, but he was taken when I was, well, a kid."

"Oh, I'm so sorry," she injects with all sincerity.

I shrug, "I don't know. It happened. It's over now. My mom was, well, much like your dad, I assume. She raised me to believe what… I came to believe—"

"And now everything's different?" she asks, stopping and looking directly at me.

Locking eyes with her for a moment something else breaks loose in the back of my skull like last night. A twinge, I guess. Slowly, I answer, "Yeah. Yes. Things are, progressing."

The rest of the way to the park, the conversation meanders back and forth from employment to education to favorite pets. Nothing seems right at this moment. I want to fight with her on the smallest of points but I resist for two reasons. First, I have a mission I can't give away. Second, I… kind of… don't want to disagree with her… at least not on everything… I'll need to pay careful attention to this as she's awfully convincing. Manipulative almost.

Between what we've been talking about and my own curiosity about her apparent attraction to me, I keep wanting to ask if she's a lesbian but don't know how to bring it up without it being awkward and embarrassing. So, I let it go.

We watch the dogs for a time and she pets them as they approach, taking particular interest in the Golden Retriever that keeps coming around.

"You like Golden Retrievers?" I ask.

"Oh my gosh, yes! They're such loveable dogs. Not the brightest, but they're loyal and sweet. I like that."

"I was always kind of a Beagle fan, myself," I admit.

She responds instantly, "Uck, they can be so loud, can't they?"

"Yeah. You know, now that you mention it I don't know if I like them as much."

"Oh! I'm sorry! Sometimes my mouth gets ahead of my brain – I don't want you to not like Beagles! They're great!" She genuinely feels bad about this and is covering her mouth with one hand while petting the Golden Retriever with the other.

"That's okay. I guess I'd never really thought about it. My mom just always had Beagles. Huh. Well, I get to like something new now, right?" As I say this, another twinge pings off the back of my skull and I gulp the last of my coffee. Until now I hadn't thought of it, but the bitterness stinging the edges of my tongue makes me aware I have coffee breath.

Just as all these thoughts are going through my head, she says, "Well, I do have a schedule to keep. I'm on my way to a birthday party for my friend's toddler."

"Lots of kids at this thing?" I ask, just trying to keep the conversation going.

Grumbling, she responds, "Yes. She always drags me to these things. But hey, I gotta get going," she pauses, looking down momentarily, then back up at me much like Vic did last night and adds, "Soooo, I don't mean to be too forward, but can I call you some time? I mean, are you available?"

"Available?" I ask.

"Seeing someone?" she clarifies and bites her lip, managing to avoid the hoop protruding from it.

"Me? Yeah – I mean, no. I mean, yes, I'm available – no,

I'm not seeing anyone… yeah."

She smiles, her bottom lip still pinched between her teeth then demands, "Give me your thumb," and holds her left hand out while retrieving her mobile device from her back pocket. I give her my hand and she presses my thumb to the screen. *That's* how Vic got my number! "Now, let me see yours."

I'm embarrassed and have to admit, "It's an old model I got in America. Sorry. But I can punch it in."

She moves closer to me and in a low voice relays her phone number then says, "You should call me," and without warning kisses me on the cheek and starts quickly off down the street.

"I'll do that!" I shout after her. She turns to look at me twice, smiling as she goes, almost skipping down the street.

I turn briefly to my right and see a young couple (man and woman) with the Golden Retriever. They're looking at me expectantly and the woman says, "She's cute."

"Thanks," I reply sheepishly, adding, "Nice dog."

They thank me and I turn to walk back to my apartment. Hannah. Vic. Shit.

***

I arrive back at my apartment, my head whirling from the past twelve hours and plop into my bed, contemplating whether or not to open the PC. The orange, throbbing glow emanating from it eventually goads me into moving to the chair and cracking it open. It reads:

7 MISSED CALLS

Crap. Reluctantly, I press the screen to awaken it and enter my password. The initial screen that pops up includes a list of all the missed calls and Gray's face wallpapers my desktop. I press it, leaning my head on my hand and wait for him to answer.

I don't have to wait long as he accepts the call after only a ring and a half. Angrily, he barks, "Hawley, you were to check in last night at 10:00 pm! What happened?"

Despite the fact I've had all morning to come up with something, I haven't. I struggle to blubber out, "Uh, nothing. Nothing, sir. I just, uh…"

"Well?!"

"I went out with some co-workers and ended up staying out a bit too late. Sorry about that, sir."

Without pause, he asks, "Why didn't you call when you got in?"

"I was… a little intoxicated, admittedly and I didn't want to bother you—"

"I don't care what time of day it is, you need to check in when you're scheduled to check in!"

I sit back in my seat and sarcastically reply, "Yes, mom."

Gray pounds his fist on the desk in front of him and thunders at me, "*This is not a joke, Hawley!*" I straighten up and refocus my attention as he proceeds to dress me down, "You are a valuable asset to the Department of Foreign Affairs and we expect you to operate as you are *told* to operate. Do you understand?!"

Stammering, I answer, "Yes, sir."

"You may think this is some god damned dodge…" I make the sign of the cross but do not interrupt him, "…but it is *not.*

We have invested thirty years, trillions of dollars, and thousands of lives in the operation of which you are now a part, Corwin and I will not have it compromised because you are too lax with your duties. Do you understand?"

"Yes, sir."

"Now," he coughs and tugs on the lapels of his suit jacket, "As it appears you've been working to socialize yourself into their culture, we have an assignment for you. We would have given you one sooner, but we wanted to make sure you had a good social cover before you stuck your neck out." I gulp at this, "When you're processing applications, we want you to pay special attention to the Chinese applicants and what their particular lines of employment are. We've been receiving intelligence that Gaymerica…" Inadvertently, I almost correct him here, "…is having strained relations with the Chinese government and we believe this could be a weakness. We want to know what types of people are defecting from China and what industries are gaining from the defections. In addition, we have a watch list to check those names against. If one pops up and we can apprehend them, we can bring them to America and possibly gain an edge. Is this something you think you can do, Hawley?"

Without hesitation, I agree, "I can do that, sir."

"Good. We're counting on you, Corwin. Every bit of information helps."

"I'm your man, man," I can't believe I just called him that.

Gray looks at me quizzically for a moment but shakes it off, "Whatever. Just be careful. We can't have you getting caught or giving yourself up. Keep working to fit in, Corwin.

It's good that you're socializing, but you have to play close to the vest. You can't let *anyone* know that you're not fitting in.

I dare not tell him a couple lines have already blurred for me, so I just keep it to the business at hand, "You can count on me, sir."

"Take care of yourself, Corwin. And, if you're going to be checking in late next Friday, too, send me a message from your mobile to let me know, you understand?"

"Understood."

***

In 2039, a young woman by the name of Winifred had been implanted into a community in Southern California with the responsibility of finding a weakness in the relationship between local Californian municipalities and the Northern Hispanamerican Federalis. According to Gray and a rather graphic video produced by DoFA, the woman encountered some difficulties along her journey.

Winifred found herself in a romantic tangle with a Federali and after a few months carrying on the affair, they were caught. According to DoFA, straight relationships are not allowed in Gaymerica. To protect himself, the Federali claimed he'd never met her and didn't want anything to do with the case. The local Gaymerican government, though, had been deceived by Winifred and wanted to throw the book at her.

In an attempt to seek clemency for her misdeeds, Winifred offered to spill everything she knew about the American plot to overthrow the Gaymerican government. Luckily for DoFA, her knowledge level was minimal. Every agent is given only the information they need to complete their assigned task. While DoFA can put the pieces together like a puzzle, no one by themselves can bring the organization down. Winifred did not know this, though the local officials did.

They spurned her request and extradited her to America, where she was summarily put to death as a traitor. The American government does not bask in taking the lives of its people, and so the execution of the traitor was kept from the news.

Winifred is dead. I could be next.

9

There's a dusty, used book store on the bus route between work and my apartment that I've been meaning to visit. Yesterday I jumped off the bus to sneak a peek. They had an old, but still in-tact copy of a Harper Collins Study Bible. It's not the King James version my mother raised me on, but in my eyes it's even better. It says it includes apocryphal books as well as canonical. I like this, but as I've never read it before I guess I won't know what I was missing.

Tonight, Tuesday, I'm opening it for the first time.

***

Okay, it's not exactly a page-turner, but I'm getting some good info. I am *slightly* confused, though, how in the beginning of Genesis we seem to be in the middle of a story about how the Earth was created in five days and all of mankind on the sixth (with an interesting turn of phrase saying "Let *us* make humankind in *our* image..."), when it morphs without explanation into a completely different story (the Adam and Eve one) about how mankind came to be. Did Adam and Eve and all their ancestors happen on the sixth day? That's probably it. Hmm. I'll keep reading.

***

Man, Noah's a friggin' drunk.

***

Woah, there's an awful lot of talk about foreskin.

***

Ooh! Sodom and Gomorrah! I know this one. As I'm reading, I'm vaguely remembering the stories I was told as a child about the depravity of Sodom and Gomorrah and how this is where the term "Biblical" gets applied to the word "knowledge" to mean sex. Yep, there it is. That's sick. And, he *does* offer them his daughters instead. Wow, what a dick.

***

Huh. It's Lot who's guilty of incest. Well, his daughters actually. So, maybe he wasn't wrong to offer them to the men of Sodom.

***

I would like to point out that the part of Genesis where

Jacob fathers children through his wife Leah's maid has never been told to me before. How on Earth is that remotely appropriate?

***

I go to work Wednesday and come back, stopping only to grab dinner at a Vietnamese restaurant and dive back into Exodus, right at the part where the Israelites are plundering the Egyptians on their way out of town. Also, God's kind of a dick, too. Pharaoh was actually going to let the Israelites go until God "hardened his heart" and basically told him not to. God created that situation. What the fuck? But hey, plagues! ...Ohhhhhh, *that's* what Passover means...

***

Thursday night I get to Leviticus and discover we're not supposed to eat fat or blood. What the hell good is prime rib, then?

***

Okay, now I'm not a woman, and I don't have any particular feelings toward the female "condition" or whatever it's called, but why is a woman's purification period longer after giving birth to a female than a male?

***

I think it's awesome that there's a whole section entitled *Concerning Bodily Discharges.*

***

Here we go! 18:22 very clearly states, "You shall not lie with a male as with a woman; it is an abomination." That's… not in any way vague. I almost didn't get to this section as I kept reading the part about female *nakedness* over and over again. But, I don't see anything about death. It just says that gays should be cut off from their people. Isn't that what we did?

I keep reading and *good Lord* there are a lot of obscure rules in here. I mean, I know it's a while back now, but I'm pretty sure my entire diet breaks the rules in this thing and I think the punishment's about the same as for being gay. If not worse! Wait, nope. Here it is. 20:13 "If a man lies with a male as with a woman, both of them have committed an abomination; they shall be put to death; their blood is upon them." It's in their twice – then again a lot of stuff is in their twice and the punishments seem to change depending on which version of the rules I'm reading.

The more I read this, though, the less these things seem like laws and more like guidelines. Half the shit in here is punishable by death, so why would this be any *more* reprehensible… other than that it's friggin' gross. I'm pretty sure I've touched women when on the rag before, and I *know* I've eaten shellfish – in fact I ate last night's leftover shellfish six hours ago.

I need to go to bed. I have a full day of work ahead and then another happy hour with Michael and Travis. Michael in particular has not given me a moment's rest when he's seen me this week, asking about the "mysterious lover" I met last week and absconded with. Travis just looks at me, shakes his head and says, "He *was cute*, mister."

Both have been far less apprehensive about inviting me out this week, which is a good thing. This means I'm fitting in. More important than fitting in, though, they think I'm gay. Although, I'm not sure about it anymore either after the test, Gray's admission that the test is accurate, and the fact that kissing Vic didn't completely appall me.

On the flip side, I called Hannah on Monday night, which is why I didn't dive into the Bible then. She sounded just as giddy as the day we met. Since she was busy this week, we scheduled a date next Tuesday to have some gelato and see a free outdoor concert at Buena Vista Park. I'm going to attempt not to address how I feel about this at all. That may be the safest way to handle things.

***

I'm sitting on the rooftop of the building in our outdoor lunch area munching on a turkey sandwich when my mobile beeps. There's a message from a number I don't have stored and I read it, "U goin' out 2nite?"

I reply cautiously, "Maybe. Who is this?"

"That's rite. Ur old-ass phone can't store #s."

This must be Vic, "Sorry about that."

"Whatever. It's Vic. Will I c u @ The Work House?"

I don't know how to answer that. I worry that if I push Michael and Travis too much to go back there that I'll come off as needy. To hedge my bets I send, "Maybe. @ the mercy of co-workers."

"I understand. C u if u do. Won't if u don't." It's sing-songy. I like that.

After saving Vic's number in my mobile, I finish my sandwich and return to my desk to toil away the few remaining and seemingly endless hours of my day. Batch. I love that part.

***

Instead of Quantum, we take the train to the other side of the bay and a club called Stella's to see some female artist scheduled to start at 7:30. The club is in an old limestone-front building with half of an antique streetcar fastened to it, and the main entrance cut through the middle under a plaque that reads "Desire." I don't get the reference, but it's very cool.

We carouse for a while and order some appetizers but no real food and I remain hungry. Realizing I don't want to be as drunk as last Friday, I slow down, making the occasional trip to the bar for a glass of water. The bartender giggles at me every time she hands me a water and I smile sheepishly.

The band sounds good but I can't hear the lyrics very well and I'm mostly distracted by the lead singer's multi-fabric, white sundress. It's kind of revealing, but not in the parts I'd like for it to be so I keep waiting for her to sway just right. This never happens. Luckily, my rapt attention is mistaken by the guys as interest in the band, so no one thinks otherwise of it.

Every song has an air of authenticity to it I'm not used to. Everything I've heard (at least on radio stations and on the internet in America) has been heavily produced and the sound is highly synthetic. This is more Earthy and raw with poor distortion in the guitar and bad tuning in the drums. The guys complain about it on occasion but applaud dutifully at the end of each song. I, on the other hand, am enjoying it greatly as it feels more natural and believable for some reason. *Twinge.*

Once the band is done and our tabs are paid, we shuffle out to the train platform and ride back to San Francisco. One of the guys' cousin is the bassist for the band and she'll be joining us later. Until that came out on the train I had no idea why we went to Oakland. Still, I'm glad we did and I purchase the band's album while on the train.

It's raining now and even though it was only drizzling on the platform in Oakland, it's pouring when we get to our stop in San Francisco.

"Who's up for Work House?!" Michael shouts as we hide under the platform overhang. The entire group enthusiastically replies in the affirmative and Michael pinches my cheek (a unique reversal of age stereotypes) and adds, "I know *you* do, Corwin. Let's get wet!"

And wet we get. It's late and the post-Drag dance party is in high gear when we burst – soaked – through the doors. To my surprise, there is no recoiling of the crowd at our dampness, but rather embracing of it. Big hugs, kisses… Michael's friends are near the door, which helps ease the awkwardness. I make my way to the bar for a drink.

The bartender remembers me from last week and says, "Let me guess, gin and tonic?"

"Uh, yeah. Sounds good."

"Looks like you could use somethin' to warm you up, too," he adds and slaps a shot glass down on the bar.

I shake my head, "That's really not necessary."

He wags his finger at me, pulls out a bottle of rail tequila, and pours some into the shot glass. He then slides it across the bar and eyes me expectantly. I sigh, pound the shot, and slam it back on the bar. "There we go," he shouts pridefully and finally starts pouring my gin and tonic. Actually, that should be gin and tonics, plural. There are now two of them.

I pay him, tipping heavily and rejoin the group having taken up residence on the dance floor.

The music maintains a quality of trance-inducing rhythm, enhanced by the flashing, swirling lights. It's not that I've never seen this before. Concerts in America involve much of the same lighting technology and even some of the same rhythms, but this is where the similarities end.

While at those concerts, I always felt an air of apprehension. There were lights and sound and screaming and singing along, but all of it was done with a collective knowledge that the outburst ends there. It wasn't a comfort zone, but rather the *edge* of comfort. The edge of human behavior, as if we all knew we could display the emotions we'd ramped up to, but nothing beyond. Here, there's no such understood barrier. No line that we're subconsciously instructed not to cross.

But where does the behavior end? What is outside the lines? Or are they blurred or visible only to the more seasoned citizens and I'm just not aware of them? Despite my level of experience or comfort, there's no impending sense of fear or apprehension. There's just the knowledge that there's a communal experience being had.

When it happens, fear is palpable. Get a room of people together and utter one inappropriate word and all of a sudden it's something a person could chew; it's that thick. I don't sense that here, nor do I sense that these people ever have the level of fear I do. Or did. In Chad's basement, playing cards last December, when he called me a faggot, everything changed. Or maybe it didn't change – just my understanding of it, "it" being my experience with my friends. We'd always been friends, but a simple word turned us from friends to government informants. Anyone in the room at that moment could have ratted me out to the American government. My heart was racing and I felt a pain in my chest.

But who's to say they didn't? This is the first time I've had the thought and it grips me, making it harder to dance (though I've been dancing badly, so little is lost). It was less than a month after that incident that Gray showed up on the train, but who knows how long he'd been watching me before that?

Of course Chad would have turned me in, except doing so might have required him to account for some of his own, lesser transgressions. The rest of the guys had no incentive to turn me in, for anything, since I'd done nothing to them… Dave. All at once, the thought crashes on me like a felled tree. The blood from the broken bottle he wiped in his pocket. Dave had intended to turn me over to Gray all along. But then why did Dave confide in me about his wife *after* I'd already agreed to work for DoFA? He'd been so understanding and so earnest in sharing his experiences with Janice but I didn't turn him in. The man was in gross violation of the Sexual Promiscuity and Appropriateness Act, state sex laws, and the Bible. And I didn't turn him in. Instead I encouraged him to embrace his transgression, to take comfort in his wife's slutty desires.

Was that the last test? A final check to see how well I could hold a secret? If I wouldn't even turn Dave in, then I could be trusted to keep government secrets – or was it the other way around? Was I supposed to report this to Gray the next opportunity I had? To prove my loyalty to America? I begin to wonder if Dave sensed my "aptitude" and chose to exploit it to draw attention away from himself; to relieve the burden of his own moral disobedience by placing blame on someone else. After my over-the-top reaction to being called a faggot, Dave must have sensed I was covering something up. How would he have known that, though, if even I didn't know what I was covering up? But, then again, even Chad was suspicious. Otherwise he wouldn't have said anything. They conspired to out my vulnerability.

The authorities chose to act covertly instead of making an example of me. Perhaps my zeal for moral rectitude impressed them and they sent DoFA after me instead of arresting me and proceeding with a public trial. What if I've been deported? What if this bogus shit Gray has me doing means nothing and there is no government plot to overthrow The Western Sta– Gaymerica?

I'm virtually swimming in my own fear at the moment. I've been ostracized from my own country, my own home, family, friends… my whole fucking life! Those twinges I've been feeling in the back of my head are firing a thousand times a minute now as if my brain is being loosed from its moorings, ready to sail from one reality to another in which I'm an outcast criminal instead of a self-sacrificing, patriotic hero.

I would feel sick if it weren't for the fact that I haven't had enough to drink to make me throw up. Unknowingly, I've backed myself off the dance floor to the fringes where I stand watching the sea of unafraid humanity. My fear and anger has repelled me like a magnet from the crowd.

This is what they wanted. For me to feel alone, trapped, lost, and cut off from the world. For me to be sitting in a foreign nation with the sudden knowledge that I'll never see the people I love again. For me to be questioning everything I hold dear. It could be a test, but I somehow doubt it. As these thoughts overwhelm me, I'm feeling more and more angry and embittered. It's not that I've never been disillusioned before, but there's something considerably more profound about losing one's perspective of reality than discovering there's no Santa Claus.

Out of the corner of my eye, I spot Vic dancing with Rap and a couple people I don't know. His trim figure and effortless movements jive in time with the thumping of the sound system and I find myself staring. There's something very, very wrong with this feeling.

An impulse overtakes me and I put my drink down on a ledge, march over to him, grab him by the arm, spin him around and plant a forceful kiss on his lips. He's surprised but receptive and puts his arms around my waist, kissing me back in the process. His tongue breaks the threshold of my lips and I do not protest, instead searching it with mine. This all feels terribly strange and yet common and familiar at the same time. He's better at this than most of the women I've dated.

Eventually, he stops and takes a step back, "Well, hello to you, too, Corwin." He's smiling and checking me up and down. I can feel moderate arousal and am suddenly very conscious of it.

"Hi," I respond faintly.

"You okay?" he asks. "'Cause, you look okay, you just look a little… unhappy?"

I have no desire to talk, but every desire to not be alone at the moment and I whisper in his ear, "I wanna get out of here."

He's taking a swig of his drink and almost chokes when I say it. Thumping his chest to help the beverage go down, he then replies, "You don't have to tell me twice." Vic hands his drink to Rap, tells her he's leaving, and we head outside into the rain.

We talk very little on the way back to my apartment. He's rubbing his hand on my wet arm and though I'm terribly self-conscious in the brightly-lit bus I don't stop him. Every once in a while he kisses my cheek or ear and I kiss him back, taking his hand at one point. The bus drops off a block from my apartment and we climb the stairs to my door, reigning in the anticipation with as much self-control as is reasonable under the circumstances.

I feel reckless. Lost in my passion and desire for intimacy, both of which scream against the better judgment of my raising, I open the door. Every moment that "better judgment" is pushed further into my gut, where it festers on its own, untouched by the excitement and lust propelling us from the swiftly slamming door into each other's arms.

We're kissing and my hands meander down to Vic's toned ass – I'm suddenly self-conscious about the much more aged and saggy ass I possess, but try to forget about it. He reaches up and starts unbuttoning my soaked shirt.

You shall not lie with a male as with a woman; it is an abomination.

The words rattle around in my head and I hesitate momentarily. Vic takes this opportunity to un-tuck, finish unbuttoning my shirt, and rip it off me, followed by my undershirt which then reveals my paunch. He touches it delicately and runs his hands along my abdomen. I feel compelled to apologize, "I've had a few beers over the years, Vic."

Laughing, he shakes his head, "I like it. I like a man with some meat on his bones."

I blush, and to hide my rosy cheeks pull Vic's t-shirt up over his head and off, pressing my body up against his and kissing him on the lips. He allows this for a moment before moving his lips down to my neck where he nibbles the flesh. Not knowing how to proceed, I run my hands lightly up and down his back.

In response, he grabs the lower part of my rib cage and maneuvers me onto the bed. Our lips are locked and I run my hands along his sides. Vic works out regularly and his body harbors little if any fat. I can feel his ribs, buttressed by cords of slender muscle and begin to fondle his chest and stomach, a hard shell of toned tissue.

He kisses my neck some more and starts working his way down my hairy, unkempt chest. As he does, he brings his hands to the front of my pants and he unclasps my belt. My self-consciousness takes over and I stop him, "I need a shower. Really, I've been sitting all day and…"

Vic gives me a sarcastic look and says, "For real?"

"Yeah, I'm just… I really need a shower."

"I'm not going to wait here for you," he announces, folding his slender arms in front of his chest.

I'm speechless at first, then start to reply, "Well, I… I don't want you to leave, I just want to…"

"Oh, I heard you. I just don't think it's fair that you get to get all clean and I have to sit out here smelling like a fuckin' club," he's not angry, just explicit, and his hands have gone from covering his chest to propping him up on the bed with one leg crossed and bouncing up and down in front of the other.

"You… you could take one, too, if you want," I suggest, with absolutely no ill intent.

He grins devilishly and hops up off the bed, "I hoped that's what you'd say."

You shall not lie with a male as with a woman; it is

Exciting and rash. Vic is restrained by nothing. He has no inhibitions about this process and no sense of guilt about it. I try to match his enthusiasm but my fervor for the activity is driven more by anger and lust than enjoyment and sexuality. In any case, it spurs me forward and I rush to the bathroom with a pair of pajama pants to take my shower.

Vic laughs at me and asks, "What are you doing?"

"I need something to wear," I say matter-of-factly.

He walks over to me and rests his hands on my hips, "What the hell for?" When I fail to respond, my bottom lip hung open like a swinging door, he grabs the pajama pants from my hand and throws them on the floor next to the bed. He then turns me around and pushes me into the bathroom.

"I'll be out in a couple minutes," I tell him. He nods and leans his hand on the doorway.

Closing the door, I take my pants the rest of the way off and start the water. At this hour, no one else is showering and the hot water comes quickly and easily. I jump in the claw-foot tub and start washing myself vigorously, beginning with my armpits and ending with my junk as I know I've been sweaty for much of the day at work.

The door creaks and I stop with the bar of soap in one hand on my ass and a handful of soap working my erection gently in the other. "Vic?"

The curtain slides over and Vic steps in, fully naked, "I figured I'd give you a few seconds to get all sudsy."

I haven't moved and soap is streaming down my legs from my hands and the most private parts of my body. I'm only partially conscious of this as Vic closes in on me. He takes the soap from my one hand, and helps me to stroke myself with the other momentarily before turning the soap on himself.

Dumbfounded and more aroused than I've been in a decade, I stand there, letting the water wash the soap off my body. I'm frozen. Vic takes the lead and moves up to me. Our parts touch as he does this and he rotates me around so he's in the water and can lather up with soap.

You shall not lie with a male as with a woman;

Because the parts don't fit together right. My parts, his parts, they do the same thing. Clearly, neither was built to receive the other. So why on Earth does this feel so enthralling? He wraps his hand around both of our erections briefly and turns to soap himself up. I am left standing in the dry side of the tub watching him rub the soap over his skin.

He turns around and, unable to resist the urge, I close the distance between us and run my hands over his silky body, terminating at the crack of his ass. I run my right hand down through the crevice while reaching around to touch his rippling abdominals with my left. Vic stops lathering himself to let me do this and puts his hand up against the wall on the other side of the shower head to balance himself so he can spread his legs. My left hand roams along his lower abs and starts to scan the small patch of curly hair over his well-manicured genitals. He exhales audibly which I take as an indication he's liking what we're doing. As he leans forward, the water streams down his back, washing the suds away from my right hand and his ass. Without the soap, I can start to feel more of his anatomy, my fingers gently pressing on his anus.

Flashback, Iowa – 2025.

I'm fifteen and masturbating on a daily basis because my hormones are telling me I'm supposed to be impregnating at least one human female per day. My condom contraband is accompanied by a small bottle of something called KY Jelly. My supplier is my mother, though I try not to think of this. She feels that if I'm properly prepared for sex, I'll be more willing to do it right and follow God's will. I have no idea who *her* supplier was, but neither Ida nor any girl I dated in high school or college was ever made aware of the chain of custody. No woman needs to be thinking of a guy's mother while his cock is inside her.

Mom is at work (second shift of some customer service job) and I'm in the shower at 5:25pm on a weekday. I bring the tube of KY Jelly with me into the shower as I've made a habit of jerking off and washing it down the drain.

I'm seated on the far side of the tub with the shower head aimed at the wall so as not to wash the lube away from my masturbatory activities. I squeeze the bottle and too much comes out – my zeal getting the better of me. I spread as much on my cock as possible, but a copious lump of it begins to drip down my testicles. In reaching to catch it I (only for a second) massage it into the flesh under them. A brief encounter of my lubricated fingers and my anus reveals a distinctly pleasurable experience. Without contemplating the repercussions of my actions, my hand returns to the spot (excessive lube gathered there) and begins to massage the opening until it relaxes. I take my other hand and start slowly jerking myself off while massaging my anus. The sensation increases the harder I push on the opening until my finger slips through into the rectum. A tiny yelp escapes my lips and I clamp my mouth shut to keep it from happening again.

Still not realizing I'm doing anything wrong, I allow it to happen again, then again until I retain the penetration and just start moving it back and forth in time with the other hand. The further my finger penetrates, the more sensation I feel both in the opening and beyond where a swollen lump of flesh encourages me to press just a little harder, forcing my erection even stiffer. I shudder and my thighs slap against the sides of the tub. I keep pressing my lips harder together as some unseen force is willing them apart.

A sensational three minutes pass as I bring myself to climax – not caring about where the ejaculate lands – and sink, spent into the basin with water rushing down off the wall next to my head.

I would do this once a week as a special treat until a year later when I learned the evils of masturbation and the temptations to touch "parts of the body not intended for sexual pleasure." Sex Ed was terribly vague and non-committal in its delivery. I had no idea what they were talking about but was certain my weekly penetration practice was one of the forbidden activities…

You shall not lie with a male as

I search Vic's body for the same pleasure spots, assured by biology that he has them. Before my fingers can press further into him, he turns to me, whispering, "Relax. We'll get there." The soap has not been rinsed off the front of his torso and our chests and stomachs slip together. We kiss again, his hands now running from my cheeks to my neck to my nipples where he makes a fast study of them, then proceeds on down to our erections again. Water descends down his body onto our cocks, washing the suds into the tub. As before, I try to press my lips together, but can't and the slightest sound emits from them. Vic takes the queue and drops his own penis to focus on mine for a moment, massaging it in the hot water of my ancient shower.

This goes on just long enough for me to get my bearings and reach for his when he shuts the water off and says, "Where are your towels?"

Disoriented, I reach for the built-in shelves behind the shower and grab us each a towel, glad that the two I own are clean.

Vic towels himself off swiftly, missing spots but not caring. He then takes my towel and dries me off more thoroughly. Motioning for me to exit the tub, he saunters into the other room and we make our way to my bed. He spins me around and rests me on my back on the bed. Our bodies are damp and sticky in the heat and he opens a window before returning to me. Here, Vic repeats the process he began the shower, though more completely. Instead of running his hands from my cheek, to my neck, to my body, he does this with both his hands and his lips.

I go to touch him and rub my fingers on his muscular back but he takes my hands and pins them on the bed, indicating to stop. Vic does not stop. His mouth comes to my right nipple and he sucks on it for a moment before tugging gently with his teeth.

You shall not lie with

Anyone the same way again. No one I've been with before knew of this pleasure button, but Vic found it right away. It's painful, but not in a way that makes me want him to stop, so it continues and transfers over to the other nipple. His hands have moved on ahead and are massaging my thighs and testicles… and now my cock. While his mouth is busy with my chest, he brings a hand up to meet it. Having collected enough saliva on his fingers, his hand returns to my cock, lubricates it and starts thrusting up and down. His fingers articulate individually, magically pushing in all the right places.

I'm making more sounds now but Vic still won't let me participate, instead moving his mouth farther down my torso until he reaches my cock. He asks if I'm clean and I tell him yes, only after a moment to realize what he's asking. When he's confident I know what he's asking and have answered honestly, he begins to tongue my cock, then wraps his mouth around it. I bring my hands to my face, covering it with both of them and utter unbidden, "Oh, my God," without performing the sign of the cross.

You shall not

Compare this action to any that God allows. God himself never fucked anyone, how could he know how this feels? That no woman I've ever been with was remotely aware of how to do this such that it could feel this good. How could God know that this is the best thing I've ever felt?

Vic's head moves faster now, along with his one hand while the other gently massages my testicles. I can't stop it at this point and start to mutter, "I can't... I'm going to..."

Instead of stopping or dismounting he continues more enthusiastically. I utter several other "Oh my Gods" as he brings me to the finish.

You shall

Come.

10

Vic had to run to work early Saturday morning. He works at a bank and the staff rotates who works weekends. This is his. I spend the rest of Saturday and all of Sunday just waiting for work to begin as I can't seem to wrap my head around what's going on.

Work is simple. I do my job, try to scam Chinese immigrant profiles (which is easier than I thought thanks to a screen capture function on my mobile), and take my allotted breaks and lunches. All this is quantifiable and doesn't require me to think about how it affects me. But my personal life has taken on a life of its own.

I don't know where I stand with the American government, no matter what Gray says, and my situation with Vic is difficult for me to justify. I promised myself before I came over here that I would only go through with the activities in which I was forced to partake. Other than that I wanted to stay out of the way. The reality, though, is that *I* initiated Friday night's activities with Vic. More crucial then that is the fact that I still don't find it completely repulsive. Emotionally, I'm harboring intense guilt over it and have prayed at least a dozen times since

Saturday morning for God to forgive me. I'm not asking for forgiveness about having *done* it as I can easily excuse the activity as part of my infiltration, but rather for *enjoying* it.

We Americans revile a lack of inhibitions. Every action, no matter how small, must be undertaken with caution and respect to rules of conduct and morality. I'm pretty sure I broke all of them. Fortunately, I've taken a pretty firm line of avoidance when debriefing with Gray.

I explained to him that I'd be late checking in this time, and debriefed a bit before noon yesterday. We talked about the screen shots I transmitted and about some of my extra-curricular activities (like reading the Bible, meeting Hannah, the girl rock concert) but not about what happened *after* the concert. Gray didn't ask and I told him the concert ran late which is why I had to check in the next day. He bought it and that's good enough for me.

All this being said, I know that at some point all of this information will come to the surface. They have ways of knowing what's happened and upon my reentry (if that ever comes) I'll be intensely debriefed. With every personal event that takes place I fear that debriefing more and more. It's not a matter of *if* they find out, it's a matter of what happens to me *when* they find out. So why go back? I've thought about this many a time and haven't come up with a more solid answer than that it's home.

My feet are propped up on the window sill and I scan the city lights under the retreating daylight, a slight fog drifting in and enhancing the view. I've begun drinking hard liquor instead of beer and have a mid-grade scotch balanced on my hip. I haven't decided how I feel about the stuff — it's too strong and hits in a bad place in the back of my mouth — but I drink it anyway. It's a mellow drunk and I can't drink so much of it that I get stupid or hungover, so it works for me.

I glance down at the street and the lamppost opposite my building. Next to the lamppost, is an electrical box about five feet high. Maybe it's the fog and maybe it's my affected vision, but I'd swear there's someone standing between the two. My feet lower from the window sill and I lean forward for a better look. Slowly, I reach to turn off the lamp. Sure enough, there's a man (or what appears to be a man) in a light jacket and a fedora looking in this direction.

My eyes adjust and I take a closer look. He's older, I think. Maybe fifties or sixties. His eyes meet mine, but only for a second. I watch as he breaks away and starts down the street away from the building. Hastily, I put the scotch down on the window sill and move to the next window to watch him go.

A shudder runs up and back down my spine and I close the window to ward off the cooling evening breeze. What the hell was that? Was he some kind of government spook? The urge strikes to run outside and tail him as long as I can, but I think better of it. No one needs to see me running down the street calling attention to myself. Am I paranoid? Maybe I should tell Gray about this the next time we talk... But no! What if that man is an operative of the American government as well? What if this is how Winifred was found out? Was she tailed to make sure she was doing her job?

I'm paralyzed with indecision about this and instead return to my seat to sip scotch. Then I flip open the PC and start flipping for sports programming to watch.

***

RePro is the shortened term for legislation that passed in the late teens, early twenties prohibiting certain amoral and socially inappropriate acts. Long form, the name means Revised Rules of Prohibition as Defined under the Social Morality Act. You can see why someone might shorten it to RePro. The Social Morality Act dictates that society is governed by certain moral codes to which every person is responsible for adhering. The Rules of Prohibition clearly outline the behaviors which are prohibited under the act. If I remember right, it goes something like this:

> *A citizen shall not engage overtly or covertly in any of the acts contained herein:*
> 1. *Immodest dress*
> 2. *Lewd or promiscuous behavior*
> 3. *Prostitution*
> 4. *Sexual acts in positions other than Missionary or with purposes other than procreation*
> 5. *Use of contraceptives*

These are the misdemeanor offenses. Punishments for them range up to and including jail time depending on severity, longevity, and frequency. Not surprisingly, Prostitution is the most often debated of the minor offenses. Most people in America believe that it should be ranked as a felony, but many of the higher-ups consider the felony penalties too steep.

Felony crimes included under the Rules of Prohibition are listed as follows:

> *A citizen shall not engage overtly or covertly in any of the acts contained herein:*
>
> 1. *Abortion – for any purpose whatsoever*
> 2. *Any act identified as a behavior of Gays, Lesbians, Bisexuals, Transgenders; including but not limited to: Sodomy, bestiality, incest, or polygamy*
> 3. *Ingestion, possession, or sale of drugs as defined by the Illicit Substances Schedule*
> 4. *Sedition and seditionist gatherings*

There are more items on each of these lists, but those are the ones I remember. We were required to memorize them in Junior High. Other offenses such as murder, rape, theft, robbery, etc. are all listed under the standardized penal code and are processed on a cursory basis at the state level. To maintain moral integrity, the federal government of America, specifically the F.B.I. and the Department of Homeland Security, retain jurisdiction over these lists.

I'm told that the F.B.I. and the Department of Home-land Security are holdovers from when we were named The United States, but they're far too efficient and absolute in their meting out of justice for most people to believe they were ever part of the Socialist regime. The two things a person would never want to be convicted of in America are sedition and homosexuality.

It's just the way things are.

No matter what I do for the good of my country, I'll forever be known as at least one of those, however true it may be.

***

It's about 1:30 pm on Monday and Hannah just messaged me to confirm the time of our date tomorrow night. Finishing a quick snap of some Chinese person's profile, I check the mobile. "We still on for 7:15 tomorrow?" it reads.

She writes in complete sentences so I try not to use shorthand, "You bet. Meet you there? Or you want me to pick you up?" I realize only after I send this that there's no real way for me to pick her up and feel foolish for not catching it.

She replies, "I can meet you there. Corner of Haight and Baker. See you then!"

"Great!" I reply, now suddenly self-conscious about what I might have suggested. Was it too forward to offer to pick her up? I barely know the girl, so why would I offer to pick her up? It seems presumptuous and I worry I might have turned her off. "*I can meet you there…*" Does that mean she's annoyed with me and doesn't want to have to deal with me until it's absolutely necessary? Or does it just mean she's got something else to do? Or worse, does it mean she thinks I'm a creep and doesn't want me anywhere near her apartment and she's going to ditch me tomorrow night? Perhaps I'm being a little paranoid. In any case there's nothing I can do about it until tomorrow night, so I take the confirmation message for what it is and try to leave it at that.

Still, a creeping thought is worming its way into my head and I'm starting to wonder about... everything. I've been trying to avoid it, but I can't seem to shake the notion that meeting with Hannah may be completely useless. If I'm straight, then I could see existing in this country with a wife and maybe a family. One patently false aspect of the DoFA training has been the suggestion that opposite sex relationships aren't allowed. Knowing that makes living here markedly more tolerable.

If I am indeed gay, however, a relationship with Hannah is only a reasonable goal if I'm ever to return to America. Her openness and understanding would allow me to be honest with her and not have to be judged from both within and without of the relationship. I don't know how much fun that would be for her, though, or if she'd follow me back there. Great, now I'm talking about a relationship with someone I hardly know. I need to get my brain to shut up somehow.

***

I arrive at Haight and Baker to find dozens of people meandering toward the Northwest corner of Buena Vista Park, but no Hannah. Admittedly, I have an irritating habit of showing up early for things and Hannah doesn't strike me as the type to be very concerned with time. I haven't been to this corner of the city before and it looks a tad rundown. Still, the April air is warm and people seem in good spirits. Concert-goers are carrying picnic baskets, bottles, blankets, and folding chairs. Apparently, there are no seats here and I've forgotten to bring anything to sit on. Scratch that, I can't forget what I never knew.

Just as I'm wondering what to do about the seating arrangements, Hannah bounds from across the street and stops in front of me with a smile on her face. "Hi there, Mister. You ready for this rockin' affair?"

"Sure. One question, though. I see lots of people bringing chairs – should I have brought one?"

Shaking her head emphatically while taking my arm and starting up the street, she replies indicating the large bag in her hand, "Nope. I brought a blanket. We'll just have to sit up close."

"Great," I say. I only half mean it as I don't much care for loud concerts and am not looking forward to sitting on the ground, front row for something I've never heard before. I don't wish to show her my discontent, though and swallow it.

"How was your week?"

"It was fine. You know. Work is work, I guess," I use this dodge to avoid thinking about the bizarre sexual activity that occurred since the last time since I saw Hannah.

"I hear ya. I used to work for this insurance company doing claims adjusting. I hated it…" Hannah likes to talk. I like to listen, for multiple reasons. Primarily, I'm less likely to get myself in trouble, but also because I just enjoy the sound of people's voices. Hannah's in particular is a beautiful voice. I'm not saying she's descended from angels or anything, but it has a strong Alto vibe to it that resonates from her chest up through her mouth. She's continuing, "…and I finally got out of there and started doing the work I went to school for which was – well *is* family counseling. I finished my schooling for that at nights while I was working at the insurance company." After a brief pause, she growls as if angry about something and says, "I did it again! I swear, when I talk to you I just babble. Why do you let me do that?"

Shrugging, I answer, "I don't know. I like to hear you talk, I guess. Plus, if you're a counselor I imagine it might be nice to have someone listen to you for a change."

"Oh, sure. You say that now. I used to date this one guy – he claimed he loved to listen, but whenever it came to anything important, he was a friggin' mile away."

I feel like I know exactly what she's talking about. I can't remember the last time I had a meaningful conversation with anyone. Nodding, I reply, "Well, then I'll say 'I like to listen to you for now. I'll get bored with you later.'"

She takes the sarcasm as it's intended and squeezes my arm a bit tighter. We're nearing the corner of the park and what I mistook via our previous conversation and the messages as a band shell or outdoor concert hall of some kind is actually just a hill with some grass and a walkway. A guy and a girl with acoustic guitars and other sundry instruments are setting up on a tiny wooden stage. There are no microphones, amps, or electronics of any kind. What on Earth have I gotten myself into?

It looks crowded and I ask, "How are we going to get up near the front?"

"Here," she says, grabbing my hand and leading me through the crowd. She offers the occasional "excuse me" to people on either side and plows her way up to the front where she then commandeers a small patch of grass and lays down her blanket. Just as embarrassed by her forcefulness as I am impressed, I quickly sit down on the blanket and kick out my feet, trying to make myself comfortable. Hannah joins me after she finishes arranging her side of the blanket. Once seated, she digs back into the bag to retrieve a bottle of wine and two plastic cups. Some guy next to me laughs and starts whispering to the person next to him.

Suddenly concerned, I lean over to her and ask, "Is that allowed?"

"Wine, in a park?" There is a brief pause before, "No, I don't think so. Is that a problem for you?" she asks holding the bottle, ready to pour.

Part of me really wants to fit in, not rock the boat, and just sit here dutifully. The rest of me, though, wants to do exactly what Hannah does. After all, she's lived here and knows the ropes. If she's not presently in jail, then I'm guessing she's familiar with the rules that should or should not be broken.

Shrugging and laughing it off I tell her, "No. Sorry, it's just uh…"

"You come from the land of repression, I know. Don't worry. I won't hold that against you."

"Oh. Good." I am now thoroughly embarrassed. I do as instructed and take the wine glass, cupping it in my hands and sit cross-legged like a child on the blanket.

The concert is fun and energetic, even interactive at times. There are over a hundred people here just to watch these two goof off and it's absolutely free. I'm not sure I've seen anything like that before and it's relaxing, authentic fun. What makes it even more satisfying, though, is watching Hannah's reactions. She responds with genuine zeal at the smallest of things. Her ability to let go and appreciate what she sees is inspiring to say the least. For obvious reasons I have a tendency to approach all of my reactions with caution, but she has no such censor. I envy that.

A number of times throughout the concert, Hannah turns to me and makes pleasant but intense eye contact. She wants something. Granted, I have a pretty good idea what it is, but it's exhilarating to be around a woman who's not afraid to express it, however inappropriate it may feel. Now, I haven't had sex… at least not with a female, for over two years. More importantly, I haven't had a date with anyone for all that time and I may be wrong about the signals I'm receiving. Despite that, I still think Hannah is more open and honest about her feelings than any woman I've ever known.

Women in America are cagey, shy, and protective. Any overt flirting could be viewed as promiscuous behavior so they refuse to act out at all, forcing men to be the initiating party in every scenario. Each relationship I've had began as a result of a friendship of great length turning into something more romantic, but I never had the guts to just approach someone I was attracted to and proposition her. Here, the roles are reversed. In meeting Hannah I haven't had to step outside of myself and force the issue. She wanted to spend some time with me and initiated interaction. Inappropriate though it may be, it is also simple and forthright.

At the end of the concert, I help her fold the blanket and

pack it into the bag along with the empty wine bottle and plastic cups. It's colder now and both of us are wearing light jackets, but during the concert she even leaned on me at one point. Maybe she needed to keep warm, but I'm choosing to believe she just wanted contact. Human touch is very underrated when you haven't had it for a long time.

"Did you enjoy yourself?" she asks, taking my arm again as we begin to leave.

"You know, I didn't think I would, but I really did. They were talented and funny… and simple. I like that."

"Wow, you really must have liked it. I think that's the most I've heard you talk all night." I shrug sheepishly and she eyes me suspiciously before asking, "You do like to talk, right?"

"Sure. I guess I don't have a lot to talk about, maybe."

She gasps and throws her head back. The action almost knocks her hat off her head and she grabs it in her exasperation, "Oh, no! Don't tell me you're boring, Corwin. I had such high hopes!"

We laugh over this and I finally answer, sensing that her anticipation is real though her sarcasm masks it, "I'm guarded right now. A lot of changes lately."

"And I totally respect that. Hey, I love to talk, so for now this works out fine!" When I merely smile in response she reaffirms her apprehension. "But you gotta give me some feedback here, man."

"Sorry. I agree. This works for me for now, so I'm glad it works for you."

"Great!"

After walking a block to Lyon and Haight Street we stand

in silence for a moment before she says, "So, I had a great time tonight, and… I'd kinda like to see ya again."

"Me, too," and I'm about to make a caveat but she interrupts me.

"But I refuse to until you kiss me."

Baffled, I stumble in my response, "Kiss you?"

"Whew! Yeah, I've had a few glasses of wine, and I'm being a little forward, but I'm gonna need you to kiss me… before we go on another date. It's just a rule I have. Well, technically one I'm making up right now, but a rule none-theless."

And before I can stop myself I begin to vomit things I wish I didn't. Apparently, I'm suffering the same level of wine intoxication as Hannah and it all blurts out, "I *really* want to kiss you, and I'm about to, but I feel like I need to be honest with you first. It's just that… I went on a kind of date last Friday…" At this she is unresponsive – it's the next part that grabs her attention, "…with a guy, and I'm not sure where things stand." There is dead silence even I can't escape and the words somehow start again, "…with him. Right now. And, I just don't want to be getting into anything without, ya know, disclosure."

She blinks, flabbergasted and turns to walk away from me. After a few steps, she stops and turns back to me with a more incredulous look and says, "See, now that's a shame, because… Damn. I could have… I could have *sworn* you were straight! I swear…" I think much of this is to herself and not as much to me, "…I have the worst gaydar on the planet."

"Gaydar? I don't—" and then I catch myself, "Gaydar!

Yes, well, I'm not sure–"

"I just. Damn," she accentuates the "*damn*" and stops, tapping her finger on her lip. She's not angry, just perplexed. "A guy, really?" I shrug, not knowing how to reply. "Fuck. Well, it's been real, I guess," she says, visibly perturbed but trying to be amenable and extends her hand to shake.

I take her hand but start to protest, "I don't want—"

"Nope. I don't compete. Well, okay, I don't compete with *guys*. I mean, there are parts I just don't have, Corwin, and if you're into that, there's nothing I can do. I stopped trying to turn all the decent guys straight a long time ago, and ya know, there's a *lot* higher percentage of gay men here than anywhere else and that can be quite the project, so… no."

Twinge. Dumbfounded, I keep trying to assert myself, "Right, but I'm not… See, I don't know—"

"Really, Corwin, it's okay. I don't want to change you. There's lots of confusion going around about these things right now and I don't want to be part of your confusion."

This hits me hard and I realize she's right. I shouldn't be dragging someone else into my problems. I start to protest again, but nothing comes out. I don't want to see her go, but I can't force this, so I purse my lips and nod, staring down at the concrete.

She turns and steps over to the designated bus stop area and waits. Disheartened, I start to walk away. I get only about twenty feet, though before I hear her voice again, "You're not going to say goodbye?" I come back to her, shrugging, unable to find the right words. "You're not the assertive type. I get that. Still, if you really want something you shouldn't let it go that easily."

Hannah grabs my chin, kisses my cheek and turns back to watch for her bus. Not wanting to say the words, I simply turn around and walk away, feeling I've lost a real opportunity at something.

***

As my mother used to say, when it rains, it pours. My mobile has been on silent and I'm a mile into my walk of penance before I decide to check it. It's blinking with an unread message from half an hour ago. Vic: "U busy?"

Despite my desire to be alone, I seem to have a noteworthy problem with assertiveness and reply, "Nope."

"Meet 4 drinks?"

"Sure." Shit. I should have said no.

"Savvy in 20!"

I have no idea what or where Savvy is so I do a quick search, the battery on my mobile limping woefully along. It connects me to the location and guides me to a nearby bus line before beeping at me to plug it in.

***

Savvy is a low-key nightclub on the edge of the business district with a backlit Plexiglas doorway. Normally, a bouncer of some sort would be here letting people through a rope but as Tuesday is a slow night, there's no need. I enter, surveying the establishment. There's a petite stage occupied by a mediocre jazz group and a cocktail seating area several steps down from the bar and restaurant. The backlit Plexiglas appears to be a theme that recurs in the design of the bar, steps, and stage. It's a little much for me, but the lights are low and mostly unobtrusive.

Vic comes quickly up behind me and plants a kiss on my cheek, surprising me. I try to respond cordially, but I'm uncomfortable with the public display and it's awkward. He recognizes my discomfort, looks around, slaps me on the arm and says, "Come on, Mister uptight, let's have a seat at the bar."

I order and pay for us. Vic thanks me cordially then continues the conversation, "So, you're not comfortable being seen with another man in social situations?" Of course, he dives right into something I'm already uncomfortable with and right after the dressing down from Hannah, so I'm rendered speechless. "Scratch that. That's not fair, I guess. You're still getting used to civilized culture."

Defensively and already a bit tipsy I respond, "Civilized?"

"Oh hey, don't get me wrong. I'm sure all those cage fights and car races you had were the most civilized of their kind, but something tells me you're happier here, no?"

He's being sarcastic, assuming I'm on his side and somewhere deep down I know that but I'm fighting intoxication and fragility, "I *like* those cage matches, damn it. Besides, what's so civilized about a couple of lousy guitar players in a park?"

"Okay, you had me with the cage matches – two burly men all greased up, fighting for my favor – you lost me on the hippie shit, though," and with that he takes another swig of his drink. I take large gulp from mine and turn my attention to the band. "Hey," he starts inquisitively, "You okay? You seem… irritable."

"Irritable?" I ask, training my attention on the band.

"Yeah. Like someone just pissed in your Corn Flakes. If you don't wanna talk about it, that's cool, I just want you to know it's okay to share."

I swing myself around to face him, "What's with everyone wanting me to share? What if I just don't want to talk?"

"That's fine. Then you don't have to. You know, you could have declined my invitation."

I wave that off, "No, I'm just…"

"Irritable."

Reluctantly, I nod, "I think I had a rough day and I'm a little confused about some things." Why am I telling him this? What the hell business is it of his?

"So, spill. What are you confused about?"

"You wouldn't understand."

Shaking his head and leaning in, he answers, "Honey, I realize you come from a long way away, both geographically and culturally, but don't think for a second I don't understand what it is to be *confused*."

"Do you? And how do you know what I'm confused about?"

Vic is taken aback, "Oh, so we're getting serious, huh? Well, let me see. You come from a sexually repressed, morally superior country where you're allowed to be as mean to people as you want but you're not allowed to be expressive with your emotions, am I right?" I don't answer, but my silence rings affirmative, "All right. Then you come here. You're *not* judged for who you are. People genuinely want to know what you feel, and you're spooked. It all seems a little disingenuous because you're expecting some government guys to come from out of nowhere and whisk you away to a hefty prison sentence. Right?" He's almost laughing by the time he finishes this.

"I don't expect to be arrested, I just..."

"What? Hate yourself?" Again, I am silent, shoving my drink in my face. Vic continues after finishing his drink, "Look, man, you're right. You *are* confused, but you gotta understand no one's gonna solve it for you. You're gay. Or bi, I guess, but that's the way it is. There's nothing wrong with that. If you don't start accepting yourself as you are, you're just going to hate yourself for the rest of your life and, I gotta tell ya, you're not going back there."

Struggling to control my impulses I respond, "Well, what if I *do* want to go back there?"

"I know you're not serious, Corwin."

"No? I have family. Friends. I had a life there, and really what's so bad about it?"

"Okay, I don't think 'irritable' was quite the word I should have used. '*Lunatic*' might be more appropriate."

"Because I want to go back to my homeland? That makes me a lunatic?"

He shakes his head incredulously and puts his hand up to stall me from speaking again, "Listen. First of all, you don't have a homeland. It's not like there's a Corwinville, Scandinavia beckoning you to return for the bicentennial family reunion. Second, *yes*! If you want to go back to Chicago, or Iowa, or wherever the hell they think people like you are an abomination, then you are most definitely a lunatic."

I can't think of anything to say that won't result in shouting and losing my cool, so my response is silence. It speaks volumes while not speaking at all. He's right, though not for the reasons he thinks he is. Everyone seems to think they know what my problems are, but how could they? No one knows my circumstance and they can't.

Trying not to break open, I proceed cautiously, "I just feel that there's an awful lot of ignorance and anger pointed toward a country very few people here know much about."

Vic opens his mouth to say something, but instead smiles, pushes his glass away from him on the bar and stands up, "I don't really have anything to say to that, so I'm gonna go home. I want you to call me but, not tonight. Okay?"

I start to answer, but when nothing comes out, he shakes his head and leaves. I remain, ordering another scotch and listening to the mediocre jazz while watching the battery die on my mobile.

11

By train it's about an hour from San Francisco to Sacramento including stops. Michael wasn't interested, but Travis and I (along with a couple women from the department) are joining a group of "activists" from San Francisco at the capitol for a demonstration. We each burned two hours of vacation time to get out of work early and join a protest that's been going on since noon.

It's May and I've been in the country long enough, Gray thinks, that I should start getting more involved to enhance my cover. Had he not suggested it, I probably would have declined Travis' invitation. Supposedly, there's a dissident faction of citizens planning to protest the government's relations with China. Considering sedition is a felony crime in America, I'm understandably apprehensive about being seen with sedition-ists. But, Gray insists I'll be in no immediate danger at this particular event. Perhaps safety in numbers is the key here.

Travis explained to me that it's common for people to protest actions they believe are not in line with the best interest of the people. I'm dizzied by the conversation between Travis and his friend Jessica while on the train. Initially, the three of us are engaged in the conversation but as they start arguing, I drop out for safety's sake.

"See, Corwin, in a democracy you can't just do whatever you want. As a government, you're subservient to the people, and if the people get together and say, 'Hey! China's in violation of human rights,' the government has to listen—" Jessica is cut off by Travis.

"Except that we're not in a democracy, Jess."

"Oh, picky picky."

"Well, you wanna argue the point – the reason we're only demonstrating what we want the government to do is because we have a representative government. If we really were a democracy, then everyone would vote on everything."

Defensively, Jessica asks, "So why the hell are we going then?"

"Because. The only two times you have a say in what your representative government does is when you vote and when you shout at them. We're on our way to shout at them," Travis asserts.

Vote?! I think back to all the times growing up when I was told that the Queen Supreme reigned at all times. There are no elections in Gaymerica. I break in, "Wait, vote? You vote?"

"Uh, yeah? I mean, not all the time obviously – as is the point here, but for our elected officials, yeah," Travis clarifies. This is no less shocking news.

Jess turns to me, "My girlfriend hates Travis because he's always got to pick at things. He's so damned particular."

"That is not true. Violet hates me because I killed your plants while you were on vacation."

"See my point?" she asks. I purse my lips, trying to feign a grin and the conversation goes on without me.

Travis senses he's being targeted and tries to redirect the conversation, "My point is that using the term 'democracy' has a false connotation. Democracy is a very specific type of government that just isn't feasible—"

"Fine, fine, mister smarty-pants. So we're not going to the capitol to tell the government what to do. We're going there to tell the government that if they don't do what we want them to do, we'll vote them out of office next chance we get."

Travis looks at me and gestures toward Jessica, "With a little refinement, that about sums it up."

Travis and Jessica (Naomi is mostly silent – working on making signs while the rest of us talk) tell me that Sacramento is more changed than any of the other cities in the Western States Republic since secession. Interesting side note – no one here really calls it secession. I use that word because it helps me to remember my DoFA training, but everyone here just calls it "separation."

Sacramento is now the capital of an entire country of nearly one hundred million people. Prior to secession it was the capital of California, a state in the U.S. of only forty Million. Much of the infrastructure of Sacramento had to be built anew to accommodate the added administrative responsibilities placed on its locale. Some administrations and departments still have headquarters in other areas of the country, but most of the government is here. Each province also has its own seat but as the country isn't that large in area, there is more of a centralized, federal government, with weaker state governments in each province. This is precisely the opposite of how America is run. In America, each state is given its own authority to govern with final authority over the most important matters decided at the federal level.

There are elevated bridges and roads going into and out of the city over what I'm told is the confluence of the Sacramento and American Rivers. That irony is not lost on me. Supposedly, the river was named that before secession and no one saw a need to change it. Where the rivers meet, there is a plaque commemorating the secession and dedicated to Gaymerica's "...brothers and sisters who fight for freedom behind the walls of tyranny." I fully plan on informing Gray of that bizarre phrase.

The capitol, just West of a vast park occupying twelve city blocks of space, is actually the same building that used to be the capitol of California. Seeing no need to rebuild it when the building itself was sufficient for governance, the city planners left it alone. Most of the administrative buildings are adjacent anyway, and the capitol is more ceremonial than anything. I'm told that the Prime Minister (the term Queen Supreme has *never* been used in my presence) has her office several blocks from the capitol and is not on our list of people to accost while demonstrating.

We pull into the train station at a little after 3:00pm and walk to the capitol where a large demonstration involving hundreds, if not thousands of people has clearly been underway for some time. The crux of the demonstration is this. The Western States Republic apparently still does substantial business with China, despite their supposed human rights violations. Now, I'd never heard of human rights violations while I lived in America, so this is news to me. I do know that Hawaii was sold to China for nearly one trillion dollars to help bolster the American economy right around the time of secession. Since then, America has been doing business with China like any other country.

The people of the Western States, on the other hand, seem undecided on whether China is safe to do business with. Some people believe China is too big to be ignored and that doing business with them is essential both for the economy and for technological advancement. Others believe that no amount of economic security or technological gadgetry is worth the violation of human rights, among them:

"Bridget Merriman!" Travis points to the stage where the attractive, well-dressed woman from the cover of the magazine is speaking.

"...and we have a responsibility as an industry to forward thinking. Isolationism solves nothing and in fact causes regression instead of progress. We have seen this before..." there are chuckles from the audience, though I'm not sure what it means, "...China is a force of nature, we are told. Not to do business with them is suicide. But in one small industry, we have proven that we don't have to do business with China to be innovative, forward moving, and global." Ms. Merriman pauses here for applause. There's something magnetic about her presence. I've never seen a woman in an authority role like this before. She speaks and people respond. No one questions her right to be here, and with the treble of her voice I find it hard to think otherwise either. "But one industry isn't enough.

Much as we loosed ourselves of the oil barons of the twentieth and early twenty-first centuries, we now need to loose ourselves of influences that would call into question our concept of basic human dignity. Moreover, this country has, in all other things, been a world leader in equality and justice. For us to choose relations with one country, however economically influential they may be, over our own basic standard of life is counter to everything we stand for." More applause and this time some deafening screams and whistles.

"Today, we are gathered to send a message to our representatives. That message is, 'Tell China No!' No more will we purchase goods built by underpaid, overworked, and frequently underage workers. No more will we be reliant on their financial influence. No more will we sacrifice our own morals for the benefit of money," she has a calm but firm tone and one that resonates regardless of my feelings about the issue. As a result, I keep forgetting that her speech is likely seditionist propaganda, and that we're right here in the open where we can be identified by authorities. Suddenly, the thought floods back to me and I begin looking around, terrified that my presence at such a public event could compromise my mission. As she continues, I walk casually to the back of the crowd.

"Now, I run a company. I'm not a representative of the government and I don't wield any particular political authority. But, in a way, we all do. We have a choice in who we do business with and how we move that business forward. Merriman Enterprises has taken great strides to push the graphics industry to new heights and to free ourselves of the influences other industries struggle to shrug off. This is my plea to you, to business owners and industry leaders, and to our government. Get innovative! Resting on what we've always done in the past ensures that we'll keep doing the same things. This isn't good for business, it's detrimental to the concept of human rights, and it's just plain counter to progress…"

I'm now towards the back of the crowd and standing in a patch of grass next to a flower bed, listening, but panicking at the same time. I hear my mobile beep and read the message, "Where r u?"

I respond to Travis, "Had 2 get some air. Near the rhododendrons." Luckily for me, my mobile spelled rhododendrons for me. Before I have too much more time to sweat, Travis shows up and taps me on the shoulder, nearly scaring my bowels loose – and I cannot stress enough how much that statement is not hyperbole.

"You doin' okay, there Corwin?" he asks casually, as if nothing's wrong.

I look back to the two uniformed police officers at the far corner of the walkway and ask, "Are we gonna get in trouble for this?"

"For this? For what?"

"Sedition! I mean, there's two cops back there and I'm sweating like a damn pig. What if we get arrested?"

"For what, dude? For standing here? Cheering a public speaker? She is good by the way, isn't she?"

"Very moving, yes, but that's not my point."

Travis looks at me, only half listening to what I'm saying, "Are you planning on starting a tussle?"

"What?! No! I just… Where I come from you don't speak out against the government. And, you *certainly* don't do it in public, man."

Shrugging, he replies, "Good thing we're not there, then." Bridget has said something else noteworthy and the crowd applauds. Travis joins them. Among the foliage to the left of me is an older man. He's watching me one moment, but when I hold his gaze he turns back to the podium and folds his arms to continue watching the speaker. I keep looking to see if he'll look back again. His face looks familiar, like I've seen him around town in San Francisco before but I can't place him. When he looks back at me and realizes I'm still watching, he steps away and obscures himself behind the crowd. When he moves, the top of his head comes out from behind a branch and I see the fedora again. This is the man that was outside my window. My anxiety level is reaching a point of critical mass and my hands start to shake. I look to Travis to see if he's paying attention but he's fixed on the presenter and not looking at me or my stalker at all.

Behind the crowd, the man's face appears and he's looking at me again. This time, I turn away but not to escape the man's gaze. Rather, I'm checking to see if the cops are moving toward me. They aren't and when I look back, he's gone. I scramble to my feet and make my way around the flower patch between where the man was standing and the two uniformed cops. A vague familiarity strikes me as I lurch from place to place, looking for the man.

Flashback. Chicago, 2042.

I'm walking down North Broadway after scarfing down a

sizeable burger. Moving past a vacant storefront I trip on a piece of upturned sidewalk and nearly go down. In doing so, I've discovered that my shoe has come untied and I bend down to tie it. It's a quiet neighborhood, so few noises go unnoticed. The footsteps are definitely there, but stop seconds after mine. I turn, laces in hand but see no one. Shudder. I finish tying my shoes and start walking again, being careful to step lightly so I can hear if the other footsteps pick up again.

Half a block later I reach the light at Belmont and stop for a cross signal. Not waiting to hear the steps again, I turn swiftly and see a man in a dark jacket duck into a doorway. I take a step toward him but see the light change and opt to go back to the apartment. When I turn back to do so, a large, clean-cut SGOC policeman is standing in my way. My veins freeze and my face turns white. "What have I done?" I think, nearly out loud.

"You okay, sir?" the officer asks me in a dull tone.

I stammer, "Y-yes. Yeah, I'm fine. I just… need to get home." Seeing the light about to change again, I maneuver around him and on to the other side of the street. I look back only once to verify that the cop has moved on. Once in my apartment building, I stand in the lobby doorway for no less than twenty minutes waiting for the man in the dark coat to come by, but he never does…

As I stumble through the crowd, sweating like a wild animal, that thought keeps coming back to me. Who was the SGOC cop after? Me or the man in the dark coat? I nearly knock a man over and have to apologize. Finally, I reach the edge of the park beyond the last row of trees, but no one is there. At least not my mysterious follower. I look back through the crowd and see nothing but a sea of people holding clever signs. Frustrated, anxious, and embarrassed, I make my way back to Travis and the others.

The incident has left me shaken and I can't take my mind off it the whole ride home. I am able, however, to at least listen to the group's conversation along the way. One of Violet's signs made a big splash, reading, "No China? No Whine-a!" Travis beheld its brilliance as both accurate and self-deprecating to the cause.

Thinking back on Ms. Merriman's speech, something struck me and the words are still ringing in my head, causing varying sizes of twinges, "...but the critical distinction here, is this: by abandoning business relations with China, we cannot abandon the Chinese people. We have to make it clear that we wish to do business with the people of China, but not on the same playing field on which their government wishes to play. We need to establish that our morals will dictate the field of play, not their bottom line!"

Morals. I used to think I knew what that word meant. God says something is morally correct or incorrect and therefore, it is. But now, *people* are deciding what morals are with no mention of God's intent or authority. How can morals exist without God? I mean, I agree that a ten-year-old shouldn't be working in a factory, and I agree that that is a moral imperative. But the spiritual grounds by which that conclusion is reached are absent. At least what I would perceive as valid grounds are absent.

Bridget Merriman is a force to be reckoned with. She

commands the respect of thousands, if not millions of people here and it leads me to wonder who the real Queen Supreme is. They have a Prime Minister, but she certainly isn't the loudest speaker among these people. In fact, she remains business-like and professional at all times. The only opportunity she's taken to address the China issue is to say it's the responsibility of parliament and the Minister of Commerce to draw up the legislation. Once there is documentation to review, she'll address it at that time.

On the way home, Travis and Jessica have another spirited debate about how that stance is decidedly weak and consists of nothing but non-answers. I, on the other hand, feel it's a perfectly legitimate viewpoint to take considering she (as I have now learned) was elected and not appointed to her job. Travis argues that having no answer means she is complicit, "If she really believed that China was in the wrong, she'd push for more sanctions, and work through the U.N. to make them stronger."

"But this sort of thing has to be agreed upon," Jessica digs back at him, "People have to *know* that it's wrong and if you lobby or legislate over their heads, then they won't be getting it, just swallowing it."

They argue like this the entire way back to San Francisco.

***

When I get home, I pop open the PC, sweating from the hurried walk from the bus, and call Gray. It's past midnight where he is, but I don't care.

"Corwin?" he asks, surprised.

"Yes, it's me. Hey, I went to that demonstration you told me to attend."

"You did? Good. Anything interesting?"

I try not to let my panic show, "There's this woman, Bridget Merriman, have you heard of her?"

"Grumblings, nothing big. Was she there?"

"She was the keynote speaker, and a damn good one from what I can tell," I say, trying to sound impressed by her style, not her content.

"What did she say?"

"Apparently, she's leading a movement to cut business ties with China. There was a bunch of stuff about how they have some obligation to do business ethically and morally. Since when is doing business with an entire country so complicated?"

Gray looks at me gravely and answers, "Don't worry about that Corwin, you did the right thing. We'll work on that information, you don't have to. You've been doing a great job of forwarding those profiles to us. Are you being careful about your work?"

I nod, masking my curiosity about the China issue.

"Good. Anything else of note?"

"Well, I was a little surprised that no one was arrested. I was spotted by a couple of cops, but they never did anything… to anyone."

Gray sighs and unbuttons the top button on his shirt, loosening his tie, "Demonstrations are common in Gaymerica, Corwin. People like to complain about things and the government never stops them. They don't have the respect for their leaders we do, remember that. I guess it's not necessarily a bad thing. They let people get their sense of indignation out and be done with it."

"Are they put on a list or something?"

"I would imagine so. This Merriman woman is most certainly on a list, but she's also pretty public about her opinions, so that wouldn't surprise anyone."

There is a pregnant pause and Gray looks expectant, "Anything else?"

Since the moment it happened, I've been debating whether to tell Gray about the strange man, but at this point I don't feel it could hurt anything. "There was this guy. I don't know who he was, but I kinda recognized him. I've seen him around the neighborhood a couple times and he was…"

"Yes?"

"He was staring at me. Like he was watching me or something. Then he walked away and stared at me from somewhere else – behind some of the crowd."

Gray folds his arms and leans them on the desk in front of his console, "Interesting. But you say you got a good look at him?"

"Yeah."

"So, you'd be able to identify him if you had to?"

Shakily, I reply, "Yeah. Do you have any ideas who it may be? Like, would it be a government informant or something?"

"What did he look like?"

I think carefully, "Middle-aged. Gray hair, but not balding. His face is a little rounder than yours, but he was generally pretty thin."

"What was he wearing?"

"Nothing unique. Jeans, a thermal shirt and a grungy vest. Oh, and a hat. He looked pretty casually dressed, actually."

"Hunh. Doesn't sound like a government agent at least. They're usually more well-funded."

Finally exhaling, I ask, "So should I confront him? Do you think he's part of some group?"

"I wouldn't confront anyone, Corwin. Remember, you're there to blend in, not to stir the pot. Any actions you engage in could compromise your position, particularly if they're actions that end up being caught by authorities. Suppose the man assaults you," Gray seems intent on making sure I don't confront him and I can understand his reasoning, so I nod my head in acknowledgment of his message. "Discretion is the better part of valor, Corwin. Always remember that. If you see him, try to get an idea of where he's going, but do not confront him until we have a better picture of who he is, understand?"

"Yes, sir."

We end the call, but something seems wrong with all of this. Actually, that's an understatement. Something seems wrong about *everything* these days. I've been here almost four months now and I feel like I've accomplished nothing. In fact, I feel like I've moved backwards.

Aside from sending immigrant profiles to Gray, I haven't really done anything of note. Instead, I've started to become assimilated into their culture – enjoying their music, consorting with their citizens, attending rallies, having gay sex, and worse, watching soccer. Admittedly, it can be quite hypnotic to watch the men (or women as the viewing schedule allows) run back and forth kicking that fucking ball.

The worst thing of all, however, isn't the *things* that I've done, but rather the things I've *thought*. With the exception of my interaction on the train today and the confrontational barista at Beane Wilde, I've not been around anyone who was particularly vocal about their opinions on things. Well, I suppose I could include my confrontation at Savvy with Vic, but I chalk that up to a personal dispute instead of an ideological one.

There seems to be a general consensus here that things just are the way they are. Unlike in America, I don't have ideologies constantly repeated and rammed down my throat. So, even though I disagree with many of them, their quiet insistence is infectious. Seeing things from a different side – a different perspective, rather – has been strange to say the least. I feel like a traitor every time I see something and end up believing it from any perspective other than an American one.

The individual little twinges fire in the back of my head and it feels like rapid fire TNT in the bedrock foundation of my beliefs. I've never questioned anything before. I've never looked at the things I believed and asked, "why?" I never had a reason to. Now, I'm looking at things differently and I don't like it. I don't like the feeling of being wrong.

Something about being wrong is oddly relieving, though, and I can't quite place what it is.

12

My alarm goes off ten minutes earlier today. I've been trying to think of ways to throw off my stalker. I've seen him once more since the demonstration last week and I'm starting to get nervous. He most certainly knows where I live, but what if he knows where I work and where I frequent?

I try to remain calm. Sometimes I forget about him completely. I'll be going to work or walking back from the coffee shop and all of a sudden it'll hit me. I'm in a compromised position in this country and I can't afford to be taking risks and letting this guy get the drop on me. Whatever that means. At any rate, I set the alarm early today so I could get out the door before he had a chance to follow me. True, I don't know when he's following me or where to, but if there's one very important phrase I learned from my mother's crazy father it's this: just because you're paranoid doesn't mean they're not after you.

In addition to my stalker issues, I've been messaging off and on with Vic. He apologized for going off on me at Savvy, but I've been stalling on seeing him again. Conversely, I've messaged Hannah a couple times yielding minimal response since she doesn't seem to want to see me unless I'm sure I want to see her. Every time I ask myself that question I realize it's a damned good one and that she's making an excellent point. It doesn't change the fact that I'm drawn to her, though, and I struggle with the entire situation.

I finish throwing my clothes on, duck out the back door of the building, and head down the alley to a side street that connects me to a different bus line. Also, I'll be able to go to a different coffee shop where the barista doesn't want me dead. A bus pulls up just as I reach the stop and I hop on. As I look back, mindlessly swiping my mobile over the fare box, I swear I see someone else standing at the stop. They don't look immediately familiar, so I proceed to a seat and look around the bus to make sure I'm alone. Now, I realize there are other people *on* the bus, but I'm making sure I wasn't followed and that I don't recognize anyone here. I don't, so I pop my ear buds in and listen to the band we heard at Stella's. I'm really getting into this girl rock.

***

After work, I decide to walk home. I've been exercising more as the weather's gotten nicer – if you consider walking to be exercise. I didn't used to, but with the terrain around San Francisco, a simple walk can turn into an epic event, so I'm giving myself the full credit.

I'm about half way up a large hill when my mobile rings and I check it. It's Vic. "Hello!" I answer, possibly a little too eagerly. I haven't seen him in a few weeks and he's starting to wonder. I can't say I blame him.

"Hello, mister. What are you up to these days?"

"Oh, you know. Work. Stuff."

"Stuff?" he asks, "What exactly is 'stuff?'"

I shake my head at myself, "Sorry, there wasn't any hidden meaning to that. I just... I don't know, I've been to a few demonstrations, rallies, things like that. No hidden meaning, though."

"I see. Look, Corwin, I wanna apologize for what happened at the bar. That wasn't..." He pauses and I almost speak but he starts again, "I don't just go to bed with every guy I meet at the club, ya know? So, I was a little annoyed that you sounded so... American, I guess."

Here's the truth. The *real* truth. I've been questioning my loyalty lately. All those twinges in the back of my head have begun moving forward and with every rally, demonstration, or even something so small as a trip to the grocery store they become more cacophonous. I know I owe loyalty to Gray because he's given me the opportunity to do something with myself, but now I'm not so sure that the opportunity is turning out as it was intended. Vic is right. I, of all people, had no right to be defensive of America. Though, to be fair, I wasn't defending it from him – I was defending it from my experiences, my current state of being, and me.

"Well, it's hard to change sometimes, but you're right. I need to get over it I guess." This phrase is as much to pacify him as it is to bide time against complete loss of foundation in my brain. If I can hold onto my roots just the slightest bit, maybe I can still go back.

"I get that. Hell, I've dated an American before and he was way more defensive than you've been. Then again, you don't talk much, so maybe you just haven't taken the chance."

"No, I think you're probably right – I'm not *that* defensive. I was having a bad day, though." We say nothing for a moment, then I realize it's my responsibility to say something here. He offered a piece of information and it's my turn to call or fold. After all, poker's my game, "I don't just... hop in to bed with people either. Actually, it's been two years since I was with a... well, anyone."

"A woman?" he asks.

"Um, yeah, actually. I've never been with a man before, Vic. Sorry I didn't tell you that."

"Oh, you didn't have to..." I completely deserved that, "I am *so* sorry I said that. It's just..."

To save him embarrassment, I add, "I'm a rookie, I know. I don't have much ego to bruise, there."

After an uncomfortable silence, he continues, "What do you say we go on a date soon? Like, an actual, dinner and a movie *date*?"

"I think I would like that."

"Good. So, I'm booked this weekend, but we could do it next weekend, maybe?"

Finally reaching the top of the hill, I nod triumphantly, "Yes. I'll add it to my calendar."

"Great! I'll give you a call next week and we'll hammer out the details."

I'm involuntarily smiling. Vic made me smile. Why does this have to be so fucking complex? Gray sent me here to spy on and burn the fags and now I'm grinning like a schoolgirl over having a date with one – none of which I've ever told Gray. What would he say if he knew these people were converting me? If he knew how this altered reality is getting under my skin and into my head?

There's a new kind of fear coursing through my body. I used to just feel the kind of fear you get when a police officer is right around the corner. Like someone was always watching over my shoulder. Now, the sense of fear I get isn't that someone's watching me – well, other than the creepy old guy who *is* watching me – but rather that *I've* stopped watching me. That something's being eaten away from within. I don't know what it is, but the loss of it makes me feel lighter, cleaner. It makes me feel like I've dropped some baggage. That's not it. I don't know what it is, but my thoughts aren't lining up like they used to.

There used to be a clear definition of right and wrong. Black and white. Them and us. Now, the only word that makes sense to me in those equations is the "and."

***

I've been shirking my duties at work. Well, not actually work duties, but my duties of forwarding immigrant profiles. Gray scolded me for it on the last check-in, but as I'm holding back on information about both Vic and Hannah, I'm happy to get flack for the lesser things. Hannah and I have a date tonight and I'm having trouble focusing on work as it is, let alone photographing files without getting caught. I batch and head out the door.

Maybe the word "date" goes a little too far. It's not a date so much as a talk. She agreed to meet me and have coffee again. Do some catching up. By the time I get to the coffee shop, she's sitting in the corner by the fireplace, which is handy today since it's raining and chilly out. And I say chilly even for San Francisco in May. I'm used to Chicago where it can get stifling hot in May, but rarely chilly.

Luckily for me, the barista who hates me works the morning shift only, so I'm able to order my drink in relative peace. I've expanded my tastes recently, taking advice from other baristas and some of my friends at work and today am ordering a Chai. It's a bit sweet for my taste, but then it's late in the day and I don't need to be up all night with black coffee anyway.

I walk over to where Hannah is reading a book and put my jacket down on the chair next to hers. She smiles cordially and says, "Hi. Good to see you."

"Good to see you, too," I reply, then after a moment add, "I'm waiting for my drink, so I'll be back in a minute."

She nods and I meander back to the counter to await my drink. Something seems amiss. I mean, I know what it is, but it still gives me a feeling of disappointment and disappointment irritates me. Now I'm looking forward to the caffeine to give me a little boost. The barista hands me my drink and I claim my seat next to Hannah.

Putting her book down, she smiles at me again and asks, "So, how's work? You still diggin' the job?"

"Yeah. I think I've really started to get the hang of it. Kinda feel like I'm helping people in some small way, I guess."

"Good. It's always important to enjoy your job."

I start to sip the Chai but it's too hot and I put it down on the side table. "What about you? How's work going with you?"

"Oh, it's been rough lately. Family counseling doesn't happen all that much with happy families, so it can be rough. Had a couple families added to my case load lately that have been difficult, but it can be rewarding. I try not to bitch."

"No, please. Bitch."

"Actually, ethically, I can't. I mean, I could tell you the circumstances and vent all day long about how people refuse to do what's best for themselves, but even that's borderline. Mostly, it's just best to leave it at the door."

"But, you have to talk to someone, right?" I can't tell if I'm saying this more to her or me. I could really use someone to talk to about everything right now and there's no one. Listening to other people complain about their lives always takes the stress off of realizing I can't complain about mine. I try not to beg her to complain, and fortunately for me, she finds a way to do so that appeases her ethical sensibilities.

"It's just that… Okay, did you have a close family? Wait, no, you didn't. Your dad died when you were young, right?"

"No, my family wasn't close. I mean, I minded my mother like I was supposed to, but I never got the impression I was of much concern to her other than to go through the motions of parenting."

Hannah nods at this, "But she went through the motions, right?"

I shrug, "She did her best, I guess."

"And see, that's what gets me are the people who don't want to go through the motions. They come home, they have dinner, they ask the kids, 'Did you do your homework' and then they're done. They're tapped out – no motivation to be an active parent. It's the minority of cases, I know, but it's still blindingly irritating," she seems genuinely frustrated and all I can think to do is placate her.

"But people are like that everywhere, I think. I guess not everyone's cut out to be a parent."

"What about your mother? Do you think she was cut out to be a parent? Or, do you think parenting involves more than just going through the motions."

"I think a man and a woman have a responsibility to their kids and if they can't be invested in it, they shouldn't do it," I say – a canned response from my former life.

She backs away, looking at me oddly. "A man and a woman?"

"Yeah. I mean, child-rearing shouldn't be a one-person job—"

"Back up, there, cowboy. A man and a woman? A one-person job? What kind of bullshit is that?"

Twinge. A mooring has refused to break loose apparently. Her irritation at my response means there's still something in my head holding onto the world I used to know and it both comforts and concerns me at the same time. It comforts me because it means I'm not a completely lost cause. It concerns me because I'm not sure what it is.

"Bullshit?" I ask.

"Yeah, yeah, yeah. You seriously think that only a man and

a woman can raise kids?"

And then it hits me. This is a *major* error in my cultural understanding and she's caught me. These people don't care what kind of moral influence exists in the household, just that *anyone* is allowed to be there. I try to backpedal, "Well... Well, no. Not... Not exactly. I mean–"

She leans in, "So, this guy that you're fucking. Does he know that you think he's not allowed to raise children?"

I hadn't even thought about how the issue affects Vic, and to be perfectly frank, I don't care. Well, didn't care until now. I don't know how to address that though, "We're not..."

When I fail to finish the sentence, she packs her book quickly into her purse, "You know, this may not be a perfect place to live, but god knows we keep trying to move on, and every time one of you ignorant people defects, you drag the whole society back a few decades to when this all started in the first place."

"I'm not trying to drag—"

"Corwin, stop. Look. You're a great guy. The little bit that I've been around you, I can tell. You have a good soul. You listen, you're articulate, you have the capacity to understand things, but at the end of the day you've got all this bigoted, obnoxious baggage that I just don't have the energy to deal with anymore."

I shoot back defensively as she's putting on her coat, "Anymore? This is only the third time I've seen you and, besides, I know I'm not perfect—"

"I'm not asking you to be perfect! I'm just asking you to not have to change to..." she trails off here and I let the silence fall. Her coat settles onto her shoulders, a long, red, pleather affair that ends just above her knees. She looks beautiful in it and I'm having trouble focusing. Frustrated, her arms drops to her side, her purse nudging the side table and spilling a few sips of my Chai. "Sorry about that."

"It's okay, really. I just don't know what you mean, that's all."

She shrugs, "How could you? Look, I don't know how I feel about you. I don't know that I feel *good* about you, I just know I don't feel *bad* about you, and I guess that's something. Everyone says they want to change. No one ever does."

Twinge. But I want to change. For the first time since I've been born, I truly long for change. This thought is shooting through my mind when she adds, "I'm gonna go."

She starts to shimmy between the chair and the side table and I try to stop her. "But I want to listen to you bitch." Hoping the slight tone of humor will help crack her exterior.

"I don't," she says. "It was good to see you again and I'm glad you're well. You take care now."

I'm too confused to respond and she's out the door before anything springs to mind. I sit, sipping my Chai and watching the red coat through the window as it disappears up the hill.

13

While I have been getting better at my job, I've also been given a larger work load. I'm a bit frazzled, but nothing I can't handle. Still, my immediate supervisor told me I should probably slow down and let the work flow. If there's a little extra on my plate, we can always divert work to someone whose case load is lighter. I assured her that I would be able to handle it, but even I'm not positive that's true. She walks up to my desk only moments after I've stashed my mobile in my pocket and leans over my wall.

"Hey, what are you up to this weekend, Corwin?" Chandra asks.

I have to think. The date with Vic is next weekend. "Um, nothing that I know of. Why? You need me to come in on Saturday?"

"What? No, absolutely not. We don't really do that. No, actually, my friends are heading up to a vineyard in Willamette Province tomorrow and spending a three-day weekend. As it turns out, I'm booked so I can't use my ticket. I think you should get out of here. Take a nice, long weekend and get some rest."

"Oh, well thank you, but I have a lot of work to do—"

She stops me, "No, you should go. You need to get out and see the country. No better way to start than in wine country!"

"Believe me, I appreciate it, b—"

"Great! It's settled."

Bemused, I ask, "Settled?"

"Yep. I've already sent the ticket to your mobile. Actually, I kinda thought that's what you were looking at when I came over. Anyway, you're also off the schedule for tomorrow, so I don't want to see you back here until Monday, okay?" She says this as she's turning and walks away from me, not affording me the opportunity to protest further.

I know I've dodged a bullet since she didn't see me photographing any files and know when to count my losses. While I may not want to take a vacation, this may give me a chance to breathe and collect my thoughts.

***

Thirty hours after my argument with Hannah at the coffee shop, I'm boarding a Northbound train. It's an overnight trip that stops about six times before dropping us off in Eugene on its way to Portland. After we disembark, the three of us (Chandra's friends Michele and Juanita and myself) will take a cab for a half an hour to the vineyard where we'll be staying. As the train takes off, though, I don't see Michele or Juanita anywhere. It's too late at night to call Chandra, so I let it go and decide to worry about them in the morning.

It's not the most restful sleep and I end up researching Portland on my way there. The idea of a border town sounds exciting to me, and border town it is. It's the most populace city on the border between The Western States and America. It also has the highest crime rate of any city in the country. Apparently, despite its negative reputation in the Western States, Portland still has a lower crime rate than any major city in America. The article that information came from claims it has to do with border-jumpers and general difficulty with border control, but I find that dubious. Anyway, the history beyond its existence as a popular place for Americans to cross over bores me and I eventually fall asleep.

When I wake up, it's at the hands of a gentle, yet firm attendant who's tapping me on the shoulder, "Sir? We'll be stopping at Eugene in five minutes. You'll want to gather your belongings."

"Thank you," I say, and begin to do so. The two seats across from me are still empty.

By the time I get my PC and mobile stashed in my carryon, the train grinds to a halt and it's time to get off. It's early yet, and when I step off the train I can't see much except the platform. It spits us out onto the road in front of the station and I wait for Juanita and Michele, but they never come. I'm debating whether or not I missed them when I notice a man holding a sign that reads, "Hawley, Diaz, Jones." I meander cautiously toward the man.

Recognizing that I'm looking at him, he says, "You Hawley?"

"Uh, yes?"

"Hey, if you're not, that's okay."

"No, I am. Are you expecting me?"

He nods, looking down at the sign. "That's the gist. I got a call saying the other two weren't gonna make it until later."

Suddenly, everything's making more sense and I move more swiftly toward him. "Yes, I'm Mr. Hawley."

"Kinda formal with yourself, eh?"

"Huh?"

"Nah, forget it. Throw your bag in the back. We got a long drive."

The man is curt, but efficient and I do as instructed. His cab is just as small as the rest, but when I get in, I notice one distinct difference – the smell. This man showers less than my previous cab drivers and perhaps smokes the occasional product while driving. I am less than comfortable with this, but, seeing as I don't have a choice in the matter, I resign myself to tolerate it. On the other hand, he's less chatty than the usual cabby and I'm thankful for it. We arrive at the vineyard hotel just as the sun is beginning to rise on the other side of the mountains. The sky is light as if the sun were up, but the land is still in shadow and it makes for a brilliant contrast that takes my breath away as I step out of the cab. I reach back in to press my thumb to the meter, but he stops me.

"It's already paid for, Mr. Hawley."

"I beg your pardon?"

"The ride. It's already paid for. You can just grab your bag."

"Oh." I'm confused but say, "Thank you," and close the

door, retrieving my bag from the hatch. The cab pulls away quickly and is gone.

I step into the lobby to find it empty. There's a desk, but no one manning it. The 5:30 am sun is now peaking over the mountains in the distance. When I realize the lounge to the right of the lobby is built with windows facing east I roll my carryon into the room and sit at the bar. While no one is working the lobby desk, there is staff in the lounge and I order a black coffee with cream to accompany me while I watch the sunrise.

The entire valley is laid out before this spot and I can practically watch the shadows retreat on one side while the sun rises on the other. Without question, this is the most breathtaking thing I've seen in my life and I sit, dumbfounded on my seat at the end of the bar watching it happen. These people get to watch this every day. I envy them.

I'm lost in the moment, a tear welling up in my eye when a man's voice behind me says, "You ever seen anything like it?"

"No," I admit, "Never. It's remarkable."

"I know. It's one of the reasons I came out here. To get away from all the hustle. All the business of life. It was all moving a bit too fast for me."

Still trained on the view outside I reply, "I can see how this would be a welcome change." As I finish saying it, I turn to the man. The gray hair, the strong features, the medium stature – they all come rushing up on me as I realize this is the man who's been stalking me around San Francisco. All the hair on my body stands on end and I freeze in place.

He doesn't attack me, though. He doesn't even make a move. His face is calm and poised and the look in his eyes is kind. Despite all that, my fear heightens when he says, "Hello, Corwin."

Bordering on panic, I manage to muster sound, "Who are you?" He takes a deep breath and I can see he's not fully ready to answer. Perhaps he doesn't want to have to arrest me and this is how he's stalling. Has he followed me up from the city to arrest me for treason somewhere there won't be a scene? I'm furious at Gray for letting me get myself in trouble this way but I'm cognizant enough not to give myself up right away. Instead, I add, "I mean, I know I've seen you around. Have you been following me?"

He nods, somewhat ashamedly. "For a long time, actually. Corwin, I don't really know any way to say this without it coming as something of a shock, but..." the pause is interminable, "...but, I'm Percy. I'm your old man."

"What?" is the only think I can eke out.

"Remember? That's what you used to call me when you were a child. You thought it was funny to call me 'old man.'"

He's trying to make this gentle and I appreciate it, but the news is no less ridiculous. "My father's dead."

"No, Corwin. I'm not. I'm here. I've been looking for you. For a long time."

"But you couldn't have. I've only been in this country for three months."

"I'm so sorry I had to tell you like this. I know this must be quite a shock—"

"A shock?! Is that what you call it? No, it's not, it's an

outright lie. Why are you following me?" I demand, getting up from my stool.

"Because I wanted to know you were okay. I was so happy you made it out alive that—"

I think to hit him, but instead grab my carryon and start toward the door. "Or, you could just keep lying to me."

"A friend told me you were here. Your boss, Chandra, works for a friend I used to know when I first came out here." This stops me and I turn to look at him as he proceeds, "He told me you were here and I couldn't believe it. We've been watching for your name for nineteen years – since you were old enough to leave. We bought your ticket up here and Chandra agreed to play along." As much as I don't want to believe him, the story makes sense. "Once I knew it was you, it took me a while to get up the guts to tell you…"

The face. I knew there was something about the face. It looks like mine. Older, but similar. I remember the images of when I was a child – of him sitting next to me at a baseball game in Iowa. I remember going fishing with him and seeing that face on the other side of the boat… The tears are welling up now and my anger is subsiding, "Dad? Is that really you?"

He looks more like an old photo of grandpa, but it's actually him, "Yeah, son. It's me."

I try to wipe the tears away from my eyes, ashamed at them, but he stops me and embraces me, saying, "It's okay, son. You can cry, it's okay."

We embrace for a moment and when I've gotten the tears under control, I back off so I can see his face again. I tell him, "They told me you were dead."

"I'm not, though. Heavens, they're so good at lying, they had you believing it."

"But what happened?"

"Nothing. I'm gay."

***

When I come to, I'm laid out on the sofa next to the picture windows of the lounge with my head and feet propped up on pillows. My father is sitting next to another middle-aged man on the loveseat adjacent to me, talking. They stop when they realize I'm conscious and he smiles at me, "Hey there, Corwin. How you feeling?"

The sun has only elevated a few degrees and I presume it's not a whole day later, so I can only have been out for a few minutes. Still woozy, I try to answer as coherently as possible, "I'm... all right. Kinda light-headed I guess. It was a long train ride."

"I know," the man next to my father says, nodding emphatically. "People are always so tired. We built the lounge so people could enjoy the sunrise when they get in. Sadly, most people take a later train, so not everyone gets to see it. It's the thought that counts."

"Taylor, could you get my son a muffin and some hot coffee?" My father is talking to someone behind me and he pronounces the last part as a question, looking to me to see if that's really what I want. I nod and he adds, "Yes, coffee. Thank you, Taylor." The two men are looking at me expectantly, waiting for me to say something. Instead, I just look at the man next to my father until he speaks up, "Oh, I'm sorry. Corwin, this is my husband, Alan."

My brain is mush. It is no longer moored to anything and now makes a dizzying trip around the inside of my head every thirty seconds, dancing like a drunken college boy around a cashed keg of cheap beer. Everything between my ears is foam. I have completely lost my damned mind.

"You look a little pale," Alan says.

My father slaps him on the hand. "Shush, Alan, the man's had quite a shock."

"I'll say," Alan responds.

I try to blink myself awake, but I realize I *am* awake and just try to sit up instead. My father protests, "You don't have to sit up, Corwin. You should stay lying down for a bit."

"Nope," I muster. "I'm okay. I need to sit up and see things in upright for now." When I do, I realize what I was seeing is accurate, just on a different angle. These two men are married and have spectacular matching rings to prove it. Taylor comes by with the coffee and a muffin with big, fat blueberries bulging out of it. I sip the coffee, eye the muffin, and belch inwardly.

Alan speaks up, "So, Corwin, how long have you been in the country?"

"Four months, I guess? I kinda lost track."

"Great! Well, not great that you lost track – I hope that's not for negative reasons. How are you liking it?"

"It's nice. People are friendly…" I think instantly of the barista at Beane Wilde. "…mostly. Really, I'm just kinda getting my footing for now."

Dad nods in agreement. "And you should take your time. It's certainly a culture shock."

"You people are certainly aware of that. That's been a blessing," I say. "Was it a culture shock to you?"

They look at each other uncomfortably. My father answers, "Well, not really. See, we were here when the country began… for the most part. I spent a month in prison first. Alan here got out before that ever happened to him."

"You were in prison?" I ask, concerned.

"Oh yeah. After the separation, they allocated a dozen or so minimum and medium security prisons just to hold queers. 'Course, then they realized they couldn't just execute us, so they loaded us up in trucks, dumped us off at the border with no food or clothes and drove away."

Alan puts his hand on my father's and adds, "We'd known about this practice for about six months and had started stationing lookouts near the border to spot the trucks when they came in. They'd radio back to us and we'd drive buses up to the border and pick 'em up."

"That's how Alan and I met, actually. He was working a transfer camp in West Wendover—"

"Wendover, by the way, has turned into the Wild West town of America. They're gun-happy out there, those people," Alan is friendly, but demonstrative and it's somewhat distracting.

My father is aware of it and simply pats him admonishingly on the hand while continuing, "And just the other side of the border is where Alan was working at the time. It really was just a high-altitude kind of Western town. Not exactly what you see in movies, but in a way. We'd built up our side to accommodate the influx of refugees and they let their side—"

"Including an all-too-useful airport I might add!" Alan interjects.

"—to become rather dilapidated. They only kept it up enough to be able to fly in border patrols on a semi-regular basis." My father is trying to break this all to me slowly, but Alan has no such designs.

"You would have died to know how those American border patrols behaved, it was bizarre! Half their shifts would jump the fence and help us with the effort – have affairs with the locals, things like that. The other half were liable to shoot people on site. It was ridiculous!"

My father turns to Alan and adds, "It was people being people, is what it was." Alan rolls his eyes and my father addresses him. "I think Corwin and I are gonna go for a walk now, hon' okay?"

"I know, I know, Alan gets over-excited with visitors." Alan stands to leave and smiles at me comfortingly, "You take care of that head, Cor, and we'll have some better breakfast for you when you get back."

My father and I both reply, "It's Corwin," and look at each other amusedly after.

Alan covers his mouth, "Oops! Sorry about that – I get carried away with the nicknames." With that, he exits through the lobby.

"Alan's right, he can be excitable."

I reply quickly, "He's a good man. He means well."

***

Dew is slowly evaporating off the leaves of the plants and trees in the vineyard as my father and I walk slowly among the rows. He's trying not to rush me and instead is telling me all about the wine business he's gotten into. He uses the profits to help people escape and find homes in the Western States. This is all very surreal to me, and I don't understand the wine talk much, so I try to redirect the conversation.

"Do they still drop people off at the border like they used to?"

Slowly, he shakes his head, "No. They've become somewhat more civilized now. Actually, the funding I was telling you about helps in that process. It's a lot more covert now. Then again, I guess it's more logistically feasible for it to be covert at this point. Back then, they had masses of people to deport. Now, it's just the people they don't want to make examples of. Some people are still executed for it... But, you know that," I nod without making eye contact. "The ones who aren't made into examples are deported in a lot of different ways. Athletes die of 'overdoses' and 'car accidents' while competing overseas. Family men and women fail to return from 'business trips.' Politicians are the tough ones. For the most part, they get the death sentence. The more that happens, the more difficult it becomes to find allies in their ranks, but we still try. There are other methods, too, but now that I'm strictly on the funding end of it I'm a little more out of the loop." We walk a ways longer, taking in the sights and air before he speaks again, "I heard you came from Chicago."

"Yeah. I was working at a law firm there."

"Do you miss it?"

I stop in my tracks and a few steps later he does as well and turns to me. With some difficulty, I answer, "Yes. But not as much as I did. Actually, I'm not even sure what I miss anymore – everything's so… murky, I guess."

"It's a difficult thing to give up, Corwin, don't be hard on yourself."

"What is?"

"That sense of knowing. That feeling that there's a clear understanding of who you are, and where you belong, and… right and wrong being so well defined. To be taken out of that. It must be a shock."

I take a deep breath, "You have no idea." When he laughs I realize my error, "Then again, maybe you do."

"Oh, no, Corwin, you're right. I don't know it as well as you. Hell, the world I grew up in was nothing *but* gray area. Before you came along and for most of your early childhood, the U.S. was in a constant state of ideological warfare about who had civil rights and who didn't. It was awful – neighbors telling neighbors they didn't have the same rights… But even with all that, I can't imagine what it must have been like to grow up in that country – where all the rules had been fixed to one particular ideology. You don't know New Yorkers, or people from Vermont, or half a dozen other states the way they used to be. They all live here, now – entire states were told they have the choice of leaving voluntarily or by force. Or worse, converting. The people who agreed with the ideology got to stay. Everyone else, whether gay, straight… they all had to leave."

"Why didn't you leave with them? Why did you stay?"

"If you ever have a child, you'll understand better, I guess, but it was because of you. You weren't born into that country, Corwin, you were born into something better that was taken away from you. I didn't agree with their ideology but I was willing to stay for you."

"Why didn't you take us all?"

He grumbles briefly. "Your mother, on the other hand, *did* agree with their ideology and refused to have you raised anywhere else. She threatened to run away with you and I knew I'd be killed if I tried, so…"

"And how did you get caught?" I ask, not wanting to see him cry.

"I didn't always know I was gay, actually. Prior to the separation, Iowa was one of the only states that allowed gay marriage, though, so we had a somewhat progressive population, I guess. I was at a bar having a few drinks with some friends and I met a guy who was like-minded and we hit it off. Just friends to start with. After the new government was voted in, though, everything changed. We barely talked, but when we did it was clear we were some of the only people left who felt that way."

"So, why did *he* stay?" I ask – the frustration over people staying where they're not wanted mounting.

"Because of me." He lets this settle in before going on. "He admitted that he was in love with me and it was like a fog lifting in my head. I realized I had feelings for him, too. Your mother caught us once – she came home early from work and you were still at school. I thought her eyes were going to pop right out of her head."

I've long suspected my mother to be a terribly unhappy woman and I know she's done some rather remorseless things, but I can't imagine she would turn in her own husband. "You don't think she turned you in, do you?"

He shrugs and exhales. "If she did, I've had too many other things to worry about to hold a grudge against her. Besides, I'm living here, now. Wouldn't have been without her if she did."

"And the guy? What happened to him?"

"He was shot trying to run."

My mother. She used to just be an absentee mother who liked to misquote the Bible and tell me to be afraid of Chicago's unseemly underworld. Now she's complicit in murder. Despite the newness of this information, I'm finding it hard to be shocked.

"You don't hold a grudge against her for that?"

"Anger's too destructive to hold on to, Corwin. Besides, if she was the one that turned us in, she's in a far worse place than either of us now. She's all full-up with guilt and hate and rage... Her husband cheated on her with another person. Not only another person, but a man. Psychologically speaking, that's hard to deal with when you're coming from a place of ignorance like she was. Though I wouldn't envy anyone being cheated on. Some people handle it better than others. I wouldn't want to be her at this point."

Nor would I. Her husband and her son both left her. Granted in different ways, but she likely feels she was undesirable in some way that made it easy for us to cast her off. I reflect on this and add, "And now she's alone."

"And now she's alone," he echoes, lolling his head up and down with a modicum of regret.

"I feel bad about that," I admit.

"Leaving her? Did she move to Chicago with you?"

"No. She's still in Mason City. Never moved. I left her, though, and I feel bad about that."

This time he stops and I follow suit, "Corwin, she left us both long before we ever left her. She was trapped by two things, and two things only. Fear and ignorance. Despite that, you should remember that she loved you. *Loves* you, and raised you mostly on her own. Have pity on her if you must, but mostly, if you harbor any anger toward her at all you should forgive her. I don't think she knew how things would turn out and I don't think she ever intended for anyone to get hurt."

He's right. She probably didn't intend anything. Perhaps her isolation was a product of guilt rather than due evangelical diligence. I can't imagine how alone she must feel, and suddenly I have the urge to see her again. To apologize for all the times I'd been difficult and cruel to her. It's at this moment that a thought occurs to me. Not only can I not go back, but I truly do not want to. Realizing what they've done to my mother and were doing to me makes me break. I have to tell someone.

"Dad, I think there's something you should know," I start, knowing I am about to commit treason of the highest order, but realizing what happened when I was a child is the clincher. This man deserves to know the truth. "I'm not here to defect. I'm not here for amnesty, or to live a better life. I'm here to spy on this country and report it to the American government."

He has a terrified look of panic on his face and he grabs onto a post to steady himself. I keep going, "They trained me to review immigrant files and send them back so we could keep tabs on this country's immigrant workforce."

"A spy?" he says, the incredulity quickening his breathing.

"But I can't do it anymore. I *won't* do it anymore – I've… I've bottomed out."

"You're a *spy*?!"

"No! Well, kinda, but no. Not anymore. I'm quitting. Now! Today."

I realize he might be about to pass out and start to try to climb over the row to catch him, but he holds up his hand and in an even more terrified manner shouts, "Not the grapes! Stay there, I'm fine!" When I remove my hand from the post and back away from the plants, he calms down. "They enlisted you to spy on us?"

I nod sheepishly. He walks a bit farther to where a ladder spans the row and sits facing away from me. I feel awful. His head is in his hands and he's shaking it back and forth and all I can think to say is, "I'm sorry. I didn't know. I never knew – I never had any idea what was going on outside of America. They tell you all these things…" suddenly I'm talking more than I have in months, "…and you can't help but believe it, you know? I mean, I still do somewhat… Or, I don't, I don't know, but I had no life there! I didn't realize it, but I didn't and they offered me this opportunity to make something of myself…"

He's mumbling, "I can't believe it…"

"…and I couldn't turn it down! It was an opportunity to do something with my life…"

Unexpectedly, his head pops up and he stops shaking it, "They must have had you in training for this right?"

"Yes."

He shakes his head again, then stands, still facing the other direction. "I mean, it makes sense. No one would suspect you – you're too old and unassuming to be a younger, more trained agent. It's actually kind of brilliant."

"I'm so sorry. I thought I was doing the right thing."

Finally, he turns back to me with a look of understanding rather than disappointment. "Of course you did," he says, "They raise you from childhood to hate people. Why would anyone be surprised that you think it's the right thing to do?"

"But I *don't* think it's the right thing to do!" I assert.

He holds up his hand, "You wouldn't be telling me all this if you hadn't genuinely had a change of heart, Corwin."

"So, you're not mad at me?" I ask childishly.

"At you?" he starts, then pauses and exhales. "No. I'm not mad at you at all, Corwin. I'm surprised, don't get me wrong. And concerned. But mad? Not at you." He seems as though he's about to add something but then shakes it off and motions for me to start walking again.

We're silent for a while before I change the subject, "Hey, I'm curious about something. You're gay, right?"

"Mm-hm."

"So, does that mean I'm more likely to be gay?"

"Actually, Corwin, it doesn't. Statistically speaking, a

person's genetic sexuality is usually tied to the mother's genes. From what I understand, there's still plenty of research to do, but that's pretty much how it goes."

"So, if I were gay, it would then – at least genetically –have come from mom?"

He grins. "Apparently."

"She would not be pleased with that."

"No, but it might force her to get over it." We walk in silence again for a bit before I finally mention something I first thought of shortly after I came to, "I never knew you were into wine."

"It's the damndest thing…"

***

The air here is chillier at night, but it's still nice enough to be outside. Behind the hotel, there is a fire pit we've been sitting around, snacking on dessert and finishing off a couple bottles of wine. I've never had a decent Pinot Noir before and the stuff he and his… husband make is fantastic. But, Alan has gone off to bed and my father and I are left alone to chat over the slowly dying fire. We finish an in-depth discussion about economics (which essentially consists of him explaining things to me I've never heard of and will likely forget) and fall into a lengthy silence.

Eventually, he breaks it, "What are you going to do?"

I've only had a day – and one with little sleep – to consider my options. Between the catching up, learning about wine and economics, and general tourist-type activities I hadn't been thinking about it much. "I don't know," I answer honestly, "I don't know what it's safe to do. I mean, I'm kinda screwed either way if I tell anyone, right?"

"Well, you certainly can't go back to America if you tell them you exposed their mission, that's for sure."

"But what happens if I tell people here? They'll deport me back to America and I'll be shot there anyway." I gulp the last of my wine. "And, if I just decide to cut off contact with Gray and the Department of Foreign Affairs altogether, they'll come and find me."

My father pours me another glass against my protestations, "You're in a conundrum, that's for sure. You know, you could stay here."

"I don't know—"

"Don't say no. You've got two more days here – think about it while you're here and we can talk about it on Sunday."

I let it go and we polish off the last of the wine before putting out the fire and going to bed.

***

The rest of the weekend is remarkable. We hike to the top of the hills and the view is astounding. I take enough photos that I start to wonder if I'll ever be able to go through them all. Alan and my father are both expert chefs and make exquisite food for me and the other guests in the lodge.

Meeting the travelers is a singular experience. Some of them are from this country, but most are from other countries and manage to speak passable American... English, whatever.

The stories they tell me of their travels are envy-inducing and I urge them on, hearing tales of places I've never dreamed I could go. We learn about wine making and the history of the region. We learn about the vineyard and its original owners over a hundred years ago. We learn about each other, and all the while my father and Alan are our guides through a fascinating experience.

By the end of the weekend, though, my conundrum is no closer to solved and I realize something critical. No matter how long I stay up here, among the grapes and hills, my issues won't be settled. I'll still be a traitor and liar.

I pack while my father tearfully tells me he's proud of me and the choices I've made. "You'll always have a home to come back to up here," he tells me.

"Thank you," I say, zipping up my carryon. "If I don't go to prison or get deported, I promise to visit every chance I get."

"You know, you get five weeks of vacation in this country. That's federal law."

"Yeah, I read the benefits info when I was hired. I just don't want you to get your hopes up that I'll be *able* to come back. I don't know what's going to happen, dad."

He covers his mouth and tears stream down his face at the sound of the word, "dad." I know that's the cause of it and embrace him to comfort him.

"I've only just gotten you back. After thirty years, and now I'm going to lose you again…"

"Maybe. But I was never there to lose before. I found me, too, ya know?" I'm starting to tear up now as well. The whole thing is actually awfully sappy and I'm trying not to let it get to me, but the old man looks so happy and sad at the same time that it's hard not to be affected by it. "I've got a lot of work to do and I've got to make this right."

"I know. And I *know* I'll see you again. I know it."

After a tearful goodbye (Alan blubbering more than the rest of us), I ride back to the train station in Eugene with a Japanese couple. They tell me about the rest of their trip, how they're travelling up to Portland then flying back to Japan and it makes me wonder; how much could I learn? How much could I see if I were afforded a life here? How much could I do? Who could I know? The last question is the most important, though. Who could I *be?* Whoever that is, I can't be him if I'm living a lie.

***

The pressure's been building for months and the thought of unloading it is enthralling and terrifying at the same time. I storm up to my apartment and open my PC, dialing Gray as soon as it comes up. At this point, I don't care that it's well after midnight in Chicago.

It rings seven times then goes to mail. I cut off the call and dial again. I do this three times until he finally answers, clad in his pajamas and a yawn. "Good God, Corwin, what the hell is going on?"

"I have to talk to you."

"It's one thirty in the morning here, Hawley, what do you need to talk about so badly?"

"I quit!"

He blinks his eyes open and leans in. "I beg your pardon?"

"I quit, Gray. I don't want to be a part of this bullshit espionage anymore. I'm going to fulfill my amnesty request and stay here."

"Now you just calm down a second, there, Hawley. Do you have any idea what you're saying?" he's becoming angry.

"I think I do. I think you people are sick. I think you have no idea what human rights actually are. You tell me go to some damn demonstration about how the Western States are pansy-asses for not doing business with China, but you have no concept of why. And, you have no concept of how you're *far* more guilty of human rights violations than China is. These people have ethics. They have standards and morals, and you know what?"

"Watch it, Hawley, I'm warning you!" he bellows through the computer.

I waiver, but finish anyway, "They're human. You. Me. The entire American government. We're all hypocrites and hateful, angry cowards, and I will not let you take advantage of my fear anymore. I don't want to be a part of it anymore. I. Fucking. Quit!"

"Cor—" he begins to shout, but I hit the escape button and end the call.

I then press the power button until it shuts down, unplug it from the wall and grab it with both hands. I then raise it over my head and smash it on the table, sending chips of wood flying across the room. At first, I'm impressed by the machine's sturdiness, but it eventually snaps and parts start flying out of it. There's a pounding on the floor, but I ignore it, in fact turning my anger on the floor itself and smashing the last unbroken pieces until my floor is littered with computer parts.

I am left propped up on my knees clutching broken shards of plastic until blood is streaming down my hands, sobbing in a heap in the middle of the floor. There's an unintelligible knocking at my door and someone asking if I'm okay... or something. I can't hear them over my sobs.

I am now, officially, completely disappeared.

14

On my way home from the vineyard I made sure to upload all of my photos, contacts, and personal data to wireless storage I purchased last month to hold all the girl rock I've been buying. Fortunately for me, the storage is multi-purpose. I dropped the mobile (after dismantling it and breaking it into pieces) into a trash receptacle a mile from my apartment and, well, the PC issue has been covered. I call Chandra to let her know I'll be late to work today, which she is almost gleeful to hear, and head out to buy a new mobile.

Gray will find me no matter what. I'm fully aware that all I'm doing is delaying the inevitable. Still, I want every advantage I can get to take care of things before it goes down, even though I have no idea what *it* will be. I haven't decided what to do about the Western States government, yet. I suppose they have a right to know I've been transmitting sensitive material over national borders for over a month and entered the country under false pretenses. Whatever bad faith measures I've taken in the past, my current intentions are good, though. At least I think they are. As there's more than one side to the argument, I realize the concept of "good faith" in my actions relies solely on my interpretation of the side I choose to follow. I could go round and round on this for weeks debating moral rectitude and no one would be able to fully counsel me on it.

While out shopping, I spend the entire time looking over my shoulder. I keep reminding myself that being obvious about it doesn't help the situation. "Be cool, Corwin," I keep saying, but to no avail. I start counting steps, trying to get farther in between each look back before I start sweating. I make it to the mobile store and stop at the door. When I spend a solid fifteen seconds surveying both employees and shoppers I finally convince myself I'm being paranoid and am able to chill for a bit.

I buy a mobile with enough memory to hold all my music, photos, info, and that again. The quality of the mobile devices here is definitely superior to what I had in America. In fact, the general technology level appears to be years ahead of American technology and I've never bothered to ask why. From the electric vehicles, to the computer consoles, to the universal thumbprint granting access to chunks of data depending on the recipient's information license, it all seems terribly simple and advanced at the same time. Ten minutes into owning my new mobile and I'm already impressed with its speed and usefulness. It's like going from using paper to using a computer, the difference is that striking. Also, the girl rock is easier to shuffle and sort on this thing.

My next step is to order a new computer when I get to work. I show up around lunchtime (taking extra note of the building security cameras on the way in) with a bag of takeout

Thai food and start browsing. Chandra stops and peeks over my wall.

"How was your weekend?" she asks, a knowing smile on her face.

"Good. It was… good," I answer.

She seems disheartened, "Good?"

"Yes. Sorry, I don't really mean to be coy, or anything. It was a little startling meeting my father, but I really appreciate the thought." I'm not being as overt in my appreciation as she'd like and it seems to have flustered her.

"Startling?"

"Actually, it was a *lot* startling. I kinda freaked out. But, it was a good thing to have happen. I had always heard he was dead, so…"

She covers her mouth in horror, "Dead?! Corwin, I'm so sorry, I had no idea! When they set this up, they never told me about that – I'm *so* sorry!"

"It's not your fault. And really, I'm okay. Thank you for sending me on the trip. It was a weekend well-needed."

"You sure?"

"Yeah, definitely. Heck, I got a new phone out of it," I say, flashing my new mobile, "And, I'm shopping for a new computer now, too. So, it was productive."

She's biting her finger and sporting an almost comically mortified look, "Well, if you're okay—"

"I'm fine. Really, there's nothing to worry about. Thank you for your concern."

She shakes her head at herself and sheepishly retreats to her desk. I watch her go and continue shopping.

***

I managed to go two years without a date and now, in the past month or so, I've had two. The first with Hannah, and now with Vic. Dinner is fantastic. He takes me to this seafood joint on the bay where we have crab, shrimp, and scallops. They're grilled, and not drenched in butter and garlic like I've had them before. Seafood in America is generally drenched in butter and garlic to hide the fact that it's not fresh. I've come to accept that where seafood is concerned, it's just better when you're nearer the source. Too much shipping time and it ends up losing its flavor.

Another thing about the food here is portion size. I've lost almost ten pounds since I came to the Western States if for no other reason than I can't seem to find a place that serves adult portions. Or, at least what I've come to know as "adult portions."

The waiter arrives with our meals and I turn to him, "Oh, I didn't order an appetizer."

"No, sir, that's your entrée." He smiles and winks at Vic who giggles at me.

I wait for the waiter to leave and say to Vic, "I'm telling you, the portion size here is killing me."

"You look like you're doing just fine, sweetie," he replies, not at all sounding like he's making fun of me, though I know he is.

"It's quite an adjustment, ya know? You're used to eating certain things, and in certain amounts, and then you go somewhere where that's all different. Does that makes sense?"

Vic has already dug into his food and swallows before answering, "Oh, totally. You used to eat crap, and now you eat this." He smiles at me and I know he's right. It's perturbing, but he *is* right. I watch him eat for a moment then join in.

Portion size aside, the dinner is, as I said, fantastic. There's a lot more flavor to food than just butter and garlic, and it's been a pleasant adjustment. Admittedly, I still long for some of the good old-fashioned greasy American food sometimes. I've found a pizza place on Dolores that makes Chicago-style pizza. The sausage isn't the same and the cheese is less fatty, but it's the closest thing in town, so I order it every once in a while to satiate my less cultivated food desires.

After dinner, we catch a film at an old movie house and sit in the front row of the balcony. The film is called *1-Up*, a picture about two soccer players who fall in love then have to play against each other in the championship and it ruins their relationship. It's not very good and Vic and I continually make fun of it throughout. We manage to enjoy ourselves as a result of our heckling, though we're shushed a number of times from a couple behind us who apparently have no taste.

Vic can no longer contain his laughter and bursts out cackling the second we hit the sidewalk, "Oh, my dear lord, that was miserable. This is one of those times I wish I still got a student discount. You'd have to pay me to watch that again."

I laugh and reply, "I can't say it's one of the better things I've seen, that's for sure…" I trail off as I see a younger man in a dark, long-sleeve shirt and a ball cap coming toward us. Vic doesn't notice, or at least doesn't care.

"When the little girl spilled ice cream on his lap, I thought 'this can*not* get more ridiculous!' and then the scene with the hedgerow happened..." I stiffen as the man closes in on us and inadvertently squeeze Vic's arm. "Ouch, what's the mat-" But Vic is cut off mid-sentence as the man's shoulder smashes into mine, knocking me off course and into Vic. He shouts back at the man, "Hey! Rude!"

I shush Vic and turn to watch the man go – rather to *make sure* he goes – and though he hesitates briefly to take stock of us, he does move on.

"Hey, you okay?" Vic asks.

"Yeah, I'm fine," I mumble, still watching the man walk away.

"What a jerk. Some people just can't control themselves I guess." I'm riveted on the stranger and Vic notices, "Hey, Corwin. You still here?" He nudges me and when I turn back to him the quizzical expression on his face urges me to respond.

"I'm fine... Just, thought I might have recognized him, that's all."

"Huh. Well, if you do, that's one questionable acquaintance you have, pal. Fuck 'em. Let's get out of here, huh?"

Vic invites me back to his apartment after the film and we go. I try to take my mind off the stranger but my apprehension crosses over into my sexual prowess. I'm apprehensive because of our last encounter in which I didn't participate much. Vic is patient enough not to get frustrated with the clumsiness that comes with my desire to do more. I go down on him, poorly, and discover two things about myself. First of all, I wasn't aware how reactive my gag reflex is. Second, there's a click in my jaw that becomes painful after more than a minute or so of this.

I apologize, but Vic isn't upset in the least. Granted, he has far more experience in these matters and has certainly had better, but he doesn't judge and instead goes down on me for a time before reaching into the drawer of his night stand to retrieve a bottle of lube. Now, I'm *really* nervous as I'm not sure I'm ready for what I think he's going to do, but I don't have the guts to speak up and simply let him proceed. However, instead of forcing himself on me all at once, he rubs the lube on his fingers and proceeds much the way I did with myself when I was a teenager. He does this with one hand while continuing to go down on me with his mouth and other hand. This is one of the most sensational things that has ever happened to me. And I don't mean as in fireworks or love or anything like that. I mean sensational as in five senses. I'd say sensual except that doesn't cover it. There's something more than just physical going on here. The twinges that have been firing all throughout my brain have now begun to move South, through my neck, to my shoulders, and eventually to all the parts Vic is stimulating. I never knew my body could feel these things, and it's pretty… well, sensational.

Vic has increased to two fingers beneath and is reaching the spot I used to engage myself. It's only slightly painful and mostly lusty and liberating. He releases my cock from his mouth and kisses my torso up to my neck and asks, "You wanna try something, Corwin?"

I know what he's talking about and I have to admit that a large part of me is wanting to say no. Still, I convince myself that if it feels right, I'm entitled to do it, so I say yes. He slowly removes his fingers and reaches back into his drawer to retrieve a condom. He bites the wrapper and opens it with one hand, rolling it on himself. I'm confused and ask, "You said you were clean, right?"

"I make it a rule to always play safe. I get tested, don't get me wrong, but until I'm officially seeing just one person, I'm a good boy." He's seeing other people. Or, at least he's not thinking of us as an item and that somehow makes me more comfortable. He applies the lube to his cock and positions it down below. I try to relax, but it's difficult at first. Again, he's terribly patient with me and eventually says, "I don't think this position's going to work for now. Why don't you roll over?"

I do as instructed. This works.

***

In the morning Vic has to go off to work again so I head home. I'm conflicted about the things that have happened and how they fit into my new life. With the exception of what I know to be a learned belief nagging in my head, it all feels right. Then again, *right* is about the extent of it. Perhaps my ability to appreciate it more is hindered by that nagging belief, but it could be a long time before I know for sure. This irritates me. Compounding that complexity is the sense of constant, impending doom I have about my situation with the American and Western States governments.

After a long, paranoid walk home I approach my door to see what looks like the corner of a piece of paper sticking from underneath. Instinctively, I look to the peep hole, only then realizing nothing can be viewed this direction anyway. Pressing my thumb to the plate, I push my door open and the paper slides underneath it as it swings. I inspect the interior of the apartment thoroughly, with the door open before returning to the entrance to retrieve the paper. Building management sends us notes on our mobiles, so I know this has to be from someone else. I'm hoping it's a neighbor whose computer is somehow incapacitated and slowly unfold it. It's hand-written and says only one thing:

"Time to come back to the fold, Mr. Hawley."

They know I won't bring this to the authorities because I'd have to admit my complicity in international espionage. This won't be the last such note, either. Panic overtakes me and sweat starts to run down my forehead and back.

My first thought is to move. It would be a solution of sorts, except that they'd find me anyway. No, moving won't solve anything. Murders and missing persons still occur in the Western States. Granted, it's a lower percentage than in America, but they have prisons for a reason. One more person showing up missing or dead won't be a red flag to anyone – just a statistic.

I could run, but where? I knew this would happen and I've been laboring over it for the last week. Moments pass by while I'm frozen in panic, the door of my apartment cracked open with a breeze gently flowing through. Virtual hours pass until my phone beeps, frightening me out of my stupor. I read the message, "You busy tonight?" It's Hannah. Now I'm really in a spin. My brain doesn't know which way is up at all. Vic,

Hannah, Gray, America, the Western States, my mother, my father... I'm torn in every intellectual and emotional way a person could possibly be torn. Unable to lie to anyone at the moment, I reply, "No. You have something in mind?"

Quickly, the phone beeps again and I'm once again unprepared for the noise, practically jumping out of my chair. It says "I think we should go out somewhere and have dinner."

We schedule a place and time and I put the mobile down to close the door, pacing for almost an hour before deciding on a course of action. Well, not really a course of *action* per se, but rather a course of inaction. I get so fed up with myself and the situation that I loudly exclaim, "Fuck it," and go about the business of doing laundry, tidying up, and napping before going out on my date with Hannah.

15

"I don't think I've been totally fair with you," Hannah says, chomping into her grilled sandwich.

I finish chewing a bite of my penne (a gloriously large bowl of it has been served me, I might add) and ask, "What do you mean?"

"Well, I'm trying to be less... I don't know, presumptive. I mean, you *told* me you were from America, and let's face it. If I really was concerned about any influence growing up there may have had on you I wouldn't have asked you out in the first place. Know what I mean?"

I've put another bite of food in my mouth and just nod casually.

She munches on a waffle fry and proceeds, "But, then I got to thinking that it's kind of high and mighty of me to just discount your background because of *where* you're from. I know how *I* feel about America, but that's like, your whole life, ya know? And here I am judging you, and it makes me feel... judgmental. I used the same word twice – but you know what I mean, right?" I nod again while chewing and am about to swallow and reply, but she continues, "And as for the gay thing… Look, if you're gay I can't be angry at you about that. Lord knows I've had my experimental phase," I find it really hard to concentrate on much after this, but do manage to struggle through it and listen to her, "…but that was back in college and I just realized that I didn't work that way. I think everyone has to do that at some point, don't you?"

"Yeah," I answer pragmatically.

"Fuck!" she exclaims, just loudly enough that someone at another table notices, "Here I am babbling again. Could you stop me some time?"

"Sorry. I just… You're right about, well, most of that. I don't think it's fair to judge yourself, though…"

"Yeah, but you don't have to let me ramble like that."

I've been wanting to discuss this with someone and it seems like the perfect moment. I swallow the last of a bite of penne, clear my throat, and lean in, "Okay, well, you're right. I may just be… experimenting. The truth is, I don't know. I've been seeing this guy and things seem okay, but I don't know. You're right, also, that things are different where I come from. Everything here is more open and accepting and it's really tempting to just take a bite out of everything," her attention is now rapt and she's making almost creepy eye contact with me so I break it every once in a while to keep my concentration, "But that doesn't mean I *know* what's real and what isn't."

When I pause, mouth agape, mid-thought she urges me on, "It's okay, I'm listening."

"I went to visit my father a week ago for the first time in thirty years. Turns out, he wasn't dead, just… deported for being gay." I say this as evenly as possible, but she reacts with horror regardless. "He's good now. He runs a vineyard up in Willamette with his husband. But seeing him there, living a real life, having a family... It made me think a lot about my perceptions of things and how everything I've ever come to know has been shaped by people who didn't necessarily have the best of intentions. And for all the blame I want to put on my mother for keeping me in a place like that, she's also the reason I am who I am. That I learned to study and read at an early age. That I can form a coherent sentence unlike most men in America my age. She forced all that on me because she thought it would help me get ahead. I imagine I must have been a disappointment to her when I managed to end up being a paper pusher instead of a lawyer, or doctor, or politician."

"Politicians don't have to be well-educated, Corwin. For the most part, they're morons here, too," she reassures me.

I'm mindlessly swirling my fork in the remnants of my penne bowl. "I know that now. Weeks ago... months ago nothing was as muddled as it is now. Everything I knew was a lie and that takes some getting used to." I stop short of admitting that I am part of the lie. I don't know that I'm ready for anyone to know this outside of my father. Though, if it were to be anyone, it would be Hannah. Vic and I have a romantic relationship, sure, but intellectually (particularly from an age and experience perspective) I have more in common with her and I sense that she understands me in ways he might not.

Hannah puts her hand on mine and I look up at her, "I can't imagine what that's like. To believe something for so long and have it questioned and violated. Regardless of what *I* may think about your upbringing and your former life, that kind of uprooting of knowledge, lifestyle… *everything* can't be easy to handle."

"But that doesn't make it right. It's one thing to learn something that *adds* to what you already know, but to find out that everything you knew is just plain wrong is…"

A silence forms around my inability to find the right words. She moves her fingers and now wraps her hand around mine, rubbing her thumb across the back of my fingers, "I won't pretend to know what you're going through, Corwin. But, I want you to know that I think you're a good man, and whatever you may have known before, it takes a really strong person to be willing to change that. And, I think it's pretty cool that you are."

"Really?" I ask.

"Yeah," she says, smiling, and retracts her hand to take another bite out of her sandwich.

We finish dinner and go for a walk along the marina. She takes my hand at one point, and despite the fact that my hands are sweaty, she doesn't let go. We reach the edge of the walkway where the evening tide waves are lapping against the sea wall and stop to look out at the Golden Gate Bridge and the bay to the North. We're silent for a few moments before I turn and notice she's been looking at me. Her face is serious but not sad. I return her gaze for a moment before she reaches up and places her hands on my cheeks. She lifts up on her toes and presses her lips to mine. The resulting kiss is long and passionate. I put my hand on her waist, then on her back, bringing her closer and she wraps her arms around my neck.

Hannah stops and pulls away enough to look me in the eyes, "Did that feel right?"

Stunned by the kiss and embarrassed by my slight arousal I answer dumbly, just nodding. In response, she moves back in to kiss again, this time pushing me up against the wall and clasping her hands on the back of my neck. The second kiss is shorter but more free and open.

When she stops this time, she takes a step back, now holding only my hands and smiling as she looks at me, "Yeah, I think so, too." I realize she's noticed I'm partially aroused and my face becomes flush. "It's late, and I need to go home so I can go to church in the morning."

"Church?" I ask. This possibility somehow never occurred to me – that Hannah would be a church goer.

"Yeah. There's a Unitarian church near my place I go to on Sundays. I don't like to miss it."

"We should probably get you on your way, then," I say, adjusting my stance and trying to calm myself down.

She drops the one hand and holds the other, starting back down the walk way, "You know, I don't mean to be too forward, but I was thinking you might accompany me home. It's late, and dark, and dangerous out."

I know she's being silly, but I play along, "You shouldn't have to walk home alone, then."

***

We're barely in the door before she throws me up against the wall, kicking the door shut behind her. This is exciting and rash. No woman in America would ever be allowed to behave this way and perhaps Hannah knows this. Perhaps she's doing this precisely to shock me out of my propriety. It's working. Even Vic was more gentle and accommodating than this. She's not just taking control of the situation, she's taking control of me.

She moves me to her couch and hops on top of me, unbuttoning my shirt as we kiss. I place my hands on her sides then begin running them up her back. She grabs my hands and brings them around front, instructing them to unbutton her shirt as well. When she's done unbuttoning mine, she rips it off me and begins kissing my neck and the upper parts of my chest. Her hands move down to my belt buckle and begin to unfasten it and the button on my jeans.

Moments later, we're fully undressed and Hannah is sitting on my lap, we're kissing, and fondling each other's intricate parts. She's wetter than any woman I've ever been with – her body heaving with our combined motion and the play of our fingers. The entire process is against my rules and I have to keep reminding myself that my rules are wrong. Granted, *everything* Vic and I have ever done is completely against the rules, but it seemed easier to digest because there were no guidelines to begin with. Sex with women is highly regulated and intended to happen in a certain way.

She bites my lip, pulling away from me as she does until it snaps back against my teeth, in pain but somehow delight as well. Lightly, Hannah slaps the side of my face checking for a reaction which comes in the form of a bemused smile. She's pleased at the result and leans across me to the night table stationed between her couch and bed.

It's a small apartment, but the pieces are arranged in a cozy, comfortable fashion. As she leans over me, I look at the curve of her back and her ass, beads of sweat gently running down the slope and I have a flashback to Dave's conversation at the bar the week before I went into DoFA training. The conversation about how his wife enjoyed sex so much in positions that weren't boring and monotonous. I start to imagine Hannah in those positions – something like the positions Vic and I have been in and more. How could Dave be so angry at me for listening to him? How could he be so angry at *himself* for enjoying this? Allowing himself to be guided by her pleasure instead of his own, and the fact that it gave him pleasure as well shouldn't be anything to be ashamed of. The look on Hannah's face as she sits over me in a position of power and enjoyment is enthralling.

She opens the condom she's retrieved from the drawer and puts it on me. I caress her breasts and sides as she slowly works me into her, shuddering once and then twice along the way, a broad smile crossing her face. She presses on my shoulders as she rolls her hips back and forth, pushing me deep inside her.

Hannah grabs the back of my neck and I move forward, pressing my face into her breasts, squeezing my hands on her back. There is less muscle than Vic's back, but her supple flesh is equally inviting and I massage it deeply with my hands while my lips and tongue focus on her breasts.

Moving more vigorously and breathing much heavier, Hannah now places her hand on the back of my head and pulls my hair. I'm not prepared for this but the pain of it is oddly enticing and I don't cry out or resist. She then, almost angrily takes my hands from her back and slams them up against the wall behind the couch, holding them there with one hand while reinitiating her grip on my hair with the other. I'm astounded by her strength and resolve as she thrusts herself upon me in an almost violent manner until her entire body shudders and quakes and she screams until eventually she collapses in a puddle on my lap, nearly suffocating me when she wraps her arms around my head. In this entire process, I have been responsible for nothing.

After what seems like a blissful eternity of sweat-filled embrace, she creates space between us, her back arched and a cat-that-swallowed-the-canary look on her face. She shakes her head, smiling, and asks, "You wanna try something?"

***

I wake up in the morning facing the edge of the bed with one wrist still tied to her metal headboard. Her arm is wrapped around my abdomen and her fingers are gently caressing my stomach. I'm sore – my back scratched and my hip muscles nearly pulled from last night's activities. It feels incredible.

As I lie here, my mind drifts back to Ida and that night we had sex on the couch in her parent's basement. This was how it should have gone. Well, at least the first part. This was what she wanted but was afraid to do. I was afraid, too. What would be so wrong about her asserting herself? Why was that such a crime that even she couldn't bring herself to commit it?

I then remember what Dave told me in the bar and I know

now why he turned on me. The night at the bar happened after I'd met Gray. Dave turned on me long before he'd confided in me about the sex he'd had with his wife, which means the government knew about it, too and they were recording the conversation to validate their selection of me as their stooge. They needed to get rid of me but needed to gather evidence. Dave helped them to lessen his sentence and possibly get himself and his wife deported. For their sakes, I hope it worked. For mine...

"I have to tell you something," I say, breaking the relative silence of birds, mild traffic, and the air flowing through our lungs. I know she's awake.

"Okay."

"You may not like it," I add.

She giggles, "Well, I better untie you then so you can get a running start."

She does so and I turn to her. Her face is soft and comforting, a gentle expression invites me to speak, "I don't know who I am. Or, actually I don't know *what* I am... I had an amazing time last night."

"Me too," she replies and gives me space to continue.

"But I don't know that I'm not gay."

She shrugs and sighs. "It's all right. At this point I don't need you to be straight, or gay, or really anything. I just need you to tell me you enjoy being with me."

"And I do!" I reply emphatically. "Believe me, I do." She smiles and starts playing with my chest hair. "I just don't know what this is, is all. I enjoy it, but I'm not sure I know why."

She exhales. "You're a submissive, Corwin."

"I'm what?"

"A submissive. You like to be controlled and not necessarily *take* control. I spotted that when we first met. I kinda find it irresistible in men. I don't know if you noticed, but I like to be in charge... just a teensy little bit." She holds her two fingers a quarter inch or so apart and kisses me gently on the lips, laughing as she does.

"Yeah, I've noticed. I like that."

"Being submissive doesn't mean you're gay, Corwin. It doesn't mean you're straight, either. Technically, all it means is that you prefer to have someone else in charge most of the time. There's nothing wrong with that."

"It's not allowed. Well, in America it's not allowed."

She rolls onto her back, sighing audibly, "Yeah, I know – those poor souls. Rules made up by a bunch of men with small dicks. The only way for them to be in charge of *anything* is to control *everything*, including sex. It's pathetic, really."

"I'm getting that. But, Hannah, that's not all," I say gravely.

"What's wrong?"

"I'm not who I've made myself out to be—"

"You'll get used to it. Sexual freedom is one of the hardest things to adjust to—"

I stop her, "That's not what I'm talking about." She turns back to me to listen. "I didn't come here to escape. I didn't... I didn't come here seeking amnesty or asylum or anything like that. I came here..." She's anticipating but she doesn't know what. I keep waiting for divine intervention, but the words escape before it comes. "...as a spy."

She blinks, the smile leaving her face, "Beg pardon?"

"For the Department of Foreign Affairs. I'm a plant."

"Corwin, I'm within swinging distance of your balls, so you better explain yourself in a hurry."

"I'm not doing it anymore. I told them I quit—"

"You *quit?*" she shouts and gets up from the bed, grabbing her robe off the hook on her bathroom door as she starts to pace, "What does that even mean, 'quit?'"

"I told my boss I wasn't going to be a part of it anymore."

"Are you a complete idiot, Corwin?"

"Um, well no—"

"How could you possibly understand these people any less than I do? I mean, are you making this up or something?!" She's got her arms folded in front of her chest protectively with the robe loosely tied beneath them

"No, I'm not! I swear to you it's the truth, but I'm not doing it anymore."

She rushes over to me and crouches down next to the bed with her face in mine. "Corwin, you can't fuck around here. If you really did this; if you really quit, then they will kill you. Do you understand that?"

"Yes, I do—"

"Then what are you doing here? Are you trying to get me killed, too?!"

I'm suddenly painfully aware of my nakedness and cover myself with the sheet, "No! I'm not trying to get *anyone* killed! Certainly not you. I just… I just needed to get out – they're sick! *I'm* sick and it needs to stop."

"Corwin, think very carefully. Who have you told about this? Who have you told that you're quitting?"

"Just them."

"Them, as in, the American government?"

"My contact with them, yeah."

"So, the only person you told is the person who's most likely to hunt you down and have you killed?" she asks. I stare at her blankly, realizing for the first time I should have cut ties with everyone I knew the second I quit. I shouldn't be here. "Do you see why I may question your motives?"

"Shit," I mutter, becoming slowly aware of what I have to do.

She stands up and resumes pacing, "Fuck, Corwin. What were you thinking? I mean, here I am – I barely know you – and I'm complicit in your... espionage, or whatever it is you're doing. What *are* you doing?"

"They had me copying immigrant employment files and sending them back to America. They were looking for dissidents, people of interest... whatever, I don't really know."

"How long did you do this for?" she asks, biting her nails.

"A month, maybe a bit more. They wanted me to have established a life here before I began any... activities."

"A life?" she asks, stopping her pacing and nail biting abruptly. "Meaning me?"

"No! Well, not exactly. You know, friends, social activities – a life, that's all. No one specific–"

Throwing her hands up she nearly shouts, "But it *becomes* specific, Corwin! I'm not just your life, I'm a person who's now wrapped up in this shit, don't you get that?"

"I can make it right, Hannah, you have to believe me," I plead.

"How?! Are you going to say, 'Just kidding! I'm going to keep doing my job,' and you think they'll buy that? After you told them to fuck off?!"

"No, I won't do that!"

"Then what?"

"I'm going to tell the government here what I've been up to – what I've been doing. Then they should be able to protect you."

Tossing her hands again, her robe slips open a bit, revealing the soft, tender skin between her breasts and I'm reminded of her vulnerability. She's trusted me with something terribly intimate and I've trusted her with nothing. I feel cheap and insincere. She asks, "Protect me how? By making me move? Change my job? Change my name? I have friends and a life here – I can't just give it all up because you feel like fucking anyone who comes along to help keep the image of your *life*."

The truth stings but it must be addressed and I don't argue with her, "I know that what I've done to you is awful and I'm terribly sorry."

"Oh, I know you are. You're sorry now, you'll be sorry later, you'll be sorry 'til the cows come home, but that doesn't change the situation."

"I will change the situation," I say assertively.

"How?" she asks, re-crossing her arms.

"I'm going to the Intelligence Administration tomorrow – first thing, and I'm going to tell them everything. I'll only tell them about you if you want me to, but they have to know what I've been doing. They have to know what the American government has been doing. No matter what happens to me, this has to be done."

"And what about me?" she asks quietly.

"I don't know. I never told them your name, just that I had a date with a girl, that's all."

"Are you naïve? You don't think they've figured all that out? You don't think they keep tabs on their own agents?"

"I don't know, Hannah, but hiding won't solve anything. Going back to the American government and telling them I change my mind will only make it worse."

I lock eye contact with her until I know she believes I mean it. She shakes her head and looks to the ceiling, breathing heavily. As she lowers her head back to me she states firmly, "Okay. You're going to change it. And I'm coming with you to make sure you do."

16

Hannah took the entire day off work and met me at our favorite coffee shop at 7am to grab some caffeine before heading to Sacramento. The train ride is agonizingly long, but we pass the time talking about our childhoods, schooling, favorite books to read – all trying to avoid my disclosing of anything which might get her in further trouble. The only thing I do divulge to her is the extent of my relationship with Vic. Her only response is, "He seems like a nice guy." I get the idea she'd rather not have asked. I wish I hadn't answered, but I don't see the point in withholding or lying anymore and I can only hope she appreciates that. I know I shouldn't ask.

The train pulls up to the station and we make the walk North to the Intelligence Administration building West of the Capitol. It's a beautiful day, which makes this all the worse. It should be 40° and rainy, not 70° and sunny. It seems incongruous with the mood.

When we reach the steps, Hannah grasps my hand affectionately but firmly and asks, "You sure you want to do this?" I don't speak, but nod and start up the steps. She resists and pulls me back down, kissing me gently on the lips before adding, "Okay, I just needed one more of those." I smile and we ascend the steps to the door of a great office building with revolving doors and large columns.

Inside is a relatively small atrium with a bubbling fountain and a front desk manned by a single individual. On either side of the desk are elevator banks guarded by the electronic turnstiles I've seen so many times before, but with an added feature – a gate poised above the elevator bank entrances ready to lock down if alarmed properly. Upon further review of the lobby, I realize there are two security guards, one on either side of the room sitting at computer consoles nearly in the dark. A pair of workers enter behind us and brush past to the turn-styles. They're talking about something but the blood in my head is thumping so loudly I can't make it out. They pass through the turnstiles and stop on the other side with their hands held out until a green light appears and they lower their arms to move on to the elevator banks. One thought keeps grinding through my head: "I'm going to die."

Our hands are trembling and sweaty but we don't let go of each other. We reach the desk and the very serious man at the counter asks, "Do you have an appointment?"

My throat is terribly dry though I'm able to faintly say, "No, but I'd like to get one with an agent soon if that's possible." I look to Hannah for assurance and she nods.

"Press your thumb to the plate, please," he instructs and I do so. It glows orange, then green. My brain is flying at a thousand miles a second – terrified of every little thing. Did the orange light go on too long? Too short? What does it mean that it's green?

I watch his face for a reaction, and perceive the slightest indication that a file has come up. Perhaps something interesting. He looks at me, I'm guessing so he can match my face to the file, though I have no idea. He then looks at Hannah. "Could you press your thumb to the plate as well?"

Her hand is shaking as she moves it up to the desk and she lets out a feeble, "Mm-hm." Hers glows green instantaneously, no stopping at orange and my mouth drops open in response. I don't feel that she's noticed anything different but when I look to her face, it's clear she has.

"If you two could have a seat over there, an agent will be with you shortly," he says as politely as a man in his position could and we move to the seating area. Neither of us has the courage to speak. We make eye contact a number of times, but the occasional caressing of each others' hands is the only constant communication we have. Fifteen minutes go by and a very business-like woman in a black suit and skirt (followed closely by another security guard) clicks without pause through the turnstiles and over to us, extending her hand. Only when she does this does she smile at all. "Mr. Hawley. Ms. Stone." We shake her hand and stand up to meet her but do not smile in return. "I'm agent Hughes. If you could follow me, please?"

It's not a question so much as an order as she doesn't wait for the answer, but rather turns to head back to the elevator banks. The security guard stays behind and waits for us to follow before joining. Her pace is brisk and we rush to keep up, neglecting to pause at the turnstiles as the previous people had done, though it doesn't detain us. We enter a waiting elevator car and stand behind Agent Hughes. Once we're all in, she presses her thumb to a plate on the wall but the elevator doesn't ask her for a floor. Instead, the doors snap shut and the car is propelled upward swiftly.

Hannah and I are now terrified beyond the capacity to even look at each other for reassurance. Our hands are practically dripping with sweat, but we cling to each other for dear life. "Why is she here?" I ask myself. She didn't have to come along. Then, when I realize I'd probably be balled up in a heap on the floor of the lobby right now (or worse, on the train platform in San Francisco), I understand why she's here, and even more amazed that she knew I wouldn't have been able to come without her.

The elevator stops and the doors rush open, revealing another desk with another security person behind the counter, this time a woman. She addresses the agent, "Agent Hughes."

"Marissa," she responds, then to us, "This way, please." She leads us to her office in the corner of the building and sits us down in the chairs opposite hers.

"Mr. Hawley, you have brought Ms. Stone with you today but she doesn't need to be here. Miss, at this point if you would like to wait out in hallway, you're welcome to do so. You may also remain if Mr. Hawley says it's okay."

We haven't even told them why we're here and she knows that I'm the guilty party. I'm utterly terrified as I look to Hannah for support. Carefully and compassionately, she replies, "I'd like to stay."

"Mr. Hawley?" Agent Hughes asks.

"I'd like her to stay."

"Well, then let's begin," she says.

The conversation takes almost an hour. Throughout, Hannah says nothing and just nods and smiles at me supportively; sometimes surprised, sometimes confused. Agent Hughes is stern, but kind and never judges or criticizes me while the questioning takes place.

Once the entire story has been told and I'm left weak and powerless in the chair she shuts down the console on her desk and addresses us directly, "If you two could remain here for a few moments, I'll be right back to tell you what we need to do for your processing, Mr. Hawley."

I have no strength and Hannah asks for me, "Processing?"

"Miss, Mr. Hawley may very well be detained, and if so it will need to happen today. I'm going to discuss the issue with my supervisor and we'll know further what his status will be." And with that, Agent Hughes' commanding presence exits the room and we hear the door click and lock behind her.

Hannah looks grimly back at the door, then at me, "Corwin, I'm so sorry. I didn't realize how you'd been used for something so ridiculous. But, only one week of training? For a spy? Don't you feel like they kind of just fed you to the wolves?"

I shrug and she leaves me alone. With barely a moment's rest, Hughes returns, the door clicking open and says, "My supervisor will see you now."

"Should I come, too?" Hannah asks.

Hughes shakes her head and answers, "Unfortunately, Mr. Hawley will need to proceed on his own. I'll be back momentarily to give you further information, Miss Stone."

Hannah hugs me tightly, then smiles, "Good luck, Corwin

Hawley. You're a good man."

"Thanks," I say. "You've been amazing about this. I'm so terribly sorry for all of it."

"If I see you again, you can apologize then," she says and gives me a peck on the cheek.

I follow Agent Hughes out the door and hear it close behind us – no lock clicking as it shuts. We travel down the hall, a seemingly endless walk though only thirty feet or so to an office on the interior of the building with no windows. I'm so terrified that I don't bother to look for a name on the door, just that Hughes presses her thumb to it and it opens. It's a set of wood double-doors that swing open to reveal a medium-sized office with a desk and numerous paintings, but other than that no decorations. There are two chairs on the near side of the desk, one on the other with a person sitting in it facing away from us looking at a second computer console with a series of screens on the far side.

"Sir," she begins, "Mr. Hawley is here to see you."

"Thank you," the man says. Hughes exits the room and the door shuts behind her.

I stand, sweating silently in the middle of the room for a few moments before he clicks the last key on his console and I watch it shut down. The chair turns to reveal… Gray. For all the things I've seen and experienced; communists, socialists, gays, lesbians, drag shows, dominant women, submissive men, trust, distrust, mistrust, health food, electric cars, high speed trains, reality, falsehood, my father, my past, my present, God, and all that was remotely understood to me before this moment, never have I seen anything that truly shocked me as the image I see before me.

"Hello, Corwin," he says casually, without the slightest hint of irony. I can speak no words and am too terrified to run, so he continues, "You look like you've seen a ghost. You know, I hate that phrase. It seems so cheap and trite. How about, you look like you've been bamboozled."

"That's a start," I mutter, my shock rapidly altering to rage.

He stands and crosses around to the front of the desk to sit on the edge nearer me, "And, since that is what's happened, I would expect no less."

"What the fuck are you doing here?" I demand quietly.

"That's certainly a fair question. And, at this point, you're entitled a fair response. So, I'll give you one. I work for the Western States Intelligence Administration as a senior operative charged with extracting individuals, whom we believe are unsafe in their current situations. Particularly from hostile zones in America."

"What?" I ask, completely confused.

"I'm a double agent, Corwin. I used to work for the American government and was approached by a senior operative here when I was arrested while on a mission back in twenty-eight."

With the same courtesy I originally gave Gray when we first met, I say, "The fuck?"

"Corwin, I know this is a lot to digest at once—"

"Ya think?!" I exclaim, mouth agape at the ridiculousness of it all. Gray holds his hand up to stop me but I don't. "You've been sending me threatening notes, telling me that I'd better join back up, sending agents to watch me, run into me even, and then you show up *here*?! What the hell am I supposed to believe?"

"Your eyes, Corwin. Nothing more. I didn't come to this job because I *wanted* it. These people had the opportunity to execute me for international espionage, but they didn't. Turns out, they don't even have a death penalty, but that's beside the point. They gave me a choice – come work for them, or go home and be reported in every way possible to Interpol. My life as a spy, or rather my entire life would have been over, but it was a choice. Do you really believe the American government would have shown me any such leniency in my failure?"

"So you switched sides, just like that?" I ask.

"No, not just like that. It took time. I'd been a spy and it took these people years to trust me enough to know that I was doing the right thing for the right motivation. There's very little of the same issue in your case, Corwin. You voluntarily told your own government where to stick it and that ranks highly on the trust scale around here."

"So if you knew you could trust me, then why all the lies? Why not just kidnap and deport me?"

"Corwin, we couldn't just tell you the truth, things don't work that way. More often than not when people believe something and are presented with evidence the contrary, their first instinct isn't to give up their beliefs. Rather, their instinct is to fight it and entrench themselves more fully in the lie. If we had just told you that everything you believed was wrong you would have told us to go to hell and our chances of bringing you around would have decreased drastically. This is the kind of thing that can only be believed if it is lived – at least from your position. We had to give you a chance to immerse yourself in the culture and see there was nothing wrong with it."

Beginning to understand, I add, "That's why you kept wanting me to fit in. To socialize."

"It wasn't for the good of America. It was just for the good of… well, you."

I have to sit down. The strain of this is too much for me and short of strangling Gray, the only other urge I have is to pass out. I look up at him sitting on the edge of the desk, smug in his knowing superiority and ask, "For me? You went through all of this trouble, for *me*?"

"Not just for you. An old friend of one of your superiors is a financier of the project," Gray admits and I suddenly think back to my father, sitting on the ladder in the vineyard. He was destroyed one second, then fine the next. It hadn't occurred to me at the time, but he seemed to get over the news that I was a spy rather quickly. Knowing what I know now, he must have realized that I was a beneficiary of a system he'd helped to create.

"But the expense? The resources? Why?"

"Because the person is the essential piece, not the money. What would you have us do, Corwin? Drop you in the middle of this country and say 'they're right, you're wrong, good luck acclimating?' How do you think you would have fared under that circumstance?"

"I don't know, but it would have been honest!"

"You would have cowered in a corner, hid from society… It would have taken you years to finally begin to socialize and even then, would you trust anyone you met?" Gray isn't pleading with me, but he clearly wants me to get that lying to me was in my best interest, "The people you've met – you got to know them as they truly are. Granted, you may have been lying to them, but in doing so, you were able to see them as they are. At no point were you outwardly engaging them in combat, verbal or otherwise, and instead of seeing these people as the enemy, you saw them as people. Though that wasn't your intent, that's clearly what happened and now you find yourself wanting to defend them from your own beliefs. That's an admirable change to see in a person, Corwin."

He's right. I could kick the fucker, but he's right. Gray lets me stew on this for a while before I ask, "You do this same thing for everyone you bring over?"

"Not at all. The process of helping an individual to defect varies on a case by case basis. Lord knows we learned a few things from your training not to repeat with others. Although, when you consider the whole package was put together in no more than a couple weeks I feel we did fairly well. Not to mention securing you a job upon arrival."

I think back to Gray's "training gaps" and am suddenly baffled at my own stupidity. Why did I not catch on sooner that something was amiss. Or, if I did, why did I not allow myself to pursue it or ask more questions. Following that train of thought, I ask, "What about the threats? Coming back to the fold and all that?"

"To drive you further away. The more the American government was a threat to you, the more you'd have to rely on the safety of the place you'd become a part of. It forced you to trust this place more."

"And so each person gets a different treatment depending on their needs?"

He nods, "Certainly. Your friend, Dave, for example…" As Gray says this, my thoughts from a day ago come flooding back to me, "…came to us. He thought he was admitting to the American authorities that he'd done something wrong, but instead he was admitting it to us. We test people, naturally, to make sure they're not trying to pull some sort of scam, but Dave was the real thing. When we told him he had the opportunity to defect he thanked us and started the process."

"He wanted to defect?" I ask.

Gray leans in to me, "He did, but he had a condition, Corwin. He wouldn't go unless we made sure to help you." This thought had never occurred to me. "He told us about you and how you dutifully followed all the behavioral rules of America. But he also told us how you refused to be part of the clique. You refused to engage in the violence and the drinking and the anger. You seemed out of place and he thought it would eventually get you killed – surprised it hadn't already. So, he risked himself to get you out."

"He risked himself?" I ask.

"That night at the bar when he told you about his wife. That was a test. We had to see the interaction to know how to present your training. To know what you believed and what you were willing to keep secret. Had that conversation been overheard by anyone other than us, or if you'd turned him in, he might have been imprisoned. And, if they tortured him and found out what he was up to, he might have been killed."

I knew what Dave did that night was risky, but until now it never occurred to me exactly how risky, "Did he make it?"

Gray leans back and stands to walk across the room, "He did, along with his wife. They live in the Northeast, in the Wallowa Province," he takes a slip of paper out of his jacket pocket and hands it to me. "He asked that you look him up if you ever get the chance."

"No mobile?" I ask, confused about the paper.

Gray laughs a bit, "It's a different way of life up there, Corwin. Where people in America who spurn technology are laughed at, here they're given an opportunity to live their lives as they choose. Dave and his wife were not fond of technology anyway..." I can't tell you how many times Dave "forgot" his mobile when coming to poker nights. "...and they, understandably, harbor a fear of the American government, particularly when living so close to the border. Still, it's a safe region and they're protected. They hike into town once a month to call me or Agent Hughes to let us know how they're doing."

"And?"

"They're well. But you should visit them some time. Now, if you don't mind, I have work to do, so you'll need to be on your way," and with that he pats me on the shoulder and returns to his seat on the other side of the desk.

I stand, taking stock of the slip of paper. Slowly, I ask, "What about me?"

"Oh yes. I suppose there is a bit left to discuss. You are, after all, a sort of traitor," the shaking returns almost immediately. He continues, "Fortunately for you, the only people who know about it work in this building. Well, and that poor, unfortunate girl you have in Agent Hughes' office. To be truthful, Corwin, it will be some time before the administration trusts you completely. We've driven you to our side, yes, but like me you have something yet to prove. At some point, the motivation of self-preservation must wear off and the motivation to do the right thing, no matter the cost, must take over. Until then, we'll have a video camera over your desk at work and will check in with you on a periodic basis to see how you're doing. But, truthfully, your life won't change much for now… Unless you wish it to."

I think on this. "And if I do?"

He smiles and rotates his chair to his rear console, firing up the computer and says, "There's always the good fight to fight. For now, Agent Hughes will get you processed and back home."

The doors open behind me and I turn to exit through them. Down the hall I find Hannah and Hughes waiting outside the Agent's door, smiling. Hughes has clearly briefed Hannah on what's going on and for this, I'm thankful. For some nagging reason, I can't seem to talk about it.

Agent Hughes greets me, "Mr. Hawley, I want you to know that the Intelligence Administration will be here for you, for as long as you need us." Because, like every intelligence agency in every industrialized nation, they never really forget you're there anyway, I think.

"Thank you," I say softly, finally slipping the paper into my pocket.

She motions for us to move down the hall back to the

security desk and the elevators. As we do, she adds, "I've sent contact information of a group to your mobile device. You are not required to attend at all, but some people have found the group to be a helpful transitioning device."

Puzzled, I ask, "Transition?"

"They're defectors, like you. They meet once a month to share their experiences, their troubles, and give each other support. Everyone's experience is unique, but they all share similarities, too. Try it out and see how you feel."

"I will. Thank you."

We've reached the security desk across from the elevators and the woman says, "Agent Hughes, are Mr. Hawley and Ms. Stone ready to check out?"

"They are," Hughes states, then winks at us. "Take care Corwin, and let us know if you need us. Miss Stone."

Hannah and Hughes nod at each other and Hughes exits to return to her office. "Well, let's get you processed then," Marissa states. The plate on her counter lights up and she adds, "Press your thumbs please."

Hannah presses hers and it glows green immediately just as before. Taking a deep breath, I press mine as well. This time, it glows green instantly and Hannah squeezes my hand in acknowledgment.

"You're both free to leave," Marissa exclaims, then presses a spot on her desk. An elevator door immediately opens and we enter it as Marissa waves, "Goodbye, now."

Hannah and I leave the building and begin our walk back to the train station. She offers to buy me lunch but I decline. Something feels off and I can't quite place it. By the time we board the train and have been traveling for twenty minutes, she can no longer contain her curiosity and asks, "What's the matter, Corwin? You seem really down for a guy that's just been given a second chance."

As I haven't quite worked it out myself, it comes with some difficulty, "It feels... hollow. I guess. It feels like it doesn't belong to me. Like I've faked my way out of some obligation."

"Of serving the American government?"

"No, that's not what I mean. I mean, like I got out easy. Like I managed to get out without paying my dues. Does that make any sense?"

She practically gasps, "I'd say thirty years is enough for dues. Maybe you shouldn't be so hard on yourself. Embrace it. Revel in it for a bit. Why not take a moment to be happy that you *are* out. That where you are, you can be who you are." I think about this long enough that she knows I won't respond and continues, "Things aren't perfect here, Corwin. This isn't some Utopia. Everyone's affected by this. Everyone left someone behind, or is missing their family, and this country is weaker for it as well. You're right that there's work to be done and that while you gain, others may lose, but at the end of the day all you have is yourself. You can make a difference. You already have to an extent."

I can't argue with her, but it doesn't make me feel much better. For now, I'm left with focusing on what I do know. I know I'm free. I know I'm able to say what I believe now. And, I know that I no longer have to pretend to be what anyone else wants me to be. I'm not one thing or another. I'm just Corwin.

Epilogue

Snow falls on the plaza creating an illuminated and serene view of Rockefeller Center. I'm standing across the street, huddled with my overpriced coffee. Almost no one in New York orders fancy lattes and the barista looked at me as if to say, "Nice choice, fruit." I winked at her suggestively and replied, "Helps keep me warm on those long Winter evenings." Now I'm sipping the overpriced espresso drink, thinking, "She was right to judge me for ordering this, because she sucks at making it." Slurp.

I've only been standing here ten minutes or so, and the view is enough to keep me around a bit longer. New York is beautiful this time of year, though you wouldn't know it by the meager populace hustling by. They seem to dart from one building to another or from car to building so fast that there's no time to stop and talk to each other. Maybe I'm soft. Maybe I've gotten so used to San Francisco that I can't fathom speeding my way through life without stopping to acknowledge at least someone, even if I have no idea who they are. Just a "Hello" every now and then can make all the difference in whether I'm having a mediocre or splendid day.

Now I recall I need to be careful with the flowery vocab. Men here shouldn't be saying things like "splendid." The two uniformed officers traipsing past help to remind me of that.

They both try to stare me down as they slowly go by and I raise my coffee to them. Eventually, they move far enough on that the panic subsides. I realize that if I were arrested I could easily be released given my special status but it's not something I want to test.

The front door opens for about the hundredth time since my shitty latte's been exposed to the cold and finally the mark comes out. He's been working overtime, I see. Poor bastard. Tossing the dregs of the latte over my shoulder, I let him get started on his way. I then dart down the stairs and onto the sidewalk along West 50th Street where I manage to keep a safe distance. A couple blocks later, he makes a right on Broadway and descends into the subway. Again, I follow, jumping on the car behind him at the last second. It's a long ride, so I find a safe place to camp out where I can see him, making sure he stays on the train.

Apparently, he's been paranoid for some time and I watch him check around every once in a while to see if anyone's following him. In this town, even with its diminished population, that's a difficult thing to weed out, though. I pull a book out of my top coat pocket and pretend to read, keeping one eye on him all the way North through Manhattan, under Central Park and the Harlem River before emerging in the Bronx just North of 149th Street. He's been standing the whole time, ready to make a run for it at any second. My eyes piercing through him have finally caught hold and he knows I'm here. To his credit, he doesn't panic and waits for his stop at Simpson Station.

I duck out the door closest to me and remain on the

platform momentarily, acting as if I'm lighting a smoke. He moves along without looking back initially, but just as I'm about to drop my hands and reveal I don't actually have a cigarette, he looks back and I'm glad I've left my hands up. He takes Simpson St. North to 169th and then onto Fox Street where he hurriedly stomps up the stairs to his walk-up. He's now fully aware of me and I make little pretense of smoking, drinking coffee, or reading at this point. But, I don't shout after him either. I've been working out and am in good shape so I'm not worried about becoming winded, but hollering at him will draw attention, so I keep a low profile until I get to the door. I know his pass code and enter it on the console.

The door opens and I can hear his footsteps pounding up to the third floor. Unless he's headed for the roof, I know exactly where he's going so I don't run to follow. I don't dawdle, either, though, as I don't want him to duck out the back on me. I nimbly ascend the stairs, hearing him slam and lock the door behind him. I give him a few moments to get his coat off and collect himself before I knock. No answer. I knock again only to elicit a distressed response, "Go the fuck away!"

I smile, knowing what he must be going through and knock again, "You don't have to open it all the way, Mr. Bell. Put the chain on the door." I say this as quietly as I can, though I'm aware other neighbors may be listening in at this point so my goal is eventually to get him to let me in." After a plaintive pause, the door opens. He's peeping around the chain, sizing me up. He's probably wondering whether he could knock me out and get past me to the door with whatever luggage he's got prepared right now. I try to be as casual as possible, "That's better."

"What do you want?" he asks angrily.

I reply, holding out my badge, "Just to talk to you."

A look of recognition and resignation flushes his cheeks and he nods, lowering his head. He closes the door and I hear the chain being removed. The door then reopens and I see him half hiding behind the wall to the kitchen as he asks, "Am I in trouble? Are you going to arrest me?" He's terrified and I can smell it.

"Not exactly," I respond. Closing the door behind me, I relish this next part with all the delight of a child on Christmas morning, "My name's Corwin Black and I'm from the Department of Foreign Affairs. We have a mission I'd like to discuss with you."

– END –

Afterward

After my marriage, I began to contemplate all the various locations in which my name would need to change. It took quite some time before I realized it would need to be changed on my novels as well. When that consideration occurred, I saw an opportunity to correct some of the errors and omissions this book possesses. I eventually pumped the breaks on that project, though, and not just because it would mean a colossal amount of work.

This book, as with all things, is a product of its time and is therefore limited to a particular context and perspective. If I were to write this today, for example, I would likely include more detail about the rise of the authoritarian regime in Corwin's America. I would likely spend more thoughtful hours crafting Corwin's intimate experiences so as not to play into potentially harmful practices like Bi-erasure or the use of rigid, binary gender pronouns. If we're going to imagine an inclusive community, it seems odd to limit a character's future experiences to the definitions of the past.

But this is all speculative because it wasn't written in the future. This afterward comes nine years after the book was written (eight years after it was first published), and the purpose of the book was never to predict such experiences, but rather to allow Corwin to have some version of them and see if he was willing to change. And this is the question asked of not just the reader but of all progressives. Are we willing to change when the world changes around us? And, more importantly, are we willing to help create that change?

In asking these questions, we must also accept that the changes we seek today may be the antiquated notions of to-morrow.

In short, I could have rewritten Gaymerica with the virtue of hindsight instead of penning this afterward. But, it would eliminate the lessons learned since that time, and the reader is encouraged to not only be more thoughtful than Corwin, but to be disappointed, yet forgiving with him and those around him when they don't do better. Expecting our fictional characters to be better than us strips them of their humanity and their need to make mistakes. It also sets unrealistic expectations on us.

I'm proud of this book for what it is; a view of one possible future from the reality of 2011. In some ways, reality has already played out more positively than I'd hoped for. In others, much worse. And this entire afterward will shortly be outdated as well.

Scot Froelich (Moore), March 2020

Acknowledgments

On a personal note, I need to thank the following people who got first peek at this thing and gave me much needed feedback:

Rachel Flynn
Mariah Christiansen
Brian Watson-Jones
Kelly Joseph
Mame Pelletier
Ruth Virkus
Becky Gebhart
Brian Joseph
Ben Layne

On a larger scale, Gaymerica owes its genesis to all those who seek equality, acceptance, and a more peaceful coexistence.

www.ingramcontent.com/pod-product-compliance
Lightning Source LLC
Chambersburg PA
CBHW050721180626
46814CB00002B/543